Look what people are saying about the Body Movers series...

"Bond keeps the pace frantic, the plot tight and the laughs light, and supplies a cliffhanger ending that's a bargain at twice the price."
—*Publishers Weekly*, starred review, on *Body Movers: 2 Bodies for the Price of 1*

"*Body Movers* is one of the most delightful series I have read in quite some time. Stephanie Bond shows her audience what a wickedly funny mystery should be all about."
—*Suspense Romance Writers*

"This series is simply splendid. Vivid, quirky, flawed, wonderful people fill its pages and you care about what happens to them. Like the prior volume, it is replete with humor as well as action. I can hardly wait to see all these characters again."
—*Huntress Reviews*

"Here's to Carlotta's future misadventures lasting a long time."
—*Romantic Times BOOKreviews*, four-star review, on *Body Movers*

"This is a series the reader will want to jump on in the very beginning. It's witty, sexy and hilariously funny. "
—*Writers Unlimited*

"*Body Movers* is signature Stephanie Bond, with witty dialogue, brilliant characterization, and a wonderful well-plotted storyline."
—*Contemporary Romance Writers*

STEPHANIE BOND

BODY MOVERS:
3 MEN AND A BODY

MIRA®

ISBN-13: 978-0-7783-2607-6
ISBN-10:   0-7783-2607-1

BODY MOVERS: 3 MEN AND A BODY

www.MIRABooks.com

Printed in U.S.A.

Also by Stephanie Bond

BODY MOVERS: 2 BODIES FOR THE PRICE OF 1
BODY MOVERS

Acknowledgments

As always, thanks to my great editors Brenda Chin, Margaret O'Neill Marbury and Dianne Moggy for your support and for the guarantee that as of this date, the series will last for at least six books! Thanks, too, to my agent Kimberly Whalen of Trident Media Group for handling the logistics, to my critique partner, Rita Herron, for your unflagging support. Chris, my wonderfully creative husband, you continue to be my rock.

And thank you to my dear, dear first-grade teacher, Miss Alice Sue DeHart, for your cover quote. Somehow you taught first and second graders every subject in the same classroom, all day, between wiping faces and tying shoes and kissing boo-boos. You made learning fun, and books special. Miss DeHart, you are still fabulous. Thank you for being a part of my life for over thirty-five years.

Carlotta Wren bumped her cast against the door frame leading from the kitchen to the living room. "Son of a..." She bit back tears as pain lit up her entire left arm. Although she was lucky the fall from the balcony of the Fox Theater hadn't resulted in more serious physical injuries, the prospect of another four weeks in this clumsy cast left her frustrated and antsy.

It wasn't enough that she couldn't do her job at Neiman Marcus at a time when she desperately needed the money (short-term disability paid only partial wages). But yesterday when Peter Ashford had brought her home from the hospital, he'd shown her a ring he'd had made for her—her Cartier engagement ring, which he'd recovered from the shop where she'd pawned it, with two more large diamonds mounted, on either side of the original stone. *The past, the present and the future.* He would keep it for her, he'd said, until she was ready to make a decision.

And on top of everything else, her brother, Wesley, was missing.

Wesley was supposed to have picked her up at the hospital yesterday in a taxi, and when he hadn't shown, his boss, Cooper Craft, had offered to go look for him. As of last night, Coop hadn't found Wesley, but Carlotta was hopeful that her brother would turn up this morning. He'd come strolling into the house, whistling, with a mouse in a jar to feed his snake, Einstein, oblivious to the fact that Carlotta had barely slept last night, worrying about him....

Worrying about Wesley seemed to be her fate in life. She'd raised him since he was nine years old, when their parents had skipped town so their father could elude charges for investment fraud. Over the past decade, they'd heard from their parents only through a handful of postcards...until recently.

When a look-alike had stolen her identity and been murdered, Carlotta had agreed to fake her own death. The D.A. wanted to try to smoke out her parents and in exchange, they'd offered to suspend Wesley's probation for hacking into the courthouse computer records. But Kelvin Lucas, the D.A. who'd been denied the chance to prosecute her father, Randolph Wren, had reneged on his deal when her parents hadn't shown.

After Carlotta had alienated Wesley for going along with the plan.

After she'd put her friends and coworkers through the traumatic ordeal of thinking her dead.

And after she'd slept with Detective Jack Terry, her temporary live-in bodyguard.

What no one knew was that Carlotta's father *had* shown up, in disguise, and he'd recognized her, even though she was also in disguise. She hadn't known it was him until later, when she'd found the note he'd slipped into her pocket: "So proud of you both. See you soon. Dad"

The scrawled words left her conflicted. During her parents' long absence, Carlotta had worked up a powerful resentment. Sometimes, she even cheerfully hated them. Leaving without saying goodbye. Leaving her to finish raising Wesley when she was just a few months shy of graduating high school and barely equipped to take care of herself. Leaving no money, only a paid-for town house in a transitional section of Atlanta that was a far cry from the palatial home in Buckhead that they had lost.

College had no longer been an option. The only real expertise she'd had was…clothes. Her father had been a wealthy investment broker; Carlotta had worn nothing but the best since she could dress herself. Thankfully, she'd been able to turn that dubious skill into a career in retail. She'd been a top salesperson for most of her years at Neiman's… until lately, when her life had seemingly exploded with complications and new relationships.

And old ones.

"Did shithead make it home yet?"

Carlotta turned to see her friend Hannah Kizer standing there, hands on hips. Dressed in pink pj's with white bunny rabbits and without her severe goth makeup, Hannah looked almost human—pretty, even.

"Not yet."

"Have you heard from Coop?"

"Not yet."

"Don't worry. Wesley can take care of himself, whether you want to admit it or not."

"I wish you were right, but history has taught me otherwise."

"How's the arm?"

"Getting dressed is an aerobic workout. Thank heaven for front-closure bras."

"Yeah, I had a broken arm once. Men wanted to jump in bed with me. I guess it made me seem vulnerable or something."

"Or less likely to eat your prey?"

Hannah gave her the finger, then dropped onto the couch, picked up the remote control and turned on the small TV. When the picture came on, it was warped. "What happened to your big-screen TV?"

Carlotta sat next to her friend and pointed to the living room window, still covered with the boards the police had tacked in place. "Taken out during the drive-by shooting. I'm waiting for a new window to be delivered and installed, but we can't afford to replace the TV. Wesley shouldn't have bought it, anyway," she grumbled. "We could've used that money for other things."

Like paying toward what he owed his odious loan sharks, Father Thom and The Carver. Or paying down their credit card debt, which had ballooned in size since her identity had been stolen. Or catching up their loan payments, or any one of a hundred other bills they were late on.

Wesley said he'd sold his motorcycle to buy the TV, but she knew the television had cost more than his bike was worth. She figured he'd been gambling again, despite his claims to her that he'd stopped.

She turned her head to look at her friend. "Where could he be?"

"A thousand safe places," Hannah assured her.

"Or a thousand unsafe places. Those thugs for The Carver who tried to force me into their van the other day said that Wesley had pulled a stupid stunt and was in big trouble. What if they kidnapped him?"

"Look on the bright side—his loan sharks probably won't kill him because they want to collect their money."

Carlotta glared at her.

Hannah's smile fell. "Sorry. Just trying to lift the mood." She flipped channels past the midmorning game shows, and stopped on a local talk show, *Atlanta & Company*, where local celebutante KiKi Deerling was being interviewed in all her silky blond, micro-mini glory, snuggling her pet pug on her lap. It was the guilty pleasure that Carlotta needed to take her mind off Wesley.

But a minute into the interview, Hannah scoffed, "Give me a break. This girl is only famous for being famous. She's a total poser."

Carlotta nodded, but nursed a little pang of envy toward the young woman who had inherited beauty, money and a last name that adorned a jewelry empire headquartered in Atlanta. "It would be fun to live her life for a day, though. No worries, just party after party." She gave Hannah a pointed look. "For once, we wouldn't have to crash."

"That girl is a waste of human skin. You'd think with all

that cash she'd buy some underwear. I've seen her twat more than my own."

"Thanks for the wholesome image."

"And you'd think she'd learn by now that if she's going to have sex with someone, she should sweep the room first for hidden cameras. I always do."

"Really?" Carlotta said. "What married man are you dating this week?"

"His name is Troy and he's a college professor."

"What does he teach?"

"Ethics."

"Oh, well then, plus ten points."

On television the starlet held up her pet pug, which she'd dressed in a T-shirt bearing the name of the camp she was promoting.

"Camp Kiki?" Hannah said. "Is that where kids go to breathe fresh air, learn to snort coke and become anorexic?"

"Cut her some slack," Carlotta said with a little laugh. "I've heard of this camp. It looks like she's at least trying to do something good for underprivileged kids."

"Underprivileged to her probably means anyone who doesn't have a driver." Hannah gave Carlotta a sideways look. "Sorry. I forgot that you used to be rich."

"Not that kind of rich."

"Are there classifications for how rich you are?"

"Sure." Carlotta used the fingers on her good hand to count them off. "There's inherited wealth, the kind that's so massive the heirs live off the interest. Then there's inherited wealth that has to be maintained, like taking over the reins of a family business. There are ranks within inherited wealth, depending on how prestigious the business—jewelry is near the top of the list. Then there's aristocratic wealth, meaning there's no cash flow, everyone just kind of exists off their family name and estate. My parents were farther down in the pecking order—they were bourgeois rich. My dad worked for his money."

Hannah lifted an eyebrow.

"Or stole it, depending on who you believe."

"And who do you believe?"

The note her father had slipped to her scratched the skin of her chest where she was keeping it in her bra. She was afraid that Wesley might find it if she left it in her bedroom. And truthfully, she just wanted to keep it close. "I honestly don't know. He was indicted for fraud, so the D.A. must have had a case, right?"

"Maybe. Maybe it was personal. What do you really know about the D.A.?"

"Just that he's a lying asshole for reneging on our deal."

"Well, there you go. Maybe he had some other motivation for charging your dad."

"So why didn't Dad stay and fight it? Why skip town and abandon his own kids?"

"I don't know."

"Would *your* parents do something like that?"

Hannah shifted on the couch, and it occurred to Carlotta that she had never talked about her parents. And frankly, Carlotta couldn't picture the people who had spawned her bizarre friend.

"Has your father called you again?" Hannah asked, neatly sidestepping Carlotta's question.

"No."

Not that it had been much of a conversation. He'd phoned her at work a few weeks ago and said, "It's Daddy." She'd been so startled, she'd dropped her cell phone—and the connection.

"And I broke my cell phone, so I couldn't even call back."

Hannah frowned and pointed to the end table. "Whose cell phone is that?"

"Mine, but…it's a new one."

"How did you afford a new phone?" Hannah asked suspiciously.

"Peter gave me an extra one that he had lying around."

Hannah picked up the sleek, razor-thin phone. "Right. This state-of-the-art gadget was just lying around. Did it belong to his murdered wife?"

"No!" At least Carlotta didn't think so.

"Is he paying for your service, too?"

"It didn't cost anything to add me to his plan," she said defensively.

"Yet. Don't kid yourself—the man plans to collect."

"Peter's been very good to me," Carlotta murmured.

"You mean the man who dumped you years ago when your parents left town? The man who's suddenly all over you when his wife has only been dead for a few weeks? Yeah, he's a real stand-up guy."

"It's complicated." No one knew that her father had also called Peter, who now worked for Mashburn & Tully, the investment firm where her father had been accused of stealing from customers' accounts. Randolph Wren had asked Peter for his help in finding an alleged file that could prove his innocence. It was a secret that bound her and Peter together.

Then there was the ring….

The sound of a car pulling into the driveway made Carlotta leap off the couch. "It's Coop," she said when she saw the white van. She watched until he got out of the van—alone. "But Wesley isn't with him."

She opened the front door and stepped out on the stoop in the early morning heat, eager for news. "Did you find him?"

Cooper Craft was tall and lean, with light brown hair and long, neat sideburns. He lifted his gaze to hers and shook his head. "No. You haven't heard from him?"

"No," Carlotta said, feeling the stirrings of true panic. "I've been calling his cell phone every hour. How far could he get on a bicycle?"

He gave her a little smile. "He'll turn up."

But she could tell by his haggard expression that Wesley's body-moving boss was worried, too. It made her sick with fear. "Come in. I'll make coffee."

2

When Coop entered the house Carlotta noticed that he was wearing the same clothes he'd had on yesterday. His hair was disheveled; his sideburns merged with an unshaved jaw. Her heart tugged when she realized he hadn't been to bed. "Did you drive around all night?"

"I checked the hospital emergency rooms and a few places I thought he might be, but no one had seen him."

"Hi, Coop."

He looked up and did a double take at Carlotta's stripe-haired friend standing barefoot and fresh-faced in her unexpectedly cuddly pj's. "Hannah?"

She flapped her eyelashes. Hannah had a huge crush on Coop. "In the flesh. Um, this isn't what I normally sleep in, in case you're interested."

Carlotta rolled her eyes as Coop smothered a smile. "Okay. Did you keep Carlotta company last night?"

"Yep."

"Good." He glanced at Carlotta, his gaze softening. "I was worried about you. How's your arm?"

She squirmed. "It's fine, thanks. How about that coffee?"

"I'll make a pot," Hannah said with a frown. "Yours is sludge." When she disappeared into the kitchen, Carlotta motioned for Coop to sit down.

He lowered his long frame into a chair, then removed his glasses and rubbed his eyes. "I'm going to throttle Wesley for making you worry so much."

Carlotta smiled to herself—for making *her* worry so much? Since Coop had hired Wesley to help him move bodies for the county morgue, he'd become a mentor to her brother. Whether Wes realized it or not, he looked up to his boss. And it appeared Coop was equally fond of him. Her heart swelled with gratitude. Wesley needed a positive male influence in his life.

Heaven knew their father had fallen down on the job.

The phone rang and Carlotta dived for it. "Hello?"

"Yeah…is Wesley there?"

Carlotta pursed her mouth, recognizing the guttural voice of a person who'd lost more than a few brain cells. "He's not here, Chance. Didn't you get any of the messages I left for you, asking if you'd seen him?"

"No."

She touched her forehead. "No, you didn't get the messages, or no, you haven't seen him?"

"I ain't seen him since the day before yesterday."

She exhaled. "Do you know where he could be?"

"Uh…no."

"With his girlfriend maybe?"

"Girlfriend?"

"Come on, Chance, he's been coming home smelling like women's perfume. Unless you've suddenly started wearing Chanel No. 5, he's been spending time with someone else."

"I would not know anything about that," Chance said woodenly.

Carlotta wanted to scream. "Chance, this is serious. He could be in trouble."

"Don't worry, my boy can take care of himself."

She gritted her teeth at the implication that Wesley was part of Chance's "posse." "If you see him, will you tell him to call me as soon as possible?"

"Sure thing," Chance said, then disconnected the call.

Carlotta sighed. "His friend Chance Hollander hasn't seen him."

"What's this about a girlfriend?" Coop asked.

"I thought you might know."

"I know he's got a thing for his probation officer."

"But she has a boyfriend—remember, we met him at the Elton John concert."

Coop gave her an amused smile. "Some women have more than one guy on the line."

A flush climbed her face. Coop and Wesley had walked in on her and Jack Terry kissing, and there had been no mistletoe—or even December—in sight. She didn't know if Wesley had told Coop that Jack had spent at least one night in her bedroom, but Coop probably suspected as much.

Coop had also met Peter and was aware of their history. All of which would have to be sorted out at another time.... At the moment she couldn't think past Wesley being gone.

Luckily, Hannah arrived with three cups of coffee, and a box of sweet rolls left over from one of her catering gigs the previous day. Carlotta took the food gratefully, her stomach rumbling from hunger.

"Wesley has to come back," Hannah said dryly. "Or you'll starve."

Carlotta stuck out her tongue, but she appreciated her friend's attempt at humor. And it was true. Wesley did all the cooking, and had done so for years. He was pretty good, too, darn his infuriating, scrawny little ass. Her eyes watered.

"Hey," Coop said quietly, putting his large hand over hers. "Wesley is a smart kid. If he's in trouble, he'll figure out something."

Carlotta nodded and inhaled a cleansing breath. If their parents' leaving had taught her anything, it was that tears didn't solve a thing. Action did.

"What now?" she asked Coop.

"I know he has an appointment to see his probation officer at eleven. I'd say if he doesn't show, then you should call the police. Considering that thug's comment to you about Wesley having done something stupid, this might have to do with the loan sharks he owes."

Her heart squeezed, but she had to consider worst-case scenarios. "You're right. He wouldn't miss his appointment with Eldora. Not voluntarily."

"Meanwhile," Coop said, pushing himself to his feet,

"try to think of somewhere he might've gone, or someone who might know where he is. I'll keep making inquiries."

"Okay," she said, following him to the door. "And Coop…" She squared her shoulders, but that only caused pain to shoot down her arm. "I hate to ask this, but have you checked the…morgue?"

His brown eyes filled with sympathy, and he nodded. "I did. He's not there."

Tears of relief filled her eyes. "Thank you for caring."

He gave her a little smile. "I can't seem to help myself." Then he turned and walked to the bottom of the steps. "You have my cell phone number if you need me."

"Yes," she called after him, waving with her good hand until he drove away.

Carlotta looked to her left and saw their neighbor Mrs. Winningham working in her yard. They weren't the best of friends, but the woman had called 911 a few days ago when two of The Carver's thugs had tried to drag Carlotta into their van. So she went down the steps and crossed to the fence that separated the yards of their respective town houses. "Hi, Mrs. Winningham."

"Hello," the woman chirped. "And you're welcome."

"Pardon me?"

"I said you're welcome for the get well card I sent to you through your brother. He said you managed to only break your arm." The woman sniffed. "Although I must say you made a spectacle of yourself, dangling half-naked from the balcony of the Fox Theater."

"Yes, I'm good at that," Carlotta said cheerfully. "I'm

sorry, but I haven't seen Wesley yet to get your thoughtful card. May I ask when you gave it to him?"

The woman looked perturbed. "I gave it to him yesterday morning. He said he was going to meet you at the hospital and bring you home in a taxi. Then he rode off on his bike."

"And did he seem okay to you?"

"'Okay' is a relative term where your family is concerned, but yes, reasonably so."

"Thank you," Carlotta said as pleasantly as she could manage. "I'll let you know when I get your card, Mrs. Winningham." Her stomach rolled as she went back to her house.

"What's wrong?" Hannah asked.

Carlotta told her about her conversation with the neighbor. "So Wesley didn't just get wrapped up in some marathon poker tournament and forget. He was planning to meet me at the hospital like he said. Something bad has happened, I know it now."

"Shh, you don't know that for sure," Hannah said. "Wait to see if he shows up at his P.O.'s office. Do you have the phone number?"

"There's a business card on the bulletin board in his room."

"Want me to get it?"

"Would you?"

"Want me to feed Einstein while I'm in there?"

"Please," she said. The last time the massive python had gone unfed for too long, it had found its way out of Wesley's room and into Carlotta's bed.

When she returned, Hannah tried to entertain Carlotta

by coaxing her to the back deck to stick her feet in the kiddie pool Wesley had bought for her—to make up, he'd said, for the lavish life she'd given up with Peter in order to raise him. The cool water felt good between her toes, but it only made her miss Wesley more.

"I'm sorry I have to leave," Hannah said later, standing with her hands on her hips, back in full goth garb and makeup, the barbell in her tongue clicking against her teeth. "But I can't get anyone to cover me on this corporate luncheon."

"Go," Carlotta urged, shin-deep in the pool and clutching the phone. "You've done enough hand-holding for a lifetime."

"Call me to let me know what you find out. I should be finished in a couple of hours or so."

Carlotta waved her off, and attempted to relax, trying to find some solace in the beautiful sunny day and the fact that the neighborhood that she'd hated living in was looking quite pretty today. When the trees were leafed out, they hid the shabbiness of most of the homes, their's included. The gay couple that lived on the other side of them, whom they'd only seen and not met, had made upgrades to their house. Now that she thought about it, she decided her neighbors probably didn't extend themselves because the Wren place was, as Mrs. Winningham had so often reminded her, "a blight on our good street."

Ironically, Carlotta had vowed to update their place and make some badly needed repairs just before she'd broken her arm. For extra money, she had even contemplated joining forces with Hannah to go on some body-moving jobs for Coop—much to Hannah's great delight. But that, too, would have to wait until after Carlotta's arm healed.

"Come home safe, Wesley," she whispered. "I have plans for us. You can't leave me, too."

In that moment, her hatred for her parents was a palpable black mass in the air around her. She shouldn't have to deal with this alone. What if something happened to Wesley? Life without her brother was just too impossible to comprehend. She realized with a start how he must have felt when he thought she'd taken a dive off that bridge, before they had learned it was someone pretending to be her.

Their parents' abandonment had forced them into a closeness that probably wasn't healthy. She wondered if they would forever be emotionally dependent on each other, or if either would someday make room in their life for someone special. Wesley was particularly resistant to change—he still refused to allow her to take down the aluminum Christmas tree in the living room that their mother had put up mere days before she'd skipped town with their father. So it sat there in the corner, a sagging, tarnished emblem of their family, complete with little gifts underneath that had never been opened.

Except by Jack Terry, when he'd stayed at their house doing "surveillance" in case her parents showed up for the fake funeral. He'd thought he might find clues in them as to their parents' whereabouts. He'd rewrapped the gifts, but Carlotta had been furious when she discovered what he'd done. Had been hurt. Confused. Torn.

With Jack, everything was muddy.

Meanwhile, the hands on the clock seemed to crawl. The phone didn't ring. Wesley didn't materialize. When she called the number on his probation officer's business card at five minutes after eleven, she was nauseous.

"Eldora Jones speaking."

"Eldora, this is Carlotta Wren, Wesley's sister. We met a couple of nights ago at the Elton John concert."

"How could I forget? Are you out of the hospital?"

"Yes, thanks, and feeling much better. I'm calling about Wesley. Did he make his appointment today?"

"As a matter of fact, he didn't."

Carlotta's heart sank to her ankles. "Did he call to say he wouldn't be there?"

"No, he didn't. May I ask what this is about?"

"I hope it's nothing, but my brother seems to be missing."

"Missing?"

"He hasn't been home, no one's heard from him since yesterday, and he isn't answering his cell phone."

The woman paused, then said thoughtfully, "I did receive a call from a Richard McCormick saying that Wesley had impressed him in his interview yesterday morning. He's set to start his community service with the city computer-security department next Monday."

"He was supposed to meet me at the hospital after the interview, but he didn't show."

"Have you called the police?" Eldora asked hesitantly. Carlotta thought she detected more than professional interest in her tone.

"That's next on my list."

"Will you have Wesley phone me as soon as you…see him? He'll have to make up the missed meeting."

Carlotta promised she would, then hung up and put her head between her knees to relieve the light-headedness that suddenly overcame her. *Please, God.* She reached for the phone again and dialed Detective Jack Terry's number from memory.

Jack had arrested Wesley for hacking into the courthouse computer. He'd reopened their father's case. He'd investigated a couple of little murders that Carlotta had gotten involved in accidentally. And in between, he'd given her one or three mind-boggling orgasms. Theirs was a lust-hate relationship. After the fiasco at the Fox Theatre, during which he'd broken her fall, she was hoping she wouldn't have to call him anytime soon.

Here we go again.

"Jack Terry," said the rough-hewn voice over the line.

It was so unexpectedly comforting, Carlotta's throat choked with emotion.

"Hello?" he said. "Is anyone there?"

"Jack," she cried.

"Carlotta? What's wrong?"

"It's Wesley," she said, openly sobbing now.

"Are you at home?"

"Yes," she blubbered.

"I'm on my way."

3

Six minutes later, Detective Jack Terry walked through her door. Carlotta had pulled herself together and had promised herself she'd behave professionally with Jack, just like anyone else would report a potential crime to any police officer.

Instead, she went into his arms and pressed her wet face against his ugly tie. He just held her and rubbed circles on her back.

"You have to give me something to go on here," he finally said into her hair.

She sniffled and lifted her head. "Wesley's missing."

He fished a handkerchief from his pocket and handed it to her for an awkward one-hand nose blow. "Let's sit down and you can tell me what's going on."

They settled on the couch and she relayed what she knew, from how Wesley hadn't shown up at the hospital the previous day to the fact that he'd missed the meeting with his probation officer.

Jack's expression was serious, but not concerned. "So he's been missing for less than twenty-four hours."

"Yes, but something's wrong, I know it."

"Has he ever disappeared before?"

Carlotta hesitated. "This is different."

Jack's face relaxed. "Probably not. He could be with a buddy, hanging out, or maybe he found a card game."

"His friend Chance Hollander called here. He doesn't know where Wesley is."

"That's the guy who gave us the tip in the Angela Ashford murder, isn't it?"

She nodded. "I don't trust him. I think he's into something illegal."

"His friend could've been covering for him. Maybe Wesley was right in front of him, stoned, or sleeping off a hangover. Doesn't Wesley have more than one buddy?"

"Not really," she said, then frowned. "Not that I know of. But there's a woman."

"A woman?"

"I don't know who she is, but sometimes he comes home smelling of expensive perfume."

"I think I caught a whiff of that myself the night of the drive-by shooting," he said, nodding. "That could be where he is." He winked and thumbed away a tear from her cheek. "See, nothing to worry about."

"But remember what those guys you arrested here said about Wesley being in trouble with The Carver."

"I remember. I also remember telling you that if Wesley

has gotten himself in deep with these guys, he's going to have to figure a way to get out of it."

"But what if they hurt him?"

His mouth twitched downward. "He's young. He'll heal. And maybe a beating is what he needs to convince him that these aren't people he wants to do business with."

She gasped. "But what if they kill him?"

"That's not likely. An intelligent young guy like Wesley is more valuable to them alive."

That made her smile slightly. "You think he's intelligent?"

"Yeah. Unfortunately, he's not very smart."

"He's only nineteen."

"He's not a kid, Carlotta. When I was nineteen, I'd traveled halfway around the world."

"In the military?"

He nodded. "Don't baby him. If you do, you'll never have a life of your own."

"So you're telling me there's nothing I can do?"

"Legally, not until he's been missing for twenty-four hours. Off the record, though, I'll do a little nosing around."

She smiled. "Thank you, Jack." She reached up to stroke the bruise around his eye. "I see your shiner is fading."

"Yeah." He caught her hand and folded it into his.

His eyes were the color of amber, bright and direct. Sexy.

"How's your arm?" he murmured in a husky tone that implied he was asking how incapacitated she was.

"My arm…" She felt the pull of his body on hers, like a force field. But she remembered too well the negative fallout the last time she'd given in to that attraction. Besides, if the note from her fugitive father fell out of her bra, it would probably kill the mood. "My arm is itching, actually." She made a face and wiggled her finger under the edge of the cast.

He smiled, and the surface tension dissipated. He pushed himself to his feet. "I should go. I'll call you if I find anything. Meanwhile, if Wesley shows up, let me know."

"Okay. I'm sorry for the drama," she added sheepishly.

"Don't mention it," he said. "Wesley's lucky to have someone who cares about him. I'm not sure he deserves it."

"Do any of you male types deserve it?" she asked lightly.

"Touché." He left, grinning.

Carlotta stood at the edge of the window and watched him drive away, wishing she could put her finger on her feelings for the man. Then she shook her head at the futility of such an exercise. The next time she and Jack crossed paths, they could be at each other's throats.

But he had made her feel better…and empowered to do something more than wait to get a call from Wesley—or the morgue.

She called Hannah, who answered after the third ring. "Any news?"

"No. But I was wondering if you'd like to take a little field trip when you got off work. I need your muscle."

"You got it. Pick you up in an hour."

She was waiting outside, holding a fire extinguisher, when Hannah pulled up in her refrigerated catering van.

"Are we going to a fire?" Hannah asked, looking like the Goth Chef in her white smock.

Carlotta tossed the extinguisher on the floorboard, then climbed in awkwardly. "No, but it was the closest thing I had to a weapon. Chance Hollander is into all kinds of shady stuff. I just want to be prepared in case we have to fight our way out of there."

"Gee, if it's a weapon you need, I have an arsenal."

Carlotta squinted at her. "I don't think I want to know that."

"Knives, I mean. I've got a bagful in the back—from paring to cleavers, straight edge, chisel ground, hollow edge, serrated." She bounced in her seat with excitement. "Who are we going to hurt?"

"No one, hopefully. But I want to question Chance Hollander to his smarmy face, and who knows what kind of people I might run into at his place."

"So I should arm myself."

"*One* knife, Hannah. Just one. And let me do the talking."

They parked in the visitor lot for his building and climbed out. "We need to grab some empty food boxes so we look like we're catering a party," Carlotta said. Hannah stacked empty boxes on a handcart and wheeled them toward the entrance. Carlotta followed, carrying the fire extinguisher. The concierge buzzed them in.

"We're catering a party for Chance Hollander," Carlotta said, then smiled apologetically. "But I've forgotten his unit number."

The concierge not only gave her the unit number, but held the elevator door for them. She tipped him five dollars.

"Nice work," Hannah murmured.

"All the party-crashing subterfuge we've learned occasionally comes in handy."

They got off on the top floor and Carlotta took in the upscale decor with a twinge of envy.

"Wow, Wesley's friend must be wealthy," Hannah remarked.

"Chance Hollander is a trust fund baby, with lots of idle time on his hands." They found his door. Carlotta rang the doorbell and pushed Hannah in front of the peephole. "If something's going on, he won't open the door to me. Try to look friendly."

Hannah's attempt at a smile looked more like a grimace, but a few seconds later, Chance Hollander greeted them, dressed in a short Hefner-esque paisley robe. He was blond and tanned, with the chuffy body and casual posture of a person who enjoyed excess.

"Yeah?" As soon as he spotted Carlotta, he tried to shut the door, but he was no match for Hannah. She shoved him so hard he stumbled backward and landed on his ass on a zebra-striped rug shaped like an animal hide, in the middle of a room crammed with black leather furniture.

Carlotta rolled her eyes. Why was it that people with money usually had no taste?

They walked in and Carlotta closed the door behind them. "We just want to talk, Chance."

"I don't know where Wesley is," he said.

Carlotta narrowed her eyes at him. "You know something, you little shit. And you'd better tell me."

He got a surly look on his face as he reclined on his elbows. The robe had fallen away to reveal baggy briefs and a spare tire. "Or what?"

She handed the fire extinguisher to Hannah. "Would you pull the pin, please?"

"Here, trade me." Hannah pulled a gleaming twelve-inch cleaver from a box. "This only takes one hand."

Carlotta's eyes widened, but Chance's startled yelp vanquished the reprimand on the tip of her tongue.

She hefted the heavy cleaver while Hannah aimed the hose at Chance's dingy briefs. "Christ, what is it with you rich people and underwear? A three-pack of Hanes at Target for ten bucks—give it some thought."

Chance grinned. "Where did you get the dog, Carlotta? I kind of like her."

Hannah blasted his crotch with foam, eliciting a scream from him. When the dust settled, Hannah leaned closer. "The cleaver is next, fat boy. Start talking."

"It was Wesley's idea."

Carlotta's stomach churned. "What was his idea?"

Chance sat up, defeated. "He thought The Carver was behind the drive-by shooting at your place. He was scared that you were going to get hurt. So he came up with a plan to blackmail the guy."

"Blackmail The Carver? How?"

Chance grinned. "It was genius, really. We got a transvestite to go to a strip club with us where the guy was hanging out with his cronies. When he went to the can, we sent in our himbo, and got some incriminating photos. Wesley told The Carver if you got hurt, the photos would be posted on the 'Net."

Carlotta shook her head in confusion. "But the man responsible for the drive-by shooting is in jail. He had nothing to do with The Carver."

Chance winced. "I know. That part kind of sucks."

Carlotta exchanged a horrified glance with Hannah. "We have to go."

Chance slowly got to his feet and struck a cocky pose. "Hey, Goth Girl, can I persuade you to stay?"

Hannah blasted him with the extinguisher again, then grabbed her handcart and followed Carlotta out. They sprinted back to the van, where Carlotta punched in Jack's number with a shaking hand.

4

Wesley twisted his handcuffed wrists to glance at his watch. He'd been locked in this bathroom for twenty-four hours. He'd missed the meeting with E., his probation officer. Carlotta was probably worried to death.

He was sitting in a grimy green bathtub, his head leaned back against the cool tile on the wall. No matter what he did, he seemed to screw up. He'd thought he was protecting his sister when he and Chance had embarked on the Great Strip Club Caper. Instead he had humiliated one of the most dangerous men in Atlanta for no reason—a man he still owed a great deal of money.

Wesley gave a little laugh. They'd just had a fake funeral for Carlotta, and his parents hadn't bothered to show. He'd told Carlotta that their father had smelled a setup, but with so much time on his hands to think in this grimy, stinky john, he'd begun to wonder if Carlotta had been right all these years—that their parents didn't give a damn about them, and wouldn't risk apprehension even if one of their kids *was* lying in a pine box.

No, he told himself with a mental shake. The fact that he was doubting his father was just proof of how isolation and lack of food could mess with your mind.

It was his own fault if The Carver decided to carve him up and scatter his parts all over the city. He'd come to the shabby warehouse office in East Atlanta with a peace offering—the memory chip holding the photos he'd taken of the man with Cherry, a well-endowed transvestite, and a payment of nine hundred dollars on his loan. But before he could state his good intentions, he'd been hauled off his bike, relieved of his wallet, handcuffed, then tossed in this box.

They hadn't fed him, but he'd drunk from the sink faucet to keep from becoming dehydrated. Mouse, The Carver's collections man, told him they were keeping him until the boss decided what to do with him.

Wesley surveyed the tub he was in, wondering how many other people The Carver had dissected here, allowing their blood to run down the drain before gathering their limbs in garbage bags and disposing of them with the junk mail.

A scratch sounded at the door. Wesley glanced at the crack at the floor to see the shadows of two sets of shoes—Mouse had brought company this time. Wes's heart jumped to his throat.

The dead bolt slid open, then the knob turned and the door swung wide. Mouse and another man walked in and unceremoniously hauled him up out of the bathtub.

"What's new, fellas?" Wesley asked congenially.

"Shut up," Mouse told him as they half dragged him out of the room and down a hallway. The floor was concrete and the studded walls had been gutted of drywall. "The boss wants to talk to you."

"I can talk better with my hands," Wesley said. "How about uncuffing me?"

Mouse clocked him up the side of the head. "I said shut up."

Wesley blinked until the starbursts faded, and decided to take Mouse's sage advice. They deposited him in an office—if thugs had offices. It was pretty much just a windowless room with a rickety straight-back chair and some menacing-looking stains on the concrete floor. There was a drain in the corner—just in case the room had to be hosed down, he guessed.

They slammed him into the chair and left, closing the door behind them.

He concentrated on not sweating, visualized glaciers and avalanches and other cold scenes. Ice fishing…igloos…polar bears…Klondike bars.

But when the door burst open, so did his pores. The last time he'd seen The Carver, the man had been inebriated and sitting on the john with his pants around his ankles, a piece of duct tape over his mouth, his wrists bound with a cable tie.

He had recovered well.

The loan shark was impeccably groomed, his skin tanned and glowing, his salt-and-pepper hair smoothed back from his face, every strand in place. Wesley didn't know much about clothes, but the brown suit and collarless shirt looked expensive, as well as the square-toed shoes. The only thing that hinted the man was a gangster was the thick rope of gold around his neck.

Oh, and the switchblade in his hand.

With one click, a six-inch blade appeared. Wesley leaned forward and vomited the water that had been sitting in his stomach, splashing the man's expensive square-toed shoes.

"Christ," the loan shark said, taking a few steps back. "Are you going to piss yourself next?"

Wesley lifted his head and licked his dry lips. "I hope not."

"Me, too." The Carver leaned down to get in Wesley's face. "You stupid little shit, I ought to gut you for what you did to me."

"I'm sorry," Wesley mumbled.

He looked incredulous. "You're *sorry?*"

"Someone shot up my house when my sister was home. I thought it was your guys. I was wrong."

The Carver paced all around him. Wesley tensed, expecting to feel the blade plunge into his bony body, disemboweling him. Sweat rolled off his nose and dripped onto the floor.

"I brought the memory chip from the camera to give you," he offered.

"Where is it?"

Wesley kicked off one of his tennis shoes. "Under the insole."

The Carver used the knife to lift the insole, then withdrew

the blue memory card, pierced on the tip. "This is the only copy of the pictures?"

"Yes."

The man dropped the punctured card on the floor, then stomped on it for good measure. Every time his heel came down on the chip, Wesley flinched.

When The Carver stopped, he was panting and slightly disheveled. Using his hand, he smoothed his hair back in place, then bestowed a slow smile on Wesley. "But I can understand that you were trying to protect your sister."

Wesley swallowed hard. "You can?"

"Sure. I have sisters. That's why I'm going to let you live."

Relief flooded Wesley's body.

"In return for a fee."

"Fee?"

The man began grooming his nails with the tip of the knife. "For pain and suffering."

"H-how much?"

"Twenty-five large."

Wesley felt weak again. "I don't have twenty-five grand."

"Then you need to raise it, Wesley. By five o'clock."

"I don't know anyone who has money like that."

"Think hard," the loan shark said. "Because if you don't come up with the money, you're a dead man. Then who's going to protect your sister?"

Wesley bit down on the inside of his cheek until he tasted blood.

"I'm a busy man, so you'd better be thinking of who you need to call. I'm going to have a sandwich. I'm sending

Mouse in with your cell phone—he'll make the calls for you. If you try to signal someone or get the police involved, your sister is as good as dead." He walked closer. "Here's a little incentive."

The Carver grabbed Wesley's arm and with a twist of his wrist, sliced a two-inch letter *C* into Wesley's forearm.

The pain was intense. Wesley gasped as his blood dripped onto the floor to mix with the other stains. Since his hands were still cuffed, he pressed his arm to his chest to stem the bleeding. He ground his teeth to keep from crying out in pain.

"With every phone call, you get another letter," The Carver said, his voice deadly calm. "So unless you want my entire name tattooed on your arm, you'd better make them count."

The man strode out of the room and nodded to someone. Mouse walked in holding Wesley's cell phone, all business. "Who do you want me to call?"

Wesley's mind raced.

"You don't want to keep the boss waiting," Mouse advised.

"Chance Hollander."

"Is the number in your phone?"

"Yeah." His arm was throbbing. "Can you uncuff me, man? My hands are numb."

"No can do." Mouse operated the phone with his fat fingers, then held it to Wesley's ear. "The volume is turned up so that I can hear everything. No funny stuff, got it?"

"I lost my sense of humor on the floor," Wesley said. "Watch your step."

He prayed that Chance would pick up. After two rings, he did. "Wes?"

"Yeah, it's me."

"Where the fuck are you, man? Your sister is worried sick. She came over with some pierced chick and they kicked my ass—"

"Dude, listen. I'm in a bind and I need twenty-five grand. Can you help me out?"

"Twenty-five grand, are you nuts? Have you been kidnapped or something?"

"Or something. Can you get it?"

"Yeah, sure. But it'll take me a couple of days."

"I don't *have* a couple of days. What can you scrape together in a couple of hours?"

"Bad timing, dude. I just paid my carriers, and my girls, and I bought a new hot tub—"

"How much?"

"It was a steal—a ten-thousand-dollar model, but I got it for five."

Mouse rolled his eyes and Wesley grimaced. "Not the hot tub! How much can you get together?"

"I could probably find a grand in the couch cushions, but that's about it."

Wesley swallowed against his disappointment. "Okay, thanks anyway."

"Dude, where are you—"

Mouse closed the phone. "You know what this means."

"Come on, man," Wesley pleaded. "Give me a mulligan."

Mouse frowned. "What's a mulligan?"

Note to self: Don't use golf terms when negotiating with street criminals. "A freebie. No one has to know."

"No can do." The big man went to the door, opened it and shook his head.

The Carver came in still chewing his sandwich, and sighed heavily, as if Wesley were causing him to miss his favorite TV show. He opened the switchblade. "Hold him, Mouse."

Wesley resisted, but could only look away. It took more strokes to carve an *A* into his skin, more finesse, more blood. He screamed like a girl.

The Carver used a white handkerchief to wipe the blood off his knife. "I hope for your sake your next call is more productive." He retracted the blade and left the room.

Mouse held up the phone. "Who now?"

Wesley couldn't think for the pain. His blood was everywhere.

"Come on, kid. We all want to go home. Give me a name."

"Liz Fischer. The number is in there."

Mouse dialed it, then held the phone up to Wesley's mouth.

Liz had been his father's attorney and had gotten Wesley off on probation when he'd been busted for hacking into the courthouse database. Recently they'd started banging—everything that Chance had told him about older chicks was true. Carlotta would have an aneurysm if she knew.

Liz answered on the first ring. "Wes? Are you okay? Jack Terry called me asking if I'd seen you."

So Carlotta was beating the bushes. "Uh, I'm fine…for now. But I have a situation here and I need some cash. A lot of it."

"How much?"

"Twenty-five grand."

She gasped. "What kind of trouble are you in?"

"The expensive kind."

"Wesley, you know I adore you. But I can't get involved in whatever mess you're in. I have my career and reputation to think about."

He tried to keep his voice steady. "I wouldn't ask if it wasn't important."

"I'm sorry. I just can't help you. Maybe you should call the police—"

Mouse flipped the phone shut, then sighed. "I should've worn a dark suit." He went to the door, opened it and shook his head.

The Carver reappeared, a paper napkin tucked in his collar like a bib. Wesley considered making a run for it, but he was having trouble even holding his head up. Besides, he was still wearing only one shoe. And he wouldn't get far with his hands cuffed. Mouse held him for the next carving, but Wesley didn't put up much resistance as an *R* was engraved on his arm. He didn't even have the strength to squeal. The Carver left with no conversation.

Wesley was on the verge of passing out.

"You're killing me, kid," Mouse said. "Give me a name— a good one."

With what little strength he had left, Wesley considered his options—all of them bad, but one of them viable. Objectionable, but viable.

He gave Mouse the name and hoped for the best.

5

Carlotta stood in her living room and glared up at Jack. "Why are you just standing there? Do something!"

Jack seemed to struggle for patience. "Carlotta, we can't just send in a SWAT team to storm the place. We need a warrant, and I can't get one without probable cause. I need some kind of proof that Hollis Carver kidnapped Wesley or—" He broke off. "Or that he's holding him."

"You were going to say proof that he's killed him, weren't you?"

"No."

"So that's the guy's real name—Hollis Carver?"

Jack nodded.

She threw her hands in the air, and cringed when pain zipped up her left arm. "If you're on first-name basis with this criminal, why don't you call him up and ask him if he has Wesley?"

He hesitated. "With Hollis Carver, the communication is one-way."

"Meaning what?"

"Meaning," Hannah interjected, her eyes narrowed at Jack, "The Carver is a narc. And the police leave him alone, right?"

Carlotta looked back to Jack. "Is that true?"

He scratched the back of his neck—she was starting to learn his "tells." He didn't want to say.

"Jack?"

"I can't divulge anything that might impact open and future investigations. But Hollis Carver has been helpful to the APD in cleaning up the city."

"Cleaning it up?"

He jammed his hands on his hips, feet wide. "Yes. Believe it or not, Carlotta, there are a lot worse criminals in this city than The Carver. People selling poison crack cocaine. Sickos running pedophile rings. Serial killers—as if I have to remind you. Hollis Carver lends money to foolish, desperate people. Unless he starts killing off nonpaying customers, it's his business, not the police department's."

She stepped as close to him as she could get without touching him, and lifted her chin. "So he has to kill Wesley before you'll get involved, is that what you're saying?"

A muscle ticked in his jaw. "No, that's not what I'm saying. I sent a couple of uniforms to Carver's warehouse to take a look around. If we find something that might have belonged to Wesley—his bike, for instance—then we'll have something to work with. Until then, you need to calm down." He glanced at Hannah, who was parked on the couch. "Help me out here."

Hannah scoffed. "You're on your own, Starsky." She continued flipping through TV channels.

Carlotta looked up at him, changing tack. "I'm scared, Jack."

He sighed. "Carlotta, you're not responsible for the decisions made by the men in your family."

"Why are you bringing up my father?" Her throat constricted and she self-consciously rubbed her arm over the area where the note was tucked into her bra. Her heart beat faster, then she relaxed a little—Jack couldn't possibly know about the note.

He glanced away. Another tell. He was keeping something from her.

But then, she was keeping something from him, too.

He looked back, his expression akin to pity. "I just hate to see you keep getting dragged down by other people's mistakes."

Carlotta set her jaw. "Wesley isn't 'people,' he's my brother."

Jack's phone rang and he stepped away to take the call. Her chest ached with frustration and a clump of emotions she couldn't identify. Jack's attitude was a timely reminder that they were too different, that too many obstacles lay between them. And that he had a very low opinion of her family.

"Hey," Hannah said from the couch. "You know that Kiki chick we were watching on TV the other day? She's fucking *dead*."

Carlotta turned, grateful for the distraction, even if the news was disturbing. She walked over to glance at the warped picture on the TV screen flashing Breaking News: Kiki Deerling Dead At 21. "Turn it up."

"As we first reported earlier today, Kiki Deerling was pronounced dead at a Boca Raton, Florida, hospital around three this morning, after being found unconscious by her publicist at a club during a birthday party in honor of Deerling herself. So far, authorities are being very hush-hush as to the circumstances surrounding the starlet's death. Stay tuned for more details as they are available."

Carlotta made a mournful noise for the loss of a young, vibrant life. She had never met the woman, but like millions of people, felt as if she knew her just from the hundreds of TV impressions. And maybe Kiki didn't deserve her celebrity, but neither did she deserve an abbreviated life.

"Probably drugs," Hannah said matter-of-factly. "Otherwise, why wouldn't they say?"

"Maybe the truth isn't titillating enough," Carlotta said.

Hannah glanced in Jack's direction, then lowered her voice. "Listen, considering you and the brooding detective have a history, maybe you should request that someone else work Wesley's case."

Carlotta surveyed Jack's broad back and her anger intensified. He obviously believed that whatever happened to Wesley, her brother deserved it. "Jack does seem a little too invested in the other side."

The sound of a car pulling into the driveway drew her attention. She walked to the window and her frustration spiked at the sight of the man climbing out of the luxury SUV. Just what she didn't need right now—a visit from Peter. Although it was strange to see him driving something other than his little two-seater sports car.

Then the passenger side door opened and she shrieked. "Wesley!" She brushed past Jack, who was also staring out the window, and closing his phone.

"Guess I can call off the nationwide search," he said dryly.

She shot him a hateful look, then bounded out the door as fast as her cast would allow her to move. Jack and Hannah were right behind her.

Wesley was wearing clothes she'd never seen and pulling his bike out of the back of the SUV. He looked drawn, but safe. Beneath his long-sleeved shirt, his arm seemed stiff. "Hey, sis."

"Is that all you have to say? 'Hey, sis'? Are you okay? Why haven't you called? Where have you been? Why are you with Peter?" she demanded in a rush, then gasped, seeing the cuts and bruises on his face. "What happened?"

"Relax," he said, lifting his arm to deflect her attention. "I'm fine. I had an accident on my bike and got a little scraped up, that's all. I didn't call because my phone battery died. I was close to Peter's neighborhood when it happened, so I went to his place. He let me clean up, and gave me a ride home." He tugged at the hem of the overlong shirt. "I owe him for the clothes."

"No, you don't," Peter interjected with a flat little smile. With his blond good looks and impeccable wardrobe, he could've held his own on the cover of *Hamptons* magazine. Carlotta gave him a grateful smile, then looked back to her brother. She wanted to believe his explanation but… "What were you doing all the way up in Peter's neighborhood?"

Wesley looked pained. "I rode up there to get in a card game. Sorry. The good news is that after playing all night, I broke even."

Carlotta pursed her mouth, even more suspicious now that he so readily admitted to going back on his promise to her not to gamble. She looked at Peter, who seemed to be looking everywhere but at her. She glanced at Jack, whose expression told her he didn't believe Wesley's story any more than she did. Then he shrugged, obviously willing to forget the entire incident.

She was irritated with the lot of them. "We'll talk later," she muttered to Wesley. "Meanwhile, you need to call Coop, who was out all night hunting for you, and your probation officer."

"Okay," he said. Then he went over to shake Peter's hand. "Thanks, man."

"No problem."

Okay, now she was *really* suspicious. Peter and her brother barely knew each other, but Wesley had never bothered to hide his disdain for Peter's actions when their parents left, dumping her and leaving her in the lurch. On the other hand, she had told him about their father calling Peter, so maybe Wesley had warmed toward her former fiancé. Or maybe he'd ridden to Peter's house to talk about the phone call....

Wesley disappeared into the house, taking his secrets with him for the time being. Hannah gave them a group wave. "Since the prodigal son has returned, I'm outta here."

"Thanks, Hannah, for staying with me," Carlotta said to her friend. "I'll call you."

After Hannah pulled away in her van, Carlotta was left standing between Jack and Peter, each of whom seemed to be waiting for the other to leave.

"I need to talk to you," Jack said to her pointedly. When Peter gave him a hard look, he added, "It's business."

"Can't it wait?" she asked, not in the mood for more sparring.

"No."

Peter shuffled his feet. "I guess I'll be going."

"I'll walk with you," Carlotta said, then followed him around to the driver's side of the SUV, giving them some privacy from Jack.

"Peter," she said quietly. "What really happened?"

"It happened just the way Wesley explained." But his blue eyes were evasive, his tone practiced.

Her heart swelled with gratitude. "I have a feeling that I owe you a great debt."

"You don't owe me anything," Peter said, taking her good hand and lifting it to his mouth for a kiss that conjured up images of other things he used to do to her when they were younger. "I'll always be here for you, Carly, and for Wesley."

"Thank you," she murmured. When Wesley had gone missing, it hadn't even occurred to her to call Peter. In fact, she'd gone out of her way to conceal most of the Wren family doings from him. She didn't want him to know that the warning his parents had given him ten years ago—that her family would go to the dogs—had pretty much happened.

"Don't forget that I'm holding something for you."

The ring. "I won't forget." And her heart was so full of good memories and goodwill toward Peter for helping Wesley, she would have agreed to marry him at that moment if he'd asked.

Instead he honored her previous request not to rush her, and climbed in his vehicle. She waved until the car disappeared, then turned back to Jack, whose disposition seemed to have further soured.

"What did you need to talk about?" she asked. "If it's about Wesley, I don't believe his story for a minute—"

"It's about your father," he interrupted.

Her heart stuttered. "What about him?"

"A Holiday Inn in Daytona Beach, Florida, was robbed at gunpoint a few days ago. When all the fingerprints were run, one set matched up to Randolph Wren."

Her entire body tingled. She shook her head in confusion. "What are you saying? That my dad robbed this hotel?"

"No. All I'm saying is that sometime recently, your dad was there. He could've been a guest, or visiting a guest…"

"Or he could've robbed the place," she finished.

Jack's face told her that it was a distinct possibility. "I'm driving down to take a look, but I wanted you to know. I'll let you decide whether you want to tell Wesley."

"I'll go with you," she offered.

"Absolutely not."

"But I'm off work right now—it's perfect timing."

"What part of 'absolutely not' don't you understand? Carlotta, you can't get involved in your father's case! I can't spend all my time saving you from the scrapes you get yourself into."

"But that's the beauty of it. I'll already be with you."

"No. No. *No.*"

"Are you taking your girlfriend, Liz?"

He puffed up, meaning she'd hit a nerve. "She's not my girlfriend. But…I thought I might ask her to ride along in case I bump into her client while I'm there."

"So they can have a tumble for old times' sake? That's nice of you." She squinted. "Why don't you have a partner for these kinds of things, Jack?"

"I'm on the waiting list, but the department is short of manpower."

"So when are you leaving?"

"Day after tomorrow."

She shook her head, frustrated with the whole situation. "Don't mention this to Wesley. And let me know if you bump into dear old Dad." Carlotta turned and walked stiffly toward the house.

"Carlotta, don't be like this. I didn't have to tell *you,* you know."

But she didn't look back because she didn't want him to see the abject humiliation coursing through her. Her father had left a stink on the family that they couldn't seem to get away from. It was mortifying to think that of all the policemen who could capture her fugitive father, it would probably be Jack who ultimately brought him down.

6

Carlotta gave the new living room window one last swipe, then stood back to admire the shine. But instead of crystal-clear sparkle, the glass was smeared with cloudy streaks.

"You have to use newspaper to get the best shine," Wesley said from behind her.

She turned and frowned. "You don't say? I see you decided to grace the world with your presence today. It's almost noon."

"Sorry," he mumbled. "I was up most of the night before."

Seeing the dark circles under his brown eyes, she nursed a pang of remorse. He looked so much like their father—lean, with sharp features a male model would kill for. But he didn't have their father's confidence, the ability to win over a room. Wesley was more cerebral. He preferred his books to people. She was sure he had no idea how handsome he was. "Are you ever going to tell me what you were doing?"

"I told you. I was playing cards."

"Uh-huh." She eyed his clothing. "It's pretty warm today for long sleeves, don't you think?"

He shrugged, but she could see the bulk of a bandage beneath the fabric of his shirt.

"You must have scraped your arm pretty badly," she said, fishing.

"Man against asphalt, asphalt always wins."

"Hmm. Did Peter bandage you up?"

"Yep."

Wesley still wasn't looking at her. His reluctance to talk about what had really happened cemented her decision not to mention what Jack had told her about their father. After all, the robbery in Daytona Beach could be a dead end, a mistaken identification.

"Mrs. Winningham said she gave you a get-well card for me."

"She did, but I lost it."

"When you had the accident on your bicycle?"

"Yeah. Sorry."

He was *so* lying about the bicycle accident. "That's okay, I'll tell her I got it anyway. Are you working with Coop later?"

"Not today. I have to check in with my probation officer."

"She sounded pretty worried about you yesterday."

"Really?"

It was the closest thing she'd seen to a smile on his face since he'd arrived home. "Really. And she said that you impressed the city computer guy you interviewed with. You start your community service Monday?"

"That's the plan."

"Are you going to be able to work with Coop and do your community service, too?"

"Yeah. Coop is cutting back on body retrievals for a while. He said he was doing special projects for the morgue."

"The morgue has special projects?"

Wesley shrugged and walked into the kitchen. "Want a sandwich?"

"No, thanks." But she followed him. "I'm sure Coop was relieved to hear from you last night."

"I guess."

"Wesley, he was worried. He spent the entire night driving around looking for you."

"He shouldn't have. Besides, he did that for you, not for me."

"That's not true. He's very fond of you."

"Maybe, but he's got it bad for *you*."

A flush climbed her neck. "Coop is…nice."

"Yeah, but he's not loaded like Peter."

Carlotta arched an eyebrow. "Is that an endorsement for Peter?"

He turned back to the refrigerator. "Are we out of milk?"

"Look in the back." Carlotta wondered about his sudden attachment to Peter. Something illicit had definitely transpired. She could think of only one reason Wesley would call Peter—money. What had Wesley gotten her former fiancé in the middle of?

And how would she ever be able to repay the man?

"What are you doing after you meet with your probation officer?" she asked quietly.

Another shrug. "I'll probably go hang out with Chance."

She frowned. "I don't like you spending time with that derelict."

"He's not so bad."

"Wesley, he told me what the two of you did to your loan shark at the strip club."

He paused in the door of the refrigerator for just a second. "He shouldn't have done that."

"Hannah and I kind of beat it out of him."

"It was just a prank."

"It could've gotten you killed! He said you did it to protect me?"

Her brother shrugged again.

"You don't have to protect me, Wesley."

He closed the refrigerator door, his eyes wide. "These men are dangerous, Carlotta. You don't know."

"So stop doing business with them. Get your life together. Think about college."

He looked anguished for a few seconds, then angry. "I changed my mind about the sandwich. See you later."

She knew better than to try to stop him. He was through talking. The front door banged, and she only hoped that whatever had happened the night he was gone had scared him straight.

She turned her attention back to the streaked window, attacking it with cleaner and a page of newspaper fished out of the mail basket. When she stood back, the sun shining through the spotless window was almost blinding. "You were right, you little shit," she mumbled.

Guilt plucked at her for not telling him about the note their father had left and the development in Daytona Beach. She pulled the piece of paper out of her bra and read it again. Randolph had been within arm's length of her. He could have pulled her aside, revealed his identity…given her a hug and a kiss…and an explanation. Why hadn't he?

Because he didn't trust her. He knew she'd gone along with the fake funeral to lure her parents out of hiding. Had he felt betrayed?

Anger whipped through her—he had betrayed them first. He and her mother, Valerie. Her father had left town to escape a trial and, presumably, jail time. But her mother, who always maintained a martini in one hand and a cigarette in the other, didn't even have an excuse. She had simply chosen her husband over her children. Carlotta had gotten past being angry for herself, but she would never forgive their mom for abandoning Wesley at the age of nine.

He'd slept in Carlotta's bed for a year, clinging to her, crying for his mother every night until he was too exhausted to stay awake.

Carlotta's eyes watered just remembering. No one but she knew how Wesley had suffered. He'd been a slight kid, with a genius IQ, and the creative capacity to concoct all kinds of stories about why their parents had left. Eventually he'd decided that their father was some kind of secret agent forced to go underground. She knew Wesley had outgrown the elaborate tales intellectually, but she wondered if he still entertained some of those childhood fantasies emotionally.

Over the years, she'd vacillated between hoping their

parents were found and hoping they were lost forever. But she was starting to worry that Wesley would be at dangerous loose ends until there was some resolution to the jagged tear in their family.

Was their father close to turning himself in? Was he growing tired of life on the lam? Was that why he'd gotten sloppy and left fingerprints at a crime scene? She shook her head, trying to imagine her parents as a crime duo—her dad wielding a gun while her mom walked around holding open a designer bag for everyone to deposit their wallet in.

Frankly, the most ludicrous part of it all was the thought of Valerie entering a Holiday Inn. If her mother had any say, they would hold up only five-star establishments.

No, Carlotta couldn't picture her parents as armed robbers. They wouldn't have to resort to anything so overt. Randolph Wren could charm anyone out of his or her life savings, and Valerie was the kind of woman that men threw money at. Model-thin and beautiful, with an aura that mesmerized those around her, she was movie-star glamorous, and everyone had been happy to be in her entourage. Carlotta suspected that being on the run had been hard for her mother, who was accustomed to lavish attention. But it only demonstrated how emotionally dependent she was on Randolph…and on her vodka.

The phone rang, rousing Carlotta from her dark thoughts.

"Hello?"

"It's Coop."

She smiled into the phone. "Hi, there. You just missed Wesley."

"That's okay. It's you I want."

She gave a little laugh, enjoying the easy flirtation. "In that case, what can I do for you, sir?"

He groaned. "So many things. Seriously, though, did I catch you at a bad time?"

"Are you kidding? I'm so bored, I'm cleaning."

"I figured you might be going stir-crazy being off work, so I have a proposition."

She pursed her mouth. "I'm listening."

"Well, this isn't exactly romantic, but I have a VIP body pickup in Boca Raton, and I wondered if you'd like to ride along. We could leave tomorrow and have a couple of days of fun in the sun beforehand."

"Boca Raton? Oh, my God, is it Kiki Deerling?"

"You know her?"

"Just from television. She's hard to miss."

"Yes. This trip is to pick up her body, but no one can know about it. I signed a confidentiality agreement, so mum's the word."

"Don't worry. I won't tell anyone."

"So how about it? Want to hit the road for a few days? Separate rooms, of course…unless I can persuade you otherwise."

She laughed at his teasing tone, but entertained a little shiver of excitement. A few days alone with Coop, getting to know each other, no pressure. He wasn't holding a ring for her, and he wasn't hell-bent on capturing her father. His only angle was tempting her with sandy beaches and icy drinks.

Suddenly Carlotta's mind raced to assemble disparate bits of information. "I've never been to Boca Raton and my geography is a little rusty. Would we be driving close to Daytona Beach?"

"Right through it, as a matter of fact."

A wicked smile curved Carlotta's mouth. "What time do we leave?"

7

Wesley squeezed the hand brake on his bike and grunted when pain seized the muscles under the bandage on his forearm. He'd convinced Peter not to take him to the emergency room for stitches, but that meant the wounds would take longer to heal.

His opinion of Peter Ashford had never been high. Wesley had been young when the guy had dumped his sister shortly after their parents had left town. But he remembered how Carlotta had cried herself to sleep holding Peter's picture, how the man's absence seemed to affect her more than the absence of their parents. Probably because, like Wesley, she had expected their parents to return any day. Peter, on the other hand, had apparently made it clear he wasn't coming back.

Carlotta had been devastated, and Wesley knew she blamed their folks for Peter breaking the engagement. She'd said he hadn't wanted his family name intertwined with theirs, tainted from their father's behavior. As Wesley had grown older, though, he'd blamed himself for Peter leaving. It seemed obvious that the man hadn't wanted to be saddled with a kid.

But since Peter's wife had died, he'd certainly been trying to make up for his past behavior, coming around and acting protective of Carlotta. When Wesley started to feel bad about taking advantage of Peter's guilt, he told himself that he was doing the man a favor, giving him a chance to get back into the Wrens' good graces. Peter had agreed not to tell Carlotta about the incident at The Carver's warehouse— or the money that had changed hands—and for that, Wesley was grateful.

He must have been one hell of a mess judging from the expression on Peter's face when he'd picked Wesley up at the prescribed badass corner after Mouse had counted the cash with his thick fingers. Ashford hadn't said, but he was probably glad he'd driven his luxury SUV instead of his Porsche to shuttle Wesley and his bike home. Still, it was going to be hard to get bloodstains out of leather upholstery.

To his credit, the man had asked only if Wesley wanted to go to the hospital, holding his tongue about what had transpired until after Wesley had showered and eaten a pizza that Peter had ordered. Then, while he cleaned the wound on Wesley's arm and wrapped it with a bandage, he'd extracted the story one well-placed question at a time.

The guy should've been a lawyer, Wesley thought wryly.

He wheeled into the parking lot of the building that housed the probation office to which he'd been assigned after his arrest for breaking into the courthouse computer. Once a week he checked in with E. Jones, his surprisingly hot probation officer, who cut him zero slack. His pulse picked up just at the thought of seeing E. In those dark moments when it looked as if he might not get out of that dingy, windowless room alive, he'd imagined E.'s smile and the way her red hair fell over her shoulders. She was way out of his league, but he could dream.

He locked up his bike and slung his backpack over his shoulder with his good arm. His cell phone rang. Both the movement of retrieving it and the name on the display made him wince—Liz Fischer. He connected the call. "This is Wes."

"Wes," she crooned. "It's Liz."

"Yeah, what's up?"

"I was just calling to see if you were okay. After your phone call yesterday, I was worried."

Right. "I'm fine."

"I hope you understand why I couldn't get involved, Wes."

"I do."

"Good. But I'd like to make it up to you."

His eyebrows shot up. "What did you have in mind?"

"Come over tonight."

His cock twitched. There was no denying the woman was a looker, and great in the sack. But he wasn't sure he could trust her.

Of course, she had no reason to trust him, either. He had

ransacked her files on his father's case in her guesthouse, the place where she stored her archives, as well as "entertained."

"Maybe," he said. "I'll let you know."

"Don't take too long," she said, then hung up.

He put away the phone and walked into the building, thinking he could do worse for evening entertainment. But he'd been planning to cook a nice dinner for Carlotta, considering she'd been so worried about him, and that her already pathetic kitchen skills were now further hampered by the cast on her arm.

Even though his own dexterity would be curbed somewhat by his bandage, he could outcook Carlotta using only his thumbs and elbows. It was a good thing she was so damn pretty—no man was going to marry her for her culinary skills.

He walked into the now-familiar office and nodded to the now-familiar surly woman behind the check-in desk. "Wesley Wren to see E. Jones." He scanned the waiting room as nonchalantly as possible. The Carver had once sent a man here to remind Wesley that he was behind on his payments, and the thug had punctuated the message by snubbing out his cigar on Wesley's hand. That wound was still pink and puckering. If he didn't find a way to get out of debt soon, his entire body would look like a strip of badly cut meat. Thankfully, though, no one in the room seemed to care he was there.

The old bat at the window sniffed. "You can go on back."

He walked to E.'s office door, adjusted the sleeve of his shirt so that it didn't emphasize the bandage underneath, and rapped.

"Come in."

He swung open the door and miserably pondered the tightening of his chest when Eldora Jones lifted her green-eyed gaze to his.

"Hello, Wesley."

"Hi."

"Have a seat."

He did, across from her desk. She wore a white buttoned-up blouse that might have been prim if not for the curves it clung to.

"How are you?" she asked. Her voice sounded friendly, but he'd been meeting with her long enough to know that even an innocuous question was usually leading somewhere.

"Good."

"Why did you miss our appointment yesterday?"

He shifted in his chair. "I…was with some guys, lost track of time. Sorry."

"You couldn't call?"

"Battery on my phone died."

"Your sister was really worried. She was afraid you were hurt."

"I'm fine." He smiled and lifted his hands, but the motion pulled the tightened skin under the bandage. The sudden pain took his breath away and made his arm jerk involuntarily.

"Did something happen to your arm?" she asked.

"Bicycle accident," he said, continuing with his lie. "I scraped it."

She studied his face with a half smile, her green eyes

saying she didn't believe him. "Sounds as if you were lucky. You could've been hurt much worse."

He nodded. "Yeah."

"You do realize that missing your scheduled meetings is a violation of your probation?"

Wesley wet his lips. "Thanks for letting me reschedule."

"Next time you won't get off so easily."

He nodded.

"But I'm glad you're okay," she added softly.

He glanced up sharply at her tone. She sounded as if she…cared. But E. averted her gaze, cleared her throat and opened his file folder, back to business.

"I heard from Richard McCormick. He said he was very impressed with your computer knowledge when the two of you spoke. He said if your community service work goes well, he might even consider hiring you."

Wesley knew it was meant to be a compliment, but he had no intention of toiling away in a cubicle for city wages until he keeled over. "He seemed like a nice enough guy."

"When do you start?"

"Monday."

"Is that going to be a problem with your body-moving job?"

"Nah, Coop's cool with my community service. He said he'd work around it."

She made a couple of notes, then closed his folder. "Is there anything else you'd like to talk about?"

"Thanks for the concert tickets. I heard Elton was great."

"Yeah, the show went on after they took your sister to the hospital. I'm glad she's okay."

"Thanks." He fidgeted. "Did your boyfriend enjoy it?"

A little wrinkle appeared in her forehead. "Leonard? Yes, he enjoyed the concert."

Wes's mouth watered. He wanted so badly to tell her that the concert wasn't the first place he'd met Leonard.

E. sat back in her chair. "Are you gambling?"

"No." Not at this very moment, anyway.

"Still hanging out with that drug-dealer friend of yours?"

E. had intercepted him on an errand Chance had asked him to run in exchange for money Wesley owed him. Wesley hadn't known for certain what was in the gym bag, but he'd had a pretty good idea. E. had allowed him to take the bag back to "where it came from," without any repercussions.

"He's not a bad guy," he said of his friend Chance.

"He's going to land you behind bars...or worse."

Wesley wiped his hand over his mouth to keep from telling her that her boyfriend, Leonard, was also keeping company with his drug-dealing friend. "I'll take that under advisement," he responded, standing. "Are we through?"

E. pressed her lips together, then gave a curt nod. "I'll see you next week. Take care of that arm."

Wesley left the building in a foul mood. By the time he rode to Chance's condo, his arm was throbbing.

His chuffy friend grinned widely when he opened the door. "Dude—you're alive!"

Wesley howled in pain when Chance pulled him into a choke hold hug. "Watch my arm, man."

"What happened to it?"

Wesley set his jaw against the pain, leaning over and holding his arm. When he could talk again he said, "My loan officer decided to take a pound of flesh."

"Is it broken?"

"No. I don't think that would hurt as bad." Although Carlotta might argue the point.

Chance dug into his pocket. "Here, dude, take a couple of these."

Wesley stared at the white pills suspiciously. "What are they?"

"OxyContin. It's great stuff, man. Will make you feel good fast."

"Thanks." He took one and swallowed it dry.

Chance dumped the rest into Wesley's hand. "For later, dude. If you want to feel like you've just been laid by the woman of your dreams, chew it. Want something to drink?"

"Soda, if you have it."

"Coming up. What the hell happened to you?"

"I went to try to patch things up with The Carver."

Chance's eyes bulged. "Dude! Are you suicidal?"

"I thought it was the best thing to do, under the circumstances. He was going to come after me eventually."

Chance cracked open a can of Mountain Dew and handed it to Wesley. "So what did he do to you?"

"Cut me up a little."

"Really? I always wondered if the rumors were true. Did he use a bowie knife?"

"Switchblade."

"Cool." Then his friend blanched. "I mean—fuck. That had to hurt like a son of a bitch."

"Yeah."

"And he wanted twenty-five grand?"

"Yeah. A fee for pain and suffering, he called it."

"Sorry I couldn't help you out, man."

"That's okay. I got it."

"Where?"

"Friend of the family."

"Sweet. So does that clear your debt with The Carver?"

"Hell, no. Like I said, that was just a fee to let me keep breathing. I still owe the guy, like, twelve grand. But I'm making payments."

"I'm glad you're back. I have an economics exam next week. Think you could take it for me?"

Chance's sense of self-preservation was more keen than anyone's he'd ever met. "Sure. Meanwhile, I need a game. Can you keep your ears open?"

Chance grinned. "Sure."

"I'll need a bankroll. Same deal as before—you pay the sit fee, we split the winnings?"

"Deal. I'll make some phone calls right now. Have a seat, man, and let the drug kick in."

Wesley walked into the living room—a bachelor's dream of black leather furniture and oversize electronics. Predictably, the large flat screen was showing porn, this one of a homemade variety. What the film lacked in quality it made up for in candid angles. Wesley switched the input to the latest Xbox gaming system and pulled up Poker Smash.

He settled into a chair and played a few hands. The adrenaline and the caffeine helped to speed the painkiller through his system. He glanced around at Chance's toys, conceding that his friend lived a charmed life.

His life would've been like this if his father hadn't been forced to abandon his family. Wesley remembered the piles of toys he'd had when he was little, the expansive bedroom painted with blue sailboats, the platform that had held a running train with a real switching station, the navy-and-gray uniform of the private school he'd attended. When his father had been indicted, the train had been sold along with the house. And although Wesley had been allowed to finish the year at his school, by the next fall, his parents had been gone for several months. Carlotta had sat him down and explained that they didn't have the money for private school, and soothed him with the promise that he'd have much more fun in public school, anyway.

He hadn't. He'd been a shy, smart little kid with big glasses, a prime target for bullies. And he'd missed his parents terribly. He'd saved his acting out for home. In hindsight, he'd been a real pain in the ass to his sister…and it seemed that things hadn't changed much. Ten years later, he was still getting shoved around, and was still being a pain in the ass to his sister.

A knock sounded on the door.

"Get that, will you, man?" Chance shouted.

Wesley looked up to see his friend talking on his cell phone in the kitchen and scribbling on a piece of paper. He pushed himself to his feet and got a head rush from the painkiller.

Chance was right—the OxyContin was damn good stuff. Wes walked carefully to the door and opened it, then balked.

E.'s boyfriend, Leonard, stood there, tall, dark and beefy. "Is Hollander around?"

"Uh, yeah, he's on the phone. Come on in."

When Wesley stepped aside to allow him to pass, he noticed the man was carrying a black gym bag similar to the one that Chance had asked him to deliver to some shady character in a shadier part of town—the errand that E. had thwarted. It was ironic that her boyfriend appeared to have picked up where Wesley'd left off.

He closed the door. "I'm Wes."

Leonard flicked his gaze over him as he paced. "Yeah, we've met before."

"Right. I didn't know if you—"

"Hollander!" Leonard yelled, obviously impatient.

From the kitchen, Chance held up a finger—his middle one—but wrapped up his conversation and snapped his phone closed. "Wes," he said, striding toward them, "there's a big game next Wednesday and you're in it. Five grand a seat, twenty seats, and the pot is forty large, twenty to the winner."

Wesley nodded, but glanced sideways at Leonard. He didn't trust the man with his business, and it didn't help that he pretty much hated him for being with E. in the first place, and deceiving her to boot. He looked at Chance. "I'm outta here. Call you later."

He grabbed his backpack and banged the door shut behind him. He opted for the stairs instead of the elevator, but the OxyContin slowed him down a bit. Once he got outside, though, the fresh air helped to clear his head. He was unlocking his bike when he heard the sound of heavy footsteps behind him. He recognized Leonard's hefty shadow before he could even look up. When he straightened, he half expected the guy to kick sand in his face.

"Does E. know what you do on the side?" Wesley asked, trying to look taller.

"No," the guy said through big, gritted teeth. "And if she finds out, I know where to land with both feet, *capiche?*"

Wesley bit down on the inside of his cheek. "Is that all?"

"No. Got a message for you from The Carver."

Wesley swallowed. Shit, he didn't see that coming. "You work for The Carver?"

"Listen up, dickhead, because this is the deal of a lifetime. A way to clear everything you still owe."

Wesley broke out in an instant sweat, exacerbated by the drug pumping through his bloodstream. Deal of a lifetime?

Something told him this was going to be anything but.

8

Carlotta checked her watch and tried to ignore the fierce itching under her cast. She'd been ready for more than an hour. Her suitcase sat next to the door and her heart pounded with nervous excitement. She was eager to get out of this house for a few days, and she was looking forward to spending time with Coop. Even though she knew he had a crush on her, she also knew he wouldn't pressure her, like Peter, or mess with her mind, like Jack.

And when the time came, it would be easy to slip away from Coop for a few hours. She nursed the tiniest bit of guilt over using the trip as a cover to get to Daytona Beach, but no one had to know. She would locate the Holiday Inn where her father's fingerprints had been found, and ask a few questions of her own. Maybe he was working there. If he was in disguise, Jack could easily overlook him. He could talk to him and not know it was him…her father would love that. She wasn't even sure that she would recognize Randolph, but after her brush with him at the fake funeral, she at least knew to be looking past the obvious.

At the sound of Kiki Deerling's name on the television, she turned her head to listen. Knowing that they would be bringing Kiki's body back to Atlanta made her feel more connected to the dead girl. Carlotta reached for the remote control and turned up the volume.

"Fans of Kiki Deerling are still reeling from the news of her sudden death in Boca Raton, Florida. Details surrounding the starlet's final moments are still sketchy, but initial reports are that Deerling might have suffered a severe asthma attack. Deerling's publicist, Marquita White, issued the following statement, quote, 'We are so saddened by the horrific tragedy of Kiki Deerling's passing. This is an extremely difficult time for her loved ones and we ask the media to please respect the family's privacy,' unquote.

"Meanwhile, members of the Deerling family are not talking to the press. Here's a clip showing Kiki's ex-boyfriend, Grammy award-winning singer Matt Pearson, being turned away at the door of the Deerlings' home in Boca Raton by Kiki's older sister, Kayla. You can clearly see that Kayla has been crying. They appear to exchange angry words, then Pearson leaves, stumbling twice on the way back to his car. It's widely known that she disapproved of her sister's alliance with Pearson."

Kayla Deerling was an older, brunette version of her more famous sister, except of a more normal weight, Carlotta observed wryly. She ran a restaurant in Buckhead called Diamonds, which was all the rage with the critics.

Reservations were hard to come by and the menu was way out of Carlotta's price range.

"Pearson has been arrested twice for alleged heroin use, and has been in and out of rehab in the past few months. Deerling and Pearson have not been linked romantically for over a year, and Deerling has been photographed with many other men since. Sources say that Matt Pearson wasn't on the Boca birthday party guest list, but showed up unannounced, and Kiki herself let him in."

Matt Pearson was portrayed in the media to be arrogant and reckless, and Carlotta had heard enough reports of him trashing hotel rooms and smashing sports cars that she was inclined to believe it was true. What was it about bad boys, she wondered, that made women overlook their wayward behavior?

"No memorial arrangements have been announced, but the Deerlings own a cemetery plot in their hometown of Atlanta, where the family has many business investments, including the flagship store for the Deerling jewelry empire, and Diamonds restaurant. Experts tell us if there's an autopsy, it could be a week or more before Kiki is laid to rest. Despite the initial reports linking her death to asthma, rumors abound that drugs played a part in the young woman's collapse. Stay tuned for upcoming details on the tragic death of Kiki Deerling."

Carlotta turned down the volume, shaking her head at the pointlessness. It was a very sad ending for a woman who might have gone on to more noble pursuits, but instead would be memorialized for her excessive partying and personal humiliations played out in the tabloids.

At the sound of a car pulling into the driveway, Carlotta clicked off the TV and jumped up to look out the window. Seeing Coop's white van, she smiled. "Wesley, I'm leaving!" she called. "See you in a few days!" She doubted if he heard her, since the fan in his bedroom was still running, but she looked toward the hallway in case he emerged. She had waited up until midnight last night before giving in and going to bed, but had left a note on his door telling him she was going on a road trip with Coop. Wesley was clearly avoiding her because he didn't want to discuss what had happened. And she wasn't ready to pry the truth out of Peter. In fact, she hadn't even told him that she was going out of town.

Wesley was avoiding her; she was avoiding Peter. *Round and round we go.*

Maybe by the time she returned to Atlanta, Wesley would be willing to open up. Carlotta sighed in the direction of his closed bedroom door. They seemed bound and yet separated by old and new secrets. A few days away from each other would probably do them both good.

The doorbell rang. She hurried to the door and opened it, unable to suppress her smile. Coop looked handsome and fit in a black T-shirt and jeans, dressed more casually than usual, and wearing it well. Her heart tripped ridiculously, as if they were going to the prom.

"Hi," he said with a grin, scanning her summer outfit of white pants, pink buttoned-up shirt and sandals. "You look great."

She blushed and was struck with the sudden sensation that

this trip might be laced with more sexual tension than she'd anticipated. "Thanks. But I'm so over this cast."

He wagged his eyebrows. "I'm a doctor—I think it's kind of hot."

Carlotta laughed at his foolishness and took one last look into the hallway. Then she turned back with a shrug. "I thought Wesley might come out to say goodbye."

"Are you sure he's in there?"

"Yeah, I heard him roll in about two this morning. And the note I left on the door is gone."

"He knows where we're going?"

"You said it was hush–hush, so I said we were going on a road trip for the morgue, but not where or why." She smiled. "I said that you felt sorry for me and were letting me tag along."

Coop grinned. "Somehow I doubt he'll buy that story."

"I did."

He grinned wider. "I know."

She punched him on the arm and he faked pain, then picked up her rather large suitcase and staggered. "Whoa! You got a body in here?"

"Just a few necessities," she sang as she closed the door and locked it behind them.

"How much room does a bathing suit take up? I should've been more explicit about our itinerary." He stopped. "You did bring a bathing suit, didn't you?"

"Several," she taunted.

Coop groaned. "I can't wait to get there."

Carlotta laughed, then squashed a pang of guilt and

pressed her advantage. "I was hoping we could stop for the night in Daytona."

"Fine with me. But what's the interest in Daytona? You're not going to look up an old boyfriend, are you?"

She gave a nervous laugh. "No. Um…there's a Neiman's there I want to visit."

"No problem," he said. "Daytona is about a six-hour drive. If traffic is decent, and figuring in time to stop for lunch, we should be there by late afternoon."

She glanced toward the garage and frowned. Wesley had left the door up a few inches when he'd come home last night. "Give me a minute to close the garage door, Coop. The opener must be broken—it's been making a grinding noise." She sighed. Another expense.

He looked over and held up his arm. "Let me check it out."

She followed him. After he raised the garage door, she peered into the dimly lit interior. Her blue Monte Carlo—damnable car—sat where it had been since her accident. And her beloved but broken-down white Miata convertible sat next to it. Wesley's bike stood between the two vehicles.

"Everything looks fine," she told Coop.

"I hope Wes doesn't try to drive on his suspended license while you're gone."

"He won't." She smiled widely. "I have the keys."

"Does he have the key to the garage?" he asked, pointing to the handle.

"Yes. You can lock it."

Carlotta bit her lip, wondering where Wesley had been last night, if he'd gone to see his mystery girlfriend. Or if he'd been gambling again. Maybe he'd left the garage door up because he'd been drinking. She sighed. He certainly didn't need another vice.

After securing the garage, Coop opened the middle door of the van and set her suitcase behind the driver's seat. Behind the bench seat was a mesh screen separating the passenger area from the gurney at the rear. It was hard to imagine that on the way back, they would be carrying the body of Kiki Deerling with them.

Coop opened the passenger side door and helped Carlotta climb in, since she only had use of one arm. His body language was gentle and protective. Despite Coop's flirting, she knew he'd never want to make her feel uncomfortable. But his touch on her arm and waist wasn't unwelcome.

He helped her fasten the seat belt, his proximity sending a whiff of aftershave into her lungs. Clean and natural—like him.

"All set?" he asked with a smile, his light brown eyes crinkling in merriment behind black horn-rimmed glasses. The knowledge that he was happy being with her left her a little breathless. She needed to tread lightly here…for both their sakes.

"Yeah," she said breezily. "All set."

He stepped back and closed her door. She watched him stride in front of the van, his movements sure but relaxed, a man who was comfortable with himself. Her pulse quickened in response. She could see why her brother admired

Coop. His quiet confidence was compelling…and sexy. Coop had promised her separate hotel rooms for the trip if she wanted, but at the moment, it was deliciously entertaining to think about the alternative.

Of course, after six hours together in this van, they might be ready to drown each other in the Atlantic Ocean.

9

"Great day," Coop said happily, once he settled into the driver's seat and turned over the ignition.

It was, Carlotta conceded. Another warm summer day in the South, with an intensely blue sky and one or two puffy clouds bouncing around. She smiled up through the windshield as they pulled out of the driveway, and even waved at crabby Mrs. Winningham in her yard. As they drove away from the house, she could feel the stress draining from her body. A sigh escaped her.

"You okay?" Coop asked.

She nodded, putting on white Gucci sunglasses. "It's been a long time since I've had a vacation."

He grinned. "Then I'll have to make sure you have a good time. But first, I need to make a few phone calls. Do you mind?"

"Not at all."

"Why don't you sort through the CDs in the console and pick out something you'd like to listen to?"

He turned on his blinker and merged the long van into the traffic on the I-75/I-85 connector. The multiple lanes were clogged with locals commuting to the airport and out-of-towners following I-75 to Florida. Beyond the airport, traffic thinned, but it was still a stressful stretch of road to travel for most drivers. Coop, however, seemed perfectly at ease behind the wheel of the large vehicle. He had nice hands, with long, blunt-tipped fingers. She wondered idly if he'd ever worn a wedding ring.

She opened the console between the seats and began flipping through the eclectic mix of CDs—the Beatles, Allison Kraus, Stevie Ray Vaughn, Evanescence, and some blues singers and rock groups she'd never heard of. While she loaded the CD player, she listened to Coop's voice as he talked to the microphone on his visor. He used an economy of words, but still managed to come across as friendly and warm. The people on the other end of the line all seemed happy to hear from him—especially the women. A handsome, single physician…he must have a lot of opportunities for dates, she acknowledged.

He made sure that his pickups were covered while he was gone, and handled some business for his uncle's funeral home that kept him on the phone for nearly an hour. He kept throwing Carlotta apologetic glances, but she didn't mind. It gave her a chance to study him.

Cooper Craft had a nice profile, strong and interesting, with kind eyes and a well-formed nose. He had a habit of stabbing at his glasses, and he was quick to smile. He had nice teeth, the kind that came from drinking lots of milk. She imagined him sitting at a table at home eating a grilled cheese sandwich and drinking a glass of milk…alone. For all his amiability, Cooper seemed to hold himself aloof from others, carefully guarding his privacy. Most of what she knew about his past, she had heard from Jack and from June Moody, a friend of hers who owned the cigar bar she sometimes visited. They'd given her sketchy details about Coop's fall from grace as chief medical examiner because of his drinking. Cooper seemed to have come through his personal trial intact, but wary.

She certainly knew how that felt.

He reached up to disconnect a call. "That was the last one," he said. "I'm sorry I've been ignoring you."

"No need to apologize. You're still working, after all— unlike me."

"How is your arm?"

"It's itching like crazy," she said, tapping the fiberglass cast. "But otherwise, it's fine. I have to go next week for an X-ray to make sure it's healing okay."

"Any pain?"

"The Percocet the doctor gave me has helped."

He nodded. "You have refills?"

"Yes, plenty, I think."

"It's a miracle you weren't hurt worse. It's lucky that Jack was there to break your fall."

"And that you were there to take care of me until the EMTs arrived," she added.

Coop winked. "My pleasure. I'm sorry about your friend. Have you spoken with him?"

Just thinking about her former coworker Michael Lane made Carlotta's heart squeeze painfully. "No. I heard on the news that he's being held in the psychiatric ward at North-side Hospital."

"So he hasn't been charged yet?"

"Not yet." She fingered the seat belt and changed the subject. "Will we drive on to Boca Raton tomorrow?"

"Yeah, but we won't pick up the body until the day after, Sunday morning. That will give us a little time for some R & R."

"Her death is all over the news. Have you seen it?"

"Yeah. It's sad."

"I can't believe how quickly the media coverage exploded."

"Newspapers keep updated obituaries on file for celeb-rities, just in case they die suddenly."

"Please be kidding."

"Nope. Especially for someone like Kiki, who was making the news regularly for partying hard and erratic behavior."

"Like not wearing panties?" Carlotta asked dryly.

"I said *erratic* behavior." He grinned. "If you ask me, not enough women go without panties."

She laughed and shook her head. It was nice to see this fun, flirty side of him. "I do feel bad, though. Hannah and I were watching an interview with her on TV the other day and I was actually feeling envious."

"Envious? Why?"

Carlotta gave him a wry smile. "Young, beautiful, rich, with a glamorous life. Gee, I don't know why I'd be envious."

"You're young and beautiful."

"I wasn't fishing for compliments. But please go on."

He laughed. "And your life seems pretty exciting to me. I know *my* life has certainly picked up since I met you and Wesley."

"Exciting isn't quite the same as glamorous."

"Neiman's is a pretty glamorous place to work, isn't it?"

"It has its moments," she agreed. "But most of the time I feel like I'm on the outside looking into the lives of other glamorous people."

"You have something better than glam," he said. "You have strength and character. I don't know many women who would give up everything to raise a younger sibling on their own."

She looked at Coop and shook her head. "You give me too much credit. I didn't raise Wesley out of a sense of nobility. My parents didn't leave me a choice."

"You had a choice. You could have abandoned him," he said quietly, "like they did."

"I'd never do that," she stated, her voice tight.

"Exactly. That's why you're worth a dozen of those empty girls who have too much money and too much time on their hands."

"But I used to be like Kiki Deerling," she murmured. "I guess that's why I relate to her."

"Your parents were that wealthy?"

She nodded. "Or at least they lived like they were. Wesley and I had a British nanny. My parents bought the best of everything—cars, jewelry, art, vacations. My dad had a private plane. We even had a chef."

"Wow, I had no idea."

"When the charges were brought against my father and he was fired, my family lost everything. We moved to the town house where Wesley and I live now. They put it in my name to protect it from being seized, so at least we had a place to live after they…left."

"It was paid for?"

She nodded. "But several years ago I had to take out a home equity loan to buy a new heating and air-conditioning unit, replace the kitchen appliances and get caught up on bills. I'm still paying it off."

"I didn't mean to pry."

His pained expression tugged at her heart. "It's okay. I don't know why I'm unloading on you."

"It's my big, broad shoulders," he said ruefully. "Happens all the time."

She smiled at his attempt to lighten the mood. "So when was the last time you had a vacation?"

"I can't remember. But I take off a couple of days a week to go hiking, or attend a film festival, or whatever looks fun."

"You seem content."

He nodded. "I am, mostly."

"Do you miss your old job?"

"As chief medical examiner? I see you've been informed of my checkered past."

"Just the CliffsNotes version. And none of it was told in an unkind way."

He lifted his shoulders in a philosophical shrug. "I do miss being the chief M.E. sometimes. Dr. Abrams and I didn't see eye to eye when we worked together at the morgue. Still don't. But he's been good enough to contract me for body hauling. It keeps me on the periphery of doing what I love, what I'm good at."

"Sounds like you're good at lots of things."

A sly smile curved his mouth. "You don't really expect me to brag, do you?"

"No. That's not your style."

"I have a style?"

"Yeah," she said, angling her head. "You're…understated."

"Oh, gee, that's just what every man wants to hear."

She laughed. "I meant it as a compliment."

"No, I like it," he said, pulling on his chin. "I think I'll put it on a T-shirt."

She laughed harder. From her bag, her cell phone rang. She glanced at the display screen and bit her lip. It was Hannah, who'd made it abundantly clear that she wasn't happy about Carlotta being alone with Coop all weekend at the beach. "I need to get this," she murmured, then flipped up the phone. "Hello?"

Stony silence rang over the line.

"Hello?" Carlotta said, louder.

Silence.

Carlotta sighed. "Okay, be that way." She flipped the phone closed, shaking her head.

"What was that all about?"

"Hannah. She was calling to let me know she's still giving me the silent treatment."

"Oh."

"She's got a thing for you."

"I kind of picked up on that. How long will she make you suffer?"

Carlotta gave him a teasing smile. "I guess that depends on how this weekend goes."

He grinned widely, but the moment was broken by the sound of her phone ringing again. She reached for it. "I hope she doesn't keep doing this." But when she glanced at the display screen, she scowled. *J. Terry*. She didn't want to answer. But on the chance that he had news concerning her father's fingerprints, she murmured, "Excuse me," to Coop and flipped open the phone. "Hello?"

"It's Jack."

"Uh-huh."

"Good morning to you, too."

"What do you want, Jack?"

Coop turned his head toward her, a frown tugging on his mouth before he looked back to the road.

"I feel lousy about the other day," Jack said. "You know I don't want anything bad to happen to Wesley…or to you."

He was extending an olive branch, but she didn't want to let him get close again. Not when he might be bringing her father back from Florida. "You were just doing your job," she said tightly. "Besides, Wesley is okay."

"My hands were tied."

"Well, Liz is probably into that."

An exasperated sigh sounded on the line. "I seem to remember *you* tying a pretty decent square knot from your bedpost to my ankle."

"I'm hanging up now."

"Carlotta—"

She flipped the phone closed and tucked it back into her purse.

Coop looked over at her. "How's Jack?"

"Same. An asshole."

He pursed his mouth. "The two of you seem to have some kind of love-hate thing going on."

"Not love," she said, shaking her finger. "Believe me."

"Okay." He shifted in his seat. "Wesley said that Jack has reopened your father's case?"

"The D.A. had the case reopened, but he assigned it to Jack."

"Tough spot for Jack," Coop ventured.

"He doesn't seem to think so. He's enjoying it. He's determined to find my father and drag him back to Atlanta."

"How do you feel about that?"

"About my father being captured? I'm not sure." She hesitated, then said, "But I think Jack is underestimating him."

"What do you mean?"

"My father is intelligent…clever."

"I assumed so. How else could he have eluded capture all these years?"

Carlotta pressed her lips together, wavering. She stared at

Coop's profile. She could trust him to keep a confidence, and she was desperate to share the secret she'd been harboring. "Coop, my father came to see me."

He pivoted his head, his eyes wide. "Recently?"

"Yes. It turns out he was at my funeral after all, in disguise."

"You're kidding! The cops were everywhere."

Carlotta wanted to respond, but a movement in the back of the van caught her eye. From behind the mesh partition, a sheet-covered body was rising from the floor of the van. Her eyes watered and her heart seized with terror. She pointed, gasping. At last her vocal cords rallied and a scream exploded from her throat.

10

Carlotta screamed, straining against her seat belt, pointing a shaking finger at the sheet-covered body rising in the back of the van.

"What the hell?" Coop swerved, then pulled the vehicle onto the shoulder of the interstate and brought it to a bumpy halt. He flipped on the hazard lights, then jumped and ran around to the back. With her broken arm, Carlotta moved more slowly, but still opened the door, jumped down and picked her way through the grass, her heart pounding. She rounded the corner just as Coop yanked the tangled sheet from the body struggling underneath it. Wesley sat on top of the flattened gurney, glaring at her, his hair in disarray.

"Dad came to see you and you didn't tell me?"

"Whoa," Coop said, holding up his hands. "What's going on? How did you get back here?"

Wes shrugged. "I was in the garage and climbed in when you went in the house."

Coop looked like he wanted to shake him—or worse. *"Why?"*

"Yes, why?" Carlotta demanded, crossing her arms.

Wesley looked contrite. "I needed to get out of town for a few days. When I read your note, Carlotta, I thought coming with you and Coop was a good solution."

She gritted her teeth. "And why do you need to get out of town?"

Wesley climbed out to stand in front of her. "Why didn't you tell me about Dad?"

Coop emitted a loud whistle and chopped the air with his hand. "Okay, time out. Why don't we all get back in the van before we're killed on the side of the interstate?"

Carlotta wheeled away and walked back to the passenger door, climbed inside and slammed it. Wesley slid into the backseat and slammed his door. Coop vaulted into the driver's seat and slammed his. They were all silent for a few seconds, then she erupted.

"You scared us to death. We could've had an accident!"

"Just when were you planning to make your presence known, Wesley?" Coop asked.

"When you were too far down the road to take me back," he replied.

"I think we're there," Coop said dryly. "If I haul you home in this traffic, it'll take us three hours to get back to this point." He shot Wesley a hard look. "Or I could toss your ass out on the side of the road."

They all knew that Coop wouldn't do that.

"Why exactly did you have to leave town?" Carlotta demanded.

"One of my benefactors is leaning on me."

"You mean one of your loan sharks?" she said, not bothering to hide her sarcasm.

"Whatever. I thought it was best to lie low for a couple of days."

"You couldn't lie low with a friend?" Coop asked.

"Come on," Wesley cajoled. "I can help you with the body, man. Carlotta's no good to you with her bum arm."

Coop frowned. "I didn't ask her to ride along for her weight-lifting skills."

"I know why you asked her to ride along," Wesley said pointedly. "This way I can keep on eye on you two."

"Wesley, I don't need a chaperone," Carlotta said, her face growing hot.

"Okay, okay," Coop muttered. He dragged his hand down his face. "You're here. Let's try to make the best of it. Everyone, buckle up." He leaned forward and put the van in gear, checking the side mirror for a break in traffic, then eased back into the flow.

Carlotta sat looking forward, still furious with her brother for ruining the weekend. So much for her and Coop getting to know each other.

They were all silent for a couple of miles, each one stewing. Then from the back, Wesley asked, "So are you going to tell me about Dad or not?"

She closed her eyes and heaved a sigh, then turned around. "I didn't know it was him…at the time. This elderly man—

at least I thought he was elderly—came up to me at the funeral home. He thought Jack was bothering me because Jack had raised his voice. I was in disguise at the time, so I assumed the man thought Jack was hassling an old lady. When I told him everything was fine, he walked away."

"So how did you know it was your father?" Coop asked.

"I didn't, until the day I came home from the hospital. I was sorting through the clothes I'd worn the day of the funeral, and I found a note in the pocket of the jacket."

Wesley leaned forward. "What did it say?"

"It said, 'So proud of you both. See you soon. Dad.'"

Wesley's jaw dropped. "So it *was* Dad."

She nodded. "He must have recognized me, even in disguise."

"If he was in disguise himself, he must have known what to look for," Coop said.

Wesley bounced in the seat, his eyes wide. "This is *huge!* They're okay! I knew it!" Then he stopped bouncing. "Did you tell the cop?"

"No," she said. "No one knows except you two."

"Good thing I was eavesdropping," Wesley said wryly, "or I might not ever have found out."

"You haven't exactly been home for me to tell," she retorted.

"What do you think this means?" Wesley asked. "Do you think he's watching us? That he's going to come home?"

"Who knows?" she said with a shrug. "I think it would be foolish to try to predict his next move. We might not hear from him again for another ten years." She turned back around and pushed her finger under the edge of her cast to scratch as far as she could reach, her stomach churning over whether to tell them about the fingerprints found at the hotel in Daytona.

"He's proud of me," Wesley said in wonderment.

The awe in his voice made her heart ache. No, she wouldn't mention the hotel robbery, she decided. If she told Wesley, he'd only want to tag along and complicate things. This way she could slip away, and Wesley and Coop could entertain each other while she poked around.

"Of course he's proud of you," Coop said, glancing in the rearview mirror, then over to her. "Proud of both of you, of the way you stuck together. And at least you know he's alive."

She smiled and nodded, then looked away. Knowing he was alive somehow made the pain sharper. He could've come back if he'd wanted to. All those years struggling, crying, hating…

Her phone rang again and she rolled her eyes, thinking it was probably Hannah, reminding her that she was being ignored. But when she glanced at the display, her stomach clenched. *P. Ashford.* She didn't feel like answering, but considering that Peter had brought Wesley home the other night— not to mention the fact that he'd paid for the very phone she was holding—taking his call was the least she could do.

"Excuse me," she murmured, then angled herself away from Coop slightly and flipped open the phone. "Hello?"

"Carly, it's Peter."

"Hi," she said brightly, but her voice sounded forced even to her own ears. "What's up?"

"I called to see how you were feeling."

"Oh, I'm fine. Really…fine."

"And Wesley?"

"Fine. He's fine. We're both…fine."

"It sounds like you're in a car."

She glanced sideways at Coop, then back. "I am."

"You're not driving, are you?"

"No." She wet her lips. "Actually, I'm with Dr. Craft."

"Who?"

"Cooper Craft. You've met."

"The body mover is a doctor?"

"Yes. He, um, knew I was bored out of my mind, so he, um, asked me to ride along…on a business trip."

"To pick up a body?"

"Yes."

"He has a weird idea of what constitutes entertainment, in my opinion. When will you be home?"

"Sunday."

"You're going away with this guy for the entire weekend?"

"It's an out-of-state pickup," she said. "And Wesley's with us." She felt perturbed at him for asking and even more perturbed at herself for trying to make the trip look innocent. She sensed Coop straining to decipher the conversation.

"Oh," Peter said, sounding relieved. "Well, in that case…" He cleared his throat. "I was calling to ask you to go to New York with me for the weekend, but I guess I'm too late."

"New York would've been fun," she said. "Are you going up on business?"

"Yes. I'll be back Monday."

"Okay, we'll talk then. Have fun."

"I'll be thinking of you," he said. "Goodbye."

"Goodbye." She disconnected the call, her chest tight with worry and confusion. She had feelings for Peter. She'd been heartbroken after he'd ended their engagement when she'd needed him most. There had been days when she thought she might die from missing him. And yet, now that he was back in her life and offering her everything she thought she'd ever wanted, something held her back. Was she stalling simply to make him pay for leaving her all those years ago? She glanced sideways at Coop. Or was her heart being led down another path?

"I take it that wasn't Hannah," Coop said mildly.

"No. It was Peter."

"With a better offer, sounds like."

"Not necessarily," she hedged.

"Peter's not the jerk-off I thought he was," Wesley commented.

"Oh?" Coop asked over his shoulder. "He's your new BFF?"

"The guy's loaded. My sister could do worse."

Carlotta turned around in her seat. "If I want your opinion, I'll ask for it."

Wesley shrugged. "So what's the 411 on the body pickup?"

"Sunday morning," Coop said, "in Boca Raton. We're stopping in Daytona for the night."

"Cool," Wesley said. "We'll have time to hit the beach. Just think of all those babes in bikinis. Do you think the hotel has a hot tub?" He rubbed his hands together. "This is going to be great!"

"Yeah," Coop said, his demeanor utterly defeated, "just great."

11

"Two rooms," Coop said miserably to the clerk behind the hotel desk.

"Smoking or nonsmoking, sir?"

"Smoking," Carlotta and Wesley said in unison, then looked at each other.

"I don't smoke," Carlotta protested. "I was just saying that I don't mind a smoking room if more of them are available." She swallowed weakly. "Or if they're less expensive."

"Don't you smoke?" Wesley asked Coop. "If we're bunking together, I was only thinking of you."

Coop frowned at both of them. "Two *non*smoking rooms," he clarified, then handed over his credit card.

"I can pay for my room," Carlotta murmured.

"I invited you," Coop said. "I'm paying."

From his tone, it sounded as if he was wishing he hadn't asked her to come along. She pressed her lips together to hold back a smile. It was charming that he was so irritated at

Wesley for crashing their trip. Obviously, Coop had been hoping that the two of them would have some alone time. And admittedly, she'd begun spinning a few fantasies of her own.

Their rooms were next to each other. Coop carried in her suitcase and gave her king-size bed a wistful glance before setting the big piece of luggage on top of it.

Carlotta opened the curtains to a view of Daytona Beach below. It was three o'clock in the afternoon and the beach was swarming with brown bodies. "Nice room," she commented.

"Yeah," he grunted.

She walked over and clasped his hand. "Coop, I'm sorry that Wesley intruded on the weekend. But we can still have fun."

A pained smile twisted his mouth. "I know. Just let me pout for a little while over what might have been."

She raised herself on tiptoe and planted a kiss on his cheek. "Thanks for being such a great guy."

He sighed. "Guess that'll have to hold me over for a bit. Ready to hit the beach?"

"You and Wesley go ahead. I think I'll do some shopping first and join you in a couple of hours."

"Do you need for me to drive you?"

"No, I'll get a taxi."

"I'll take my phone with me. Call me when you get back so we can find each other."

"Okay."

"Have fun." He gave her bed one last look of longing,

then left the room and closed the door behind him. Carlotta laughed to herself, then unzipped her suitcase. With the cast, it took a while to change into an Anika Brazil beaded halter bikini and cover-up, but after much contortion and cursing, she finally managed. She slid her feet into jeweled flat sandals, donned a wide-brimmed hat and sunglasses, then picked up a beach bag of supplies and headed down to the lobby.

Outside, several taxis were standing by. She slid into the backseat of the first one and said, "The Holiday Inn, please."

Daytona Beach was a tourist town, crammed with half-naked students and tackily dressed middle-aged sunseekers. Palm trees and wild birds abounded, as did plastic palms and pink flamingos. It was both quaint and vulgar, like Las Vegas, but it was a happy, vibrant place. Daytona, she decided, was an ideal setting for her parents to blend in and still maintain a carefree lifestyle. But it pained her to think that they'd been living only a few short hours from her and Wesley, that they had been frolicking in the sand while she and her brother had been scrounging for lunch money.

As always, when she thought of her parents, the pendulum of her emotions swung from frustration to fury to resentment and everywhere in between.

"This is the Holiday Inn, ma'am," the cabbie said, breaking into her thoughts. "Do you want me to wait?"

"No, thank you," she said, handing over cash for the fare. When she alighted, her heart was racing double-time at the possibility of coming face-to-face with her father. She glanced around the parking area for Jack's car, wondering about her timing. Had he already been here and left, or would she beat him to the punch? She didn't see his sedan, but then they could be in Liz Fischer's car, and she couldn't remember what the woman drove.

Something slinky and low, for sure.

Carlotta walked into the hotel and breezed through the lobby as if she were a guest, scanning for any sign of someone who could be her father. She didn't see anyone, so made her way to the hotel bar. After another unfruitful scan of the help, she climbed onto an empty bar stool and removed her hat and glasses. The male bartender noticed her immediately and approached her with a smooth smile.

"What can I get for you?" he asked her cleavage.

"Martini," she said.

"Coming right up." He began mixing it in front of her.

"I'm looking for someone," she said casually.

He grinned. "I'd be happy to fill in."

She smiled. "Two people, in fact. They're former bosses of mine who cheated me out of wages." She slipped a photo of her parents out of her purse. "This is an old picture, but it's all I've got. Can you tell me if you've seen them?"

He glanced at the photo. "Nope."

"The man might be salt-and-pepper or gray headed by now. Someone told me he might work here. Are you sure you don't recognize him?"

He picked up the photo and studied it. "Maybe." But then he shook his head. "I couldn't say. There are so many people in and out of here, employees and guests."

"Thanks, anyway," she said, fighting acute disappointment as she put away the picture.

He set the drink in front of her. "Want to start a tab?"

"No, I'll settle up with you." As she handed over cash, she leaned in. "I heard this place was robbed a few days ago."

"Yeah. Last week."

"What happened?"

He frowned. "We're not supposed to talk about it."

She pretended to pout. "I just want to know that I'm safe. Was a guest robbed?"

He glanced around as if to make sure no one would overhear them, then whispered, "No, it was the front desk. Two people came in around four in the morning and robbed the clerk at gunpoint."

She made her eyes as big as possible. "Where was security?"

"At the time, there was only one guy on the property, and he was on break. Anyway, no guests were involved, so don't worry. Besides, they've beefed up security since then."

"That's a relief. You said it was two people—two men?"

He shrugged. "I saw the security tape and they were both wearing face masks. The one who talked was a man. But I guess it's possible that the other person might be a tall woman."

Carlotta's mother was a tall woman. "Do the police have any leads?"

"I haven't heard. The cops were here for a few hours the next morning, questioning everyone. Karen was scared to death."

"Karen?"

"The desk clerk. She…" He frowned. "Hey, let me see that picture again."

Carlotta handed it to him.

He tapped his finger on the photo. "I can't be sure, but it could be."

Her throat constricted. "Could be what?"

"This woman. She could be Karen, the desk clerk who was robbed. Karen Wells."

Carlotta's heart threatened to gallop out of her chest. "Where could I find Karen?"

He handed the picture back. "She quit. Can't blame her."

"Do you know where she lives?"

"Nope. She kept to herself."

Someone at the other end of the bar whistled.

"I gotta go," the bartender said. "Hope you find your bosses."

"If you ever see Karen or this man," Carlotta said, scribbling on a napkin, "here's my number."

He grinned. "Sure thing."

He walked away and she dialed Information. No Karen Wells was listed in Daytona. Carlotta hung up and gulped the martini for courage. She had to get her hands on Karen Wells's employee file.

She left the bar and headed to the ladies' room to rifle through the various kinds of undercover garb she crammed into her beach bag. A woman had to be prepared for anything, after all. She painstakingly removed her cover-up, then changed into the blue scrubs that so many housekeeping staffs wore these days, and white tennis shoes, even though she had to stuff the laces into the sides because she couldn't tie them.

She shoved her cover-up and sandals into the beach bag and smoothed her long hair back into a ponytail. Then she carefully pulled aside the white lining of the trash can to find what she'd hoped—a stack of more trash bags at the bottom to make changing them easier. She removed one of the white liners and put her beach bag inside. Then she left the bathroom carrying the bag of "trash" and the extra liners.

From a marquee, she learned that the manager's office was on the second floor. She took the stairs and found the office, then glanced around. On a table by the elevator was a house phone. She picked it up and the operator answered.

"Yes, I'm a guest of the hotel and my purse was just snatched. I want to see the manager in the lobby immediately." She slammed down the phone, then jogged back to the manager's office and knocked on the door.

"Come in."

She stuck her head inside to find a young man in a suit standing at a file cabinet. "I'm here to take out the trash," she announced.

"Go ahead," he said with barely a glance.

His phone rang and he answered. After a few words, he hung up the receiver. "Please close the door when you're finished," he said, then left, pulling it shut behind him.

Carlotta went to the file cabinet and with her one good hand, clumsily searched for employee records, her palms sweating profusely. She found what she was looking for in the bottom drawer, and as quickly as she could, flipped through to the *Ws*. When she found a folder marked Karen Wells, she pulled it out, her blood pounding in her ears. A three-page application listed home address and phone number, plus references.

Plus ten points.

With her good hand shaking, Carlotta placed the documents on the copier, constantly looking over her shoulder to the door. The manager was probably on his way back by now. Cursing her cast, she awkwardly stuffed the originals back into the file and the folder back into the drawer.

She heard voices outside the door. With her heart hammering against her breastbone, she slammed the drawer and shoved the duplicate records into the trash bag holding her clothes just as the doorknob turned. The manager walked in, talking to someone behind him.

Detective Jack Terry.

12

When Carlotta's gaze met Jack's behind the back of the hotel manager, she swallowed a yelp. His expression went from disbelief to outrage to fury in the space of two seconds.

Carlotta tried to look contrite. "I was just leaving," she murmured, and scurried out into the hall.

"Give me a minute," she heard Jack sputter to the unwitting manager.

She broke into a sprint toward the stairs, and heard him pounding behind her. "Goddamn it, Carlotta, stop or I'll shoot!"

She veered off toward the women's bathroom and ran inside, barricading herself in the handicapped stall. He came crashing in behind her and rattled the stall door. "Carlotta, open this door!"

"I'm changing," she shouted, pulling off the scrubs.

The door shuddered, then the flimsy lock bar failed under

the pressure. The door flew open and Jack stood there, breathing like a bull who'd been poked with a sharp stick.

Carlotta gasped, not because she was afraid of him, but because she didn't want to explain her presence. Instead, she feigned modesty, using her good arm to cover her bikini. "I'm changing!"

"Cut the crap," he said. "I've seen everything you have, anyway."

She shook her finger in his face. "If you don't leave, I'll scream."

He wrapped his hand around her finger and pulled her against him. "Go ahead," he urged. "Scream."

She opened her mouth and inhaled in preparation, but he covered her lips with his, kissing her hard. For a split second her body betrayed her, responded to the familiarity of him. The scream died to a moan, then she wrenched away and covered her mouth with her hand. "What was that?"

"A way to get your attention."

She set her jaw. "You have it."

"Good. Then what in *hell* are you doing here?"

"I'm on vacation."

His look was lethal. "I'm not kidding, Carlotta. You've got three seconds to start talking, or I'm going to arrest you for trespassing and obstruction of justice." He pulled out his handcuffs and looked at his watch. "Three—"

"You don't scare me, Jack. I've been in those handcuffs and I wasn't under arrest at the time."

"Two—"

"Where's your expandable baton? We had fun with that big boy, too."

"One!"

"Okay, okay," she said, relenting. "But you already know why I'm here."

"You're trying to sabotage my case."

"No! I…just wanted to look around." She sighed and leaned against the back wall. "I don't know. I thought Randolph might be here. I just wanted to see for myself."

She watched the anger drain out of him, replaced by frustration and sympathy. He returned the handcuffs to his belt. "Okay, what did you find?"

"What makes you think I found anything?"

He rolled his eyes. "Are you going to make me say it? Because you're good at being devious."

She angled her head and grinned. "Did you just pay me a compliment?"

"No. And quit yanking my chain."

She glanced at his crotch for effect, then relayed her conversation with the bartender. "And here are copies of Karen Wells's employee records." She withdrew papers from the trash bag and extended them to him.

But Jack held up his hands. "I can't take those. They were stolen."

"Okay, I'll keep them."

He yanked them from her. "You can't keep them either, Nancy Drew." He pulled out a lighter and held a flame under the corner of the pages. He let them burn up to his fingers, then dropped the charred mess into the commode. "I can get copies legitimately."

"Now that you know what direction to go in," she taunted.

He scowled. "I would've asked for employee records for the clerk who was robbed, anyway."

"If you let me watch the surveillance tape, I could tell you if the voice is his."

"That's why Liz came with me."

"Oh, well." Carlotta made a shooing motion with her hand. "Now that you've given me a spanking, you can get on with your investigation. By the way, where is Lizbo?"

"She's at our hotel, making phone calls."

"At the spa, huh?"

He crossed his arms, legs spread wide. "You can't drive with a broken arm. How did you get to Daytona?"

"Coop invited me to ride to south Florida for a job, and I suggested that we stop here for the night."

His eyebrows shot up. "Coop?"

"That's right. It's a business trip."

"I take it he doesn't know about your little detour?"

"Um, no. I told him I was going shopping."

"Well, I guess it's comforting that I'm not the only man in your life that you lie to."

She narrowed her eyes at him. "You can go now."

"Uh, no. Get dressed. I'll be escorting you out."

She held out the swimsuit cover-up. "Would you mind helping me? This cast is such a pain."

He tightened his mouth, then held the flimsy garment

over her head. She lifted her good arm and shimmied as he pulled it down over her head and helped ease it over her shoulders, her breasts, her cast. She moved slowly, undulating into the garment. When it fell into place she looked up to find his golden eyes hooded and smoky.

She smirked at him. "Is that chain still dangling?"

He sighed. "You are so bad."

Carlotta pushed her feet into the jeweled sandals. "Oh, no. You said I was good. I heard you with my own ears." She shouldered her beach bag, plopped her big hat on her head and marched past him.

"I said you were good at being devious," he said, following her out.

She stopped to allow him to open the outside door for her, and walked through when he obliged. "You heard one thing, I heard something else."

They walked to the elevator together and Jack stabbed the down button. "So…this business trip of yours."

"What about it?"

"Are you and Coop sharing a room?"

She raised her eyebrows, then said, "Right back at you, cowboy."

"Liz and I are just friends."

"Uh-huh. I hope your shots are up-to-date."

"Meow."

The elevator dinged and the doors opened. She walked in and he followed. When they closed, he asked, "What does Ashford think about your weekend fling with Coop?"

"I didn't ask. Peter doesn't own me."

Jack shook his head. "One of these days, Carlotta, you're going to have to decide what you want."

"Are you throwing your hat in the ring, Jack?"

He looked at her, a muscle ticking in his jaw. "You know I can't."

"One of these days, Jack, you're going to have to decide what *you* want." She squared her shoulders, which sent a pain shooting down her arm. "Meanwhile, I've been alone for a long time, looking after Wesley, hanging on by a very thin thread. Forgive me if I want to explore my options and maybe even, God forbid, have a little fun before I dry up and blow away."

He was quiet for a few seconds. "I'm sorry," he said finally. "You're right. I guess I'm regretting not allowing you to come down here with me. You have a way of making me say things I don't mean."

"It's a gift," she murmured.

The elevator doors opened and they walked through the lobby in silence, his hand at her waist.

He signaled a taxi, and when it pulled up, he opened the door for her, then handed the driver a twenty-dollar bill. "Take the lady back to her hotel, please." He looked at her. "See you in Atlanta." Then he shut the door.

Carlotta rolled down the window. "Jack."

"Yeah?"

"If you find Randolph, will you at least call me before you call the D.A.?"

He hesitated, then nodded. "Count on it."

He stepped away from the taxi and she lifted her hand in

a wave, feeling oddly comforted that Jack was on the case despite their conflict. No matter how much he blustered and pounded his chest, she trusted him to do the right thing. Carlotta settled back.

Then she withdrew the extra copy of Karen Wells's employee record that she'd made.

What was the old political saying? Trust…but verify.

13

"It's about time," Coop called, waving from the big straw mat where he and Wesley sat playing cards amid hundreds of other beachgoers. Carlotta waved and smiled, but when Coop stood to brush the sand off his trunks, the breath caught in her throat.

Plus ten.

His torso was bare, his shoulders wide, his arms and chest surprisingly muscular. His skin was already brown, perhaps from those weekly hikes he referred to…which might also explain his long, lean legs.

The man was *gorgeous*.

As witnessed by all the women who had positioned their blankets and towels close to the men's mat in the late afternoon sun. Despite his bandaged arm, Wesley didn't look too shabby, either, in his long surfer trunks. With his sharp bone structure, he resembled a young Leonardo DiCaprio. But if he was aware of the women looking his way, he was too shy to act upon it.

She was betting that both men were clueless as to the stir they were causing.

"Hi," she said after threading her way through female bodies to get to the edge of the mat. "Having fun?"

"Coop is one of the best poker players I've ever seen," Wesley said excitedly.

"Is that so?" she asked, eyeing Coop.

"We're not betting," he stated quickly. "Did you have fun shopping? We were getting worried about you."

"Coop was getting worried," Wesley corrected. "I told him that you could shop for days, like a camel."

Carlotta dropped her beach bag on her brother's foot. "Sorry I was longer than I'd planned."

"How was Neiman's?" Coop asked.

She grasped for a logical lie. "Fine, but I didn't find what I was looking for." Karen Wells's address had been bogus, and the phone number disconnected. The references, too, were dead ends—all of them companies that had closed. If her mother had been posing as Karen Wells, she had disappeared again. "So tell me what I missed."

"Coop taught me to body surf," Wesley said.

"I grew up near the ocean," Coop explained, lowering himself to the mat and leaving room for her to sit next to him.

"Really? Where?" She pulled her cover-up over her head. It was much easier to get off than to get on.

Coop stared up at her, his mouth slightly agape. "I forgot."

Wesley rolled his eyes. "Oh, brother. I'm going for a swim." He tossed down his cards and jogged away.

She sat down next to Coop and his Adam's apple bobbed.

"I might have to go for a swim, too, to keep from embarrassing myself. Nice suit," he said.

Carlotta grinned. "Thanks. You don't look so bad yourself. I'm going to have to retract that 'understated' remark."

"Oh?"

"Yeah. It's all right there. Maybe I haven't been looking."

"Careful—you'll give a man hope."

She put her hand on his. "Let's just have fun, okay?"

"Sounds good."

"How long until sunset?"

He checked his watch. "It's six o'clock now. The sun will probably set around eight." He smiled. "But something tells me it'll be worth waiting for."

They watched Wesley, laughing at his antics, and talked about Atlanta (the traffic), Hannah (the paradox) and life (the meaning). They walked to the surf and Carlotta waded in the frothy water, protective of her cast, while Coop dived and surfed with Wesley. Carlotta watched them and thought how good the two looked together. It was a shame that Wesley hadn't had a father around to give him the male attention he so obviously craved.

While she walked, she compulsively checked the faces of people on the beach, especially couples. She knew the chances of running into her parents on this particular stretch of sand were next to nil, but she couldn't help it. Carlotta mentally cursed Randolph and Valerie Wren. It had taken her years to stop scanning faces everywhere she went. She didn't want to start doing that again…start hoping.

Coop emerged from the water looking like a Greek statue with water sluicing off his lean, muscular body. A jolt of sexual attraction hit her hard and she suddenly wished that Wesley hadn't come as a stowaway, that she and Coop had the weekend to themselves. That she didn't have so much emotional baggage weighing her down.

Coop caught up with her and intertwined their fingers. They walked hand in hand for a long while. It allowed her to try on the idea of being with Coop and, inevitably, to compare him to the other two men in her life. She couldn't envision Jack holding hands and walking the beach at sunset. She could picture Peter holding hands, but the beach would be the Riviera, and in his other hand would be his iPhone in case the office called.

"I lied to you earlier," Coop said suddenly.

"What do you mean?"

"When you asked how long since I'd been on vacation, I lied."

"Why?"

"Because the last time I was on vacation was when I was in rehab."

"Oh." She stopped. "Coop, you don't have to talk about it if you don't want to."

"No, I think you should know that I'm a recovering alcoholic before you fall madly in love with me."

She laughed. "Fair enough."

He grew solemn. "I've been sober for a long time, but I believe in full disclosure. When I drank, I did some pretty irresponsible things, and people were hurt because of it."

"Did Wesley ever mention that our mother had a problem with alcohol?"

"No."

"He probably doesn't remember that she always reeked of either booze or mouthwash. At least she was a happy drunk."

"I'm sorry that she wasn't a better mother to you both."

Carlotta shrugged. "I guess it was the best she could do. I'm sure Valerie found a way to convince herself that leaving us was for the best."

"Maybe she recognized you would be a better mother to Wesley than she could be."

"Or she could have sobered up," Carlotta said.

He nodded. "You're right. But if she wasn't ready to get sober, thank God Wesley had you."

"It still wasn't fair, to either one of us." She moistened her lips. "I think I might hate her for it."

"I don't blame you," he said. "And she probably expects it, as well."

"You think she's still drinking?"

"My guess is yes, or you would've heard from her by now."

"I think so, too."

He squeezed her hand. "So have I scared you off?"

Carlotta chuckled. "Considering my family issues, you're going to have to come up with something better than a measly addiction to get my sympathy."

He laughed and they continued walking. She noticed that he seemed lighter, unburdened. His past obviously weighed more heavily on him than she'd assumed. She had the feeling that there was much more to Coop than met the eye, and she hoped that he would someday share it with her.

They got back to the mat just in time to watch the sun slip out of the pink-and-red sky, on its way to another horizon for another couple to enjoy. The moon took its place, lighting the water and the beach with silvery hues. And the exchange took mere minutes.

"Beautiful," Carlotta breathed, completely relaxed for the first time in recent memory.

"Yes, you are," Coop said, and when she turned her head, he kissed her.

His kiss wasn't hard and possessive like Jack's, but an utterly romantic one. Carlotta opened her mouth to his, reveling in the taste of him, the way he drew out the kiss with slow strokes of his tongue. Her body came alive, and she pressed into him more urgently in the near darkness.

"Gawd, get a room," Wesley said, walking up to shake water all over them.

They parted and Carlotta shrieked, swatting at her brother. They packed up the mat and, on the short walk back to their hotel, talked about where to go for dinner. She showered and dressed carefully, feeling a little scared about the way things were going with Coop. It all seemed to be happening so fast.

Over dinner she looked for a way to put the brakes on their mutual attraction, but the spark that had started with the kiss seemed to smolder all evening. Over bowls of fresh shrimp and plates of polenta, their eyes met more and more often as the night wore on. Beneath the table their knees and hands brushed.

Conversely, Wesley's mood seemed to worsen. He'd gotten a sunburn in the short time he'd been on the beach, and he kept rubbing his arm.

"You should change that bandage," Coop admonished. "It's not good to have damp fabric against an open wound."

"Did I ask for your advice?" he snapped.

"Hey, watch your tone," Carlotta said. "Considering how you hijacked your way down here, you don't need to be rude."

"Sorry," Wesley mumbled to Coop.

"It's okay." Coop exchanged a glance with Carlotta, folded his napkin and excused himself to go to the men's room.

"What's wrong with you?" Carlotta asked when he was out of earshot.

"I'm tired of watching the two of you making googly eyes at each other."

"We're not making googly—" She stopped. "I thought you liked Coop."

"I do, but that doesn't mean I want you to sleep with him."

"Watch your mouth, Wesley. I don't have to explain myself to you. Coop and I are adults."

"He's my boss, for chrissake. Besides, what about Peter?"

She squinted. "What about Peter?"

"You cried your eyes out over the guy for years. Now he's available and he wants to marry you and you're ignoring him!"

"I'm not ignoring him, but I haven't made any kind of

commitment to Peter. What's so wrong with getting to know Coop?" She tossed down her napkin, flustered.

Wesley leaned forward. "Because he's in love with you, Sis. This wouldn't be just a fling to Coop. He's not like Jack Terry."

A direct hit. Carlotta bit down on her tongue until her mouth sang with pain. "How about you stay out of my personal life, and I won't ask you about the woman whose perfume you reek of when you come home?"

She thought he'd come back with some smart teenage remark. Instead, the fleeting panic on his face set off alarms in her head. What else had Wesley gotten himself into?

"So," Coop said with a clap of his hands as he reclaimed his seat, "who has room for dessert?"

With Wesley's comment about the man being in love with her reverberating in her head, she conjured up a shaky smile. "I never turn down chocolate."

"Chocolate it is," he said, signaling the waitress.

He ordered a mud pie sundae and coffees all around, but Wesley didn't eat. Instead, he merely watched over the rim of his cup, massaging his arm, while they shared the decadent dessert. Coop was animated and made her laugh, parrying his spoon with hers.

But Carlotta grew more and more edgy, mulling over what Wesley had said. His sudden partiality to Peter was puzzling. And some part of her wondered if his behavior sprang from jealousy of Coop's attention to her. Still, he'd made a valid point or two. If she slept with Coop, it could change the dynamics for all of them.

When they got back to the hotel, she and Coop lingered in front of their doors awkwardly. Wesley leaned back and studied his fingernails, making matters worse.

"Good night, Wesley," she said pointedly.

"Good night," he muttered, then looked at Coop. "You coming?"

"Later," Coop said.

Wesley frowned and disappeared into their room. When the door closed, Carlotta swallowed nervously and looked up at Coop. Everything she'd learned about him on this trip only made her like him more…and want him more. But to what end?

"I had fun today," he ventured.

"Me, too," she admitted.

"You sound surprised."

"I am, but in a good way." She moistened her lips with her tongue. "Kiss me again, Coop."

He cupped her face with his hands, then he kissed her thoroughly and well. Her limbs grew languid and her body responded, molding to his.

He lifted his mouth from hers and whispered, "Ask me to come in."

"I want to. But, Coop…I can't make any promises. I don't want to hurt you."

He put his finger to her lips. "I'm a big boy. I can take it."

She fumbled to unlock the door and they practically fell into the room. Moonlight shone through the open window, and the sound of the ocean crashing set a primitive rhythm for lovemaking. He half carried her to the bed and pulled her down on top of him in the semidarkness.

"I've wanted you since I saw you that first time in your kitchen," he said thickly.

She smiled. "I was wearing my pj's and my hair was absolutely witchy."

"You were adorable and sexy. Like now." He slid his hands down her back to cup her hips against his, leaving her with rigid proof of how much he wanted her.

Carlotta closed her eyes against the sensations bombarding her, and she had a scary feeling in her stomach that she hadn't felt in years—that this time the sex would mean something more than just stimulated nerve endings. "You have me at a disadvantage. I've never done this with one arm."

He rolled her over gently and removed his glasses. "Let me take care of everything."

Carlotta sighed. It felt good to be taken care of, to give herself over to pleasure, to submit to his ministrations.

He unbuttoned her blouse and her front-closure bra to release her breasts into his mouth. She grabbed a fistful of the bedcovers and moaned, arching against his gifted tongue. He sighed against her breasts, sending the oddest sensation of contentment through her though it left her wanting more. She used her good arm to run her hand down his spine, then pull the T-shirt over his head. When his warm skin touched hers, she gasped against the full awareness of what was to come. Once again panic licked at her…but she couldn't bear to stop.

She explored the firm muscles of his back, felt the heat left by the sun, slipped her fingers beneath the waistband of his jeans. He kissed her ribs and stomach, then undid her pants and slid them down her legs, leaving only her red thong panties. Coop groaned in appreciation, then removed them an inch at a time—with his teeth.

Plus one hundred.

She succumbed to the feeling of sliding down a slippery slope. She would deal with tomorrow when it came. A shudder of anticipation rolled over her body.

Coop parted her knees and lowered his head.

A knock sounded, and through the door Wesley said, "Coop!"

They looked at each other through her legs and sighed in abject frustration. "Ignore him," she urged.

"Good idea." Coop dipped his head.

But before he could touch down, another knock sounded, this time more insistent. "Coop! I need to talk to you now! It's important!"

"I'm going to make you an only child," Coop muttered, pushing himself off the bed and grabbing his glasses.

"Be my guest." Carlotta snatched her jeans from the floor and struggled into them. Then she turned her back to the door to awkwardly refasten her bra and blouse. She could hear the men arguing in undertones in the hall.

She turned on the light. "What's going on?"

Coop looked back from the door, his face a mask of resigned frustration. "Wesley says his arm is hurting bad. I'm going to take a look at it."

Disappointment over the interruption warred with concern for Wesley. "I'll go with you."

Wesley's face appeared in the doorway. "You don't have to, Sis. Just go on to bed."

She knew that face, knew that tone. He didn't want her to see what was under the bandage. While Coop pulled on his shirt, she grabbed her key, then followed them to their room.

"I'm staying," she told Wesley when he started to protest.

Coop used a pair of scissors from his toiletry kit to cut off the soiled and soggy bandage. Carlotta gasped at the sight of the red, swollen skin underneath and the ugly slashes in Wesley's thin arm. "You didn't get that from a bicycle accident. What happened?"

But her brother appeared to have gone deaf.

"They're knife wounds," Coop said quietly, looking at Wesley, who was staring at the floor.

"Knife wounds? Someone stabbed you?"

"Someone cut him," Coop said when her brother wouldn't answer.

She leaned closer. "Are those...*letters? C...A...R?* Why would someone cut 'CAR' into your arm?" Then she covered her mouth. "The Carver—*he cut his name into your arm?*"

"Not his entire name," Wesley mumbled.

"He speaks," Coop said dryly. "Chief, your arm is infected. You need antibiotics, pronto." He looked up at Carlotta. "We need to take him to an emergency room."

"No," Wesley said. "It'll cost a lot of money that we don't have."

"I'll pay for it," Coop said.

"No," he said. "I won't go."

"Wesley, you need medicine," Carlotta said, her maternal instincts rearing.

"Can't you write me a prescription for antibiotics?" he asked Coop. "Maybe give me a shot?"

Coop hesitated. "I could, but I'd prefer you see a doctor."

"You're a doctor."

"You know what I mean."

"Come on, man. I trust you more than some doctor I don't even know."

Coop looked up at Carlotta.

"It's your call," she said.

He checked his watch. "Okay, I'll go get what I need and be back as soon as I can." He stood and she walked with him to the door.

"I'm sorry," she murmured.

"So am I," he said with a sigh. "It might be late by the time I get back, and then I'll have to redress his arm." He scrubbed at his face and sighed. "Maybe we can try this again tomorrow?"

Carlotta smiled and nodded. But as Coop strode way, she couldn't help feeling that what might have been had just slipped through her fingers.

14

Even with his earbuds in for his iPod, Wesley could feel the silent treatment he was receiving from the pair in the front seat. He knew what he'd interrupted last night between Carlotta and Coop, and he wasn't sorry. If his sister slept with Coop, the man would become completely pussy-whipped. And Carlotta would be distancing herself further from Peter.

And he had promised Peter he'd do everything he could to help him win Carlotta back.

After Peter had forked over the twenty-five grand, Wesley had said he didn't know how he'd ever repay him.

"Don't worry about it," Peter had said, then smiled. "I do something for you, you do something for me."

"Like what?"

"Like put in a good word for me with Carly when you can, and try to keep your boss and that cop away from her."

"I can't be with her all the time," he'd told the man.

"I know. Just do what you can." Peter had clapped him on the back. "I can give Carlotta the life she deserves, Wesley. I love her and I want her back. Do this for me and we're even."

In the rearview mirror Wesley could see the strain on his boss's face, the anxious glances he shot in Carlotta's direction, the way he looked at her when he thought no one was watching. The man had it bad for his sister, but he'd get over it.

Just like he himself would get over E. Jones someday.

He removed the earbuds and stuck his head between their seats. "How much longer to Boca?"

"Another couple of hours," Coop said.

"Good, we'll have all afternoon on the beach."

"How's your arm?" Coop asked.

"Better," he said, wiggling it. "Those antibiotics must be potent." And the OxyContin was doing its thing.

"The shot was strong. But you still have to take all the pills I gave you."

"You should've gone to Coop in the first place," Carlotta said.

"I tried to call Coop when The Carver let me go, but he didn't answer. I didn't want you to see me like that, so I called Peter. I thought you'd be happy about that."

Carlotta frowned. "Why?"

"Because I know you and Peter have gotten close again," Wesley said, talking fast. "He showed me the ring."

Carlotta turned around, her eyes wide. Coop jerked the steering wheel and swerved, then corrected. "What ring?"

"Carlotta's engagement ring," Wesley said his sister. He looked at Carlotta. "You didn't tell Coop?"

"You're *engaged?*" Coop practically shouted.

"No, I'm not engaged," Carlotta said, shooting lasers at Wesley with her eyes.

"So what's all this about a ring?" Coop asked, still sounding panicked.

Wesley felt guilty watching his sister squirm.

"It's the engagement ring that Peter gave me ten years ago," she said finally. "I had to pawn it to pay bills. Peter somehow found it and bought it back."

"And upgraded it," Wesley offered. "Had a big-ass diamond mounted on either side of the big-ass diamond that was already there. It's humongous. And it's Cartier."

Coop's face was turning gray. "Where is it?" he asked Carlotta, staring at her hand.

"Peter has it," she murmured.

"He's holding it for her," Wesley confirmed, then sat back. From the way Coop and Carlotta were looking—and not looking—at each other, he had a feeling he wouldn't have to create a diversion tonight to keep them in separate rooms.

His arm twinged, so he reached into his bag to get another pain pill, but his phone rang. When he glanced at the display, his heart surged. It was E.

Playing it cool, he let it ring twice before answering. "This is Wes."

"Wesley, hi, this is E. Jones."

"Hi, E., what's up?"

"Just checking in," she said. "Where are you?"

"I'm in sunny Florida. And the beach is *fan*tastic." He hoped it conjured up images of him frolicking with lots of scantily dressed women.

"You really should tell me when you're going out of town," she said, chastising him. "I called because I received notification from the court that you didn't make your weekly payment on your fine. If you can't afford to pay your fine, how can you afford to go on vacation?"

He sobered. "I'm actually on a job with Coop."

"You're picking up a body?"

"Yeah. We're on our way to—"

Coop signaled him in the mirror with a finger to his mouth. "It's confidential."

"We're on our way…there," Wesley said into the phone.

"When will you be back in Atlanta?"

"Tomorrow evening."

"And when will you be able to make a payment to the court?"

"Monday."

"Okay, I'll let them know. But this can't happen again."

"Right. Sorry."

"Don't be sorry, Wesley. Be a man and honor your commitments."

The call was disconnected. He sat there listening to the silence for a few seconds as frustration welled in his chest. Be a man like her boyfriend, Leonard, who was up to his dick in bad news?

"Who was on the phone?" Carlotta asked.

"My probation officer."

"Sorry for interrupting," Coop said, "but this is supposed to be a quiet job. I had to sign a confidentiality agreement and that extends to the two of you."

"Who are we picking up, anyway?"

"Kiki Deerling."

"The celebrity chick with the shaved taco?"

Coop frowned. "Show some respect, okay?"

His arm was really hurting now. He pulled out one of the OxyContin pills and rolled it around in his mouth. What was it Chance had said? *If you want to feel like you've just been laid by the woman of your dreams, chew it.*

It might be as close to having E. Jones in his bed as he'd ever get. Wesley bit down on the tablet and winced against the bitter taste. But as the tablet dissolved, he felt an immediate rush of pleasure. And within a few minutes, he felt better than he'd ever felt in his life. Light. Carefree. Euphoric.

He put his earbuds back in, cranked up Stone Temple Pilots and settled back against the seat. Damn, he could get used to this.

15

Coop rolled down the window. "Smell that?"

Carlotta lowered her window and inhaled. "The ocean?"

"Money," he said with a wry smile. "Boca Raton has some of the most expensive real estate on the East Coast."

And it looked it. The buildings were higher and more state-of-the-art. The palm trees were taller and more picturesque, the grass was greener and more manicured. The streets were jammed with beautiful people sporting cruise wear and eye-popping gobs of bling.

"TV news vans are everywhere," Carlotta said, pointing out the window. "Everyone is fascinated by Kiki Deerling's death."

"With all this media, how are we supposed to get the body out of town undetected?" Wesley asked.

"The morgue told me they have extra security, with vans going in and out all the time. No one will know which van the body is in. They've even arranged to install a Florida license plate on the back when we get there in the morning so no one will be suspicious when we leave the property."

"Wow," Carlotta said, shaking her head. "The poor girl is more popular now than when she was alive."

"Death as a career move," Wesley muttered.

"I can't imagine this many people caring whether I was dead or alive," Carlotta commented. At her fake funeral, most of the people had attended out of curiosity, to see if her parents would show.

"Apparently, a lot of us would care," Coop said lightly.

She averted her gaze. She could strangle Wesley for bringing up the engagement ring, but she was actually more angry with herself for not being able to deal with all the loose ends in her life. As much as she'd yearned to have Coop in her bed last night, this morning she was relieved that nothing had happened. The news of the ring Peter was "holding" for her made her look indecisive at best. On the heels of a night of unbridled passion, it would have made her look like something else altogether.

She felt miserable every time she made eye contact with Coop.

The hotel was nicer than anyplace she'd ever stayed, and Wesley was excited that the pool area featured a half-dozen hot tubs. Despite being so irritable yesterday, he was in a great mood now. His arm had to be feeling better, Carlotta realized, thankful more than ever to Coop.

When he carried her suitcase into her room, tension still vibrated between them. "Coop, I'm sorry."

"About what?"

"About the complicated mess my life is."

He pushed her hair behind her ear. "I guess that's what makes you so irresistible."

"I feel like I've ruined this entire trip."

"Not at all." He winked. "Let's go enjoy the beach, okay?"

Her heart expanded and she nodded gratefully. "I'll put on my suit and meet you and Wesley downstairs in fifteen minutes."

He left her room and she sank to the bed, letting out a sigh. Would she ever get her act together? Inside her bag, her cell phone rang. She glanced at the screen and gave a little laugh. It was Hannah calling. She flipped open the phone. "Hello?"

Silence.

"Hannah, this is childish, don't you think?"

More silence.

Carlotta disconnected the call, shaking her head. She unzipped her suitcase and withdrew a Karla Colletto red one-piece bathing suit. With all the cutouts, it was just as skin-baring as a bikini, but was much easier to get on with her cast. She was contorting to get into it when the phone rang again. Ready to give Hannah a piece of her mind, she yanked up the cell. But the display read *Unknown*. Frowning, she answered, "Hello?"

"Hey, pretty lady, it's the bartender from the Holiday Inn. Are you still in town?"

"No," she said warily, wondering if the guy wanted to hook up.

"Too bad, because I just saw Karen Wells."

Her pulse leaped. "Where?"

"At the Pink Pony."

"What's that?"

"A strip club, honey. She's onstage right now."

Carlotta felt sick to her stomach. "Can you give me the address?" She wrote it down with a shaking hand. "Thanks so much for letting me know."

"If you come back to town, doll face, look me up."

"Will do," she lied, then disconnected the call.

She glanced at her watch and dialed Jack's number while she continued to struggle into the swimsuit.

"Carlotta?" he answered.

"Yes, it's me." She juggled the phone between her shoulder and ear, straining to stretch a strap over her shoulder. When the strap snapped out of her hand and zinged her cast, she grunted in pain.

"If you're doing what I think you're doing," he said, "I'm going to have to find a place to be alone."

"Get your mind out of the gutter," she retorted. "I happen to have a hot tip for you."

"I know, I know—get a new tie."

"Will you shut up and listen? The bartender from the Holiday Inn just called and said he'd spotted Karen Wells at a strip club called the Pink Pony."

"She's there now?"

"Yes." She gave him the address.

"The employee file was a dead end," he said.

"Uh-huh."

He sighed. "Something tells me I should have patted you down before I let you leave. Carlotta, it doesn't make sense for us both to travel the same ground."

"Well, I have to admit that I'm glad I'm not there with you to check out this particular lead."

"It might not be your mother," he said quietly.

Emotion formed a lump in her throat. "If my mother is a stripper, that would just be the cherry on top, wouldn't it?" She broke off on a choking sound.

"Don't do this to yourself." He sighed. "Look, go have fun…with Coop," he added tightly. "I'll call you the minute I know something."

She disconnected the call and gulped a couple of breaths to calm herself. Her strength renewed, she stretched the suit over her shoulders and into place. She shrugged into a red cover-up and gold metallic flip-flops, then stuffed her phone and other necessities into a beach bag and hurried downstairs.

Wesley was waiting, wearing trunks and a T-shirt. "Coop went down to rent us beach chairs and an umbrella."

"That was nice of him."

"Yeah. But isn't there some saying about nice guys finishing last?"

She narrowed her eyes at her brother as they walked through the pool area and along a boardwalk toward the beach. He seemed determined to steer her attention away from Coop. "Wesley, what was all that about Peter today? It came from left field."

He shrugged. "He's not such a bad guy, and he's crazy

about you. Don't you want the life you would've had if you hadn't been saddled with me?"

She stopped. "Wesley, that's not why Peter dumped me. His parents didn't want him near me because of what our father did. It had nothing to do with you."

"I heard what you said in the van."

"What do you mean?"

"When I was hiding, I heard you tell Coop that you only raised me because you didn't have a choice."

She bit her tongue to stave off tears. "I still think you would've been better off raised by your own mother and father instead of an eighteen-year-old who couldn't cook. But I never would've left you to someone else to raise. I only meant that Coop shouldn't put me on a pedestal, because I did what anyone would do. For me, there *was* no other choice."

Wesley's eyes looked suspiciously moist. "You didn't do such a bad job, you know."

In the wake of rare brotherly praise, she tried to look stern. "So stay out of trouble."

"I'm trying," he mumbled.

When they got to the beach, they scanned the crowd. Coop waved to them and they wound their way to the patch he'd carved out for them. His smile was a little dimmer today, but he was still his easygoing self. And his eyes lit up appreciatively when Carlotta pulled off her cover-up. If he was remembering what little intimate contact had transpired between them last night, so was she.

They played a game of spades in the shade of the umbrella. Carlotta tried to keep her mind on the play, but she kept wondering what was happening in Daytona, if Jack had located Karen Wells and if she was really Valerie Wren.

"You broke the trump suit," Wesley said.

She blinked. "What?"

"You laid down a spade and I know you still have a club."

She frowned and pulled her cards back. "How do you know?"

"I just know."

Her phone rang. Wesley was closer, so he reached into her bag and handed it to her. "It's Jack Terry," he said.

"Excuse me a minute," she said, aware that Coop's eyes were on her.

She walked out of earshot and flipped up the phone. "Hello, Jack? Did you find her?"

"Yeah, I found Karen Wells." In the background she could hear dance music.

"And?" Carlotta held her breath.

"There's a resemblance, but she's not your mother."

She exhaled. "Oh, thank God."

"Yeah. Turns out she's using a fake name because she has a couple of misdemeanor drug possession charges. I don't think she had anything to do with the hotel robbery, but I'm still looking into it."

"I forgot to ask earlier. Did Liz recognize my father's voice on the surveillance tape."

"She doesn't think it was him."

Another relief. "Okay. Thanks for calling, Jack."

"Sure thing. Now you can get back to…whatever you were doing."

She smiled into the phone. "Sunbathing."

"Wish I was there."

"You've seen everything I have, anyway," she reminded him.

"That doesn't mean I wouldn't mind seeing it again sometime."

"Goodbye, Jack." She flipped the phone closed and walked back to the chairs, feeling less burdened. Coop was there alone, reading a book.

"Where did Wesley go?"

He nodded toward the surf, where her brother was floating, waiting for a wave to ride in.

"How's Jack?" Coop asked.

"Fine and dandy."

He closed his book. "What's going on, Carlotta?"

"What do you mean?"

"For one thing, there's no Neiman Marcus in Daytona." She winced. "You checked?"

"Where were you yesterday?"

"I can explain."

"Were you with Jack?"

She closed her eyes briefly. "He was there."

"Where?"

Carlotta massaged her temples. "At the Holiday Inn."

Coop's head went back as if she'd slapped him.

"It's not what you think," she said. She looked around to make sure Wesley was still in the water, then sighed. "The night that Wesley came home, Jack pulled me aside to tell me that a Holiday Inn in Daytona had been robbed, and when the scene was processed, my father's fingerprints came up as a match. Jack was coming down to investigate."

Coop quirked his mouth. "So that's why you wanted to stop in Daytona?"

She nodded. "I wanted to check it out for myself. I thought my father might be working there, maybe in disguise."

"Was he?"

"No. But I...ran into Jack while I was there."

"I imagine he wasn't too happy to see you."

"Uh, no. But I did give him a lead to follow up on. That was him calling back to say it was a dead end."

Coop studied her. "So that's why you agreed to come with me, so you could hitch a ride to Daytona?"

"That's not the only reason," she said, but she realized how feeble it sounded. She swallowed. "If you don't mind, I'd rather Wesley not know about any of this."

He nodded, but his disappointment was transparent. The rest of the day, she was aware of the emotional wall between them, and she knew it was her fault. Wesley seemed not to notice anything was wrong—the sun and the water agreed with him, she acknowledged. He seemed cheerful, and a little color suited him. She and Coop relied on him to keep the conversation and activities going. The gold-streaked sunset was bittersweet. Carlotta remembered how happy she'd been twenty-four hours ago.

They had a casual dinner at a beachside bar, then Wesley insisted they go to the hotel hot tub. He held his freshly bandaged arm out of the water along the concrete edge.

Carlotta did the same with her cast, but conceded that the warm, bubbly water felt good everywhere else. Still, her chest ached every time she looked at Coop. Their toes occasionally touched underwater. They were sitting a couple of feet away from each other, but as time wore on, they migrated closer and closer together until their thighs touched. She wished the entire world would fall away and leave them alone to explore this powerful pull between them.

When Wesley climbed out to go to the restroom, silence stretched until Carlotta cleared her throat. "Hannah called again today to breathe into the phone."

He smiled, but it faded as quickly. "Has Ashford called again?"

"No."

"Meaning he doesn't perceive me as a threat."

"Don't go there, Coop."

His laugh was hollow. "It's true. If I planned to marry you, I wouldn't be so calm about you taking off for the weekend with some other guy."

She sighed. "Coop, the ring was a total shock to me. I didn't make Peter any promises."

"So he's like me, operating on hope?"

She met his level gaze. "I don't know what you want me to say."

"I don't want you to say anything until you know what you want." He curved his hand around her neck and pulled her mouth to his for a hard, slanting kiss that held all the passion they might have shared last night if things had gone differently. When he pulled back, his expression was unyielding.

"I'm not Jack, Carlotta, and I'm not Peter. I'm not willing to share you. But I am willing to wait." He climbed out of the hot tub and reached for a towel. "See you in the morning."

16

The one good thing about visiting a morgue, Carlotta realized, was that it made your own problems seem small. Even with her having a dysfunctional family, an empty bank account and a confused heart, every person in the crypt would probably trade places with her if given the chance.

They had passed through an impromptu checkpoint a quarter of a mile from the entrance, on the other side of which sprawled countless TV news crews. The morgue, a four-story, nondescript stucco structure, sat in a boggy area surrounded by scrub foliage—not exactly prime real estate. The inside was filled with disinfectable surfaces of linoleum and glass and stainless steel.

They were sent to the second floor, which bustled with activity. Coop was handsome in dress jeans and a sport coat over a shirt and tie, and he'd loaned Wesley a shirt and tie to look presentable. Carlotta wore slacks and a dark blouse, with her hair pulled back.

Coop's behavior to her this morning had been friendly, but cool. She had lain awake most of the night replaying his parting comment. His intensity spooked her. Part of what had attracted her to Coop was his laid-back attitude. She hadn't counted on his feelings running so deep, so soon.

Sometimes the quiet ones surprised you.

The three of them walked up to the check-in desk, and Coop flashed his credentials to the woman there.

"I'm Dr. Craft. I'm here to pick up body 3050." A code, he had explained to Carlotta and Wesley, predetermined so that Kiki Deerling's name would not be used.

The clerk frowned. "There must be some mistake. Someone else just arrived to claim that body, a tall, bald man." She checked a sign-in log. "A Dr. Talon. He's with Dr. Shores, our chief medical examiner."

"Take me to Dr. Shores." Coop turned to Carlotta and Wesley. "Stay here. The family might have changed their minds."

"I'll go with you," Wes offered.

With her broken arm, Carlotta knew she would be of little help, so she stayed behind. Although she wished she'd asked for directions to a bathroom. Her bladder was at the brim, a by-product of riding in the car with men, who never seemed to have to pee no matter how much they drank.

She crossed her legs and leaned on the counter, flipping through an entertainment magazine the clerk had left behind. Kiki Deerling was on the cover and nearly every page inside. She was—had been—stunningly beautiful, with white-blond hair, a willowy frame and a wide, sexy smile that had driven men crazy. It seemed impossible that her radiant smile had been snuffed out forever.

"Excuse me."

Carlotta looked up to see a young man, maybe twenty, with bright red hair and pale blue eyes, wearing a dark suit and a priest's collar. He carried a small ornate box.

"Yes?" she asked.

"I'm here to bless the body of Kiki Deerling."

She lifted her eyebrows. "And you are?"

"Father Albert Morgan, minister to the Deerling family."

She took in details. He wore black combat boots, not exactly what she'd expect from the clergy. And he had tattoos on his knuckles. Sure, priests could have a checkered past and make questionable fashion choices, but he did not strike her as someone the Deerling family would have sent on such a delicate errand.

Carlotta pretended to check the log behind the desk. "Your name isn't on my list, Father Morgan. May I see some identification?"

He smiled and nodded, then turned on his heel and bolted for the exit.

"Kook," she murmured. He probably had a camera in that box. And how had he gotten through security? Even their cell phones had been held at the checkpoint.

She rolled up the magazine and went in search of a bathroom, wandering down what looked to be a likely hall, since a pay phone and a water fountain sat at the end. She found the ladies' room and relieved herself. When she emerged from the bathroom, a man stood at the pay phone, his back to her. He wore the uniform of an orderly, but his shoes were Ferragamo. More strangely, next to him was a gurney, with a body bag on it—an *occupied* body bag.

"It's time," he said into the phone, talking fast. "Bring the SUV around to the west entrance *now*. Tell the helicopter pilot to stand by."

Carlotta frowned. Helicopter? The man slammed down the phone, then saw her, and his eyes narrowed to a point. He reached for her and managed to grab the end of her ponytail. She wrenched loose, minus a few hair follicles, and ran to find Coop.

She burst through the glass double doors that he and Wesley had gone through, racing down hallways, calling his name. A couple of orderlies stopped her, and she asked to be taken to the chief medical examiner, that it was an emergency. At the sound of hurried footsteps, she looked up to see Coop, Wesley, a man who fit the description of the doctor the clerk had described, and another man she assumed to be the coroner running toward her.

"The body is gone," Coop informed her quietly.

"There's a body on a gurney next to the pay phone on this floor," she said. "Hurry! I heard the guy say a helicopter is standing by."

She led them back to the phone, but the gurney and the man were gone. They took the stairs to the first floor and ran outside to see a long black SUV peeling out of the parking lot, but heading away from the paved entrance and toward an open, marshy field.

"I'll radio security," the coroner said, looking completely panicked.

Coop ran to his van. Carlotta and Wesley followed and vaulted inside. Coop turned over the engine and slammed the vehicle into gear, then turned it toward the black SUV and gave chase over the bumpy field. She and Wesley hung on while the gurney and other equipment in the back clanged noisily. Ahead of them, the SUV blew a back tire and slowed, but kept going. Coop pulled close enough to ram the back of the SUV, and sent it spinning into a shallow, sandy ditch. The driver opened the door and jumped down.

"That's the guy I saw by the pay phone," Carlotta confirmed.

Ferragamo Shoes made a run for the tree line without looking back. By the time they stopped the van and climbed out, he had disappeared.

Coop opened the back door of the SUV to reveal a body bag. He checked the tag on it and nodded. "It's her."

He unzipped the bag a few inches and his jaw hardened. Carlotta glanced at the girl's startlingly white, famous face. Her hair looked freshly washed, the only thing about her that still seemed alive. The area around her nose was swollen and irritated, probably where tubes had been inserted. Her neck was bluish, and a red circular imprint stood out on her collarbone.

Coop zipped the bag closed. "Give me a hand, Wes."

While they loaded the body into the back of the van, Carlotta heard a helicopter in the distance. She looked up and saw a chopper come into view, then veer away from the property.

Security vehicles descended on them. The shaken chief medical examiner emerged from one of the cars and verified the body was the correct one. In the melee, Dr. Talon, the other man who had come to claim the body, had vanished.

"If that was even his name," the coroner said, clearly distraught. "He said he was Ms. Deerling's personal physician, that the family wanted him to view the body. His papers seemed to be in order." Dr. Shores wrung his hands. "This is highly unusual. I'm going to need all of you to give a statement to the police."

"I understand how you feel," Coop said to the medical examiner in the same voice she'd heard him use with victims' family members. "But if the police get involved, then it's a matter of public record and will reflect badly on your morgue. Do you really want to feed the media frenzy and put the Deerling family through that? We have Ms. Deerling, and that's what's important, isn't it?"

Dr. Shores considered Coop's words, then nodded. "You're right. And the sooner she's out of my morgue, the better."

"There's just one thing," Coop said. "I noticed the body hasn't been autopsied, and I understood I was to take it directly to the funeral home. Has there been a mistake? Do I need to take it to the Atlanta morgue?"

"No," the man said. "The family objected to an autopsy, and because of the young woman's history of asthmatic attacks, I agreed to it, after examining the body. Like you said, there was no use putting the family through unnecessary suffering."

Coop nodded, but from the set of his mouth, Carlotta knew he wasn't satisfied with the doctor's explanation.

They waited another hour while paperwork was processed, the body was placed in a box with dry ice, and a Florida license plate was added to the van. Then they made the long drive back to collect their phones at the security checkpoint, and exited with two other vans. The vehicle behind them was sparkling clean, with a pink bow tied on the antenna—the decoy van.

"Don't look at the cameras," Coop said. "Don't give the vultures any footage."

They pulled away and, as hoped, the media descended on the van behind them. Coop turned toward the interstate and they were all quiet for a long while, conscious of the pop-culture significance of their cargo. Wesley, especially, was silent. He was probably thinking how close in age he was to Kiki Deerling, and realizing that a young life could end just as quickly as an old one.

Carlotta's heart was still thudding overtime in her chest. "Have you ever had anything like that happen before?"

Coop shook his head, his expression solemn. "This is a first."

"Do you think those two men were in cahoots?" Wesley asked.

Carlotta leaned over to pick up the rolled magazine she'd accidentally lifted from the check-in counter and then dropped on the floorboard during the chase. "There were three men." She told them about the nervous redheaded "priest." "Maybe they were all in on it together."

"Maybe," Coop said. A muscle jumped in his jaw.

"What would someone do with a body?" Carlotta asked.

"All kinds of bad things," he replied. "There are a lot of sickos out there, especially when a celebrity is involved."

"What are the penalties for stealing a body?" Wesley asked.

"Abuse of a corpse is a felony," Coop said. "Stealing a corpse, receiving it illegally, all felonies."

"So if those guys were caught, they'd go to prison?"

"For several years," Coop confirmed.

"What paparazzo would risk going to prison?" Carlotta asked.

Coop shrugged. "Someone who was going to be paid well for photos, or for the body itself."

"That's so vile," she said. "Coop, you saw the body. Did it look like she'd had an asthma attack?"

He answered without looking at Carlotta. "I don't have enough information to form an opinion."

"But why was her neck so bruised?"

He shrugged. "She could've fallen and bruised herself during the attack. Or it could have been caused by someone in the hospital holding her down, or a piece of equipment they used to try to resuscitate her. There are a lot of possible reasons."

"What happens during an asthma attack?"

"The muscles in a person's airways start to spasm, and

to make matters worse, the respiratory system produces a thick mucus."

"Why?"

"There are many different triggers, some of them environmental, such as chemicals."

"What about pet hair? She had a pug."

"That can be a trigger, too, and pugs are notoriously heavy shedders. Drugs can also be a trigger, both over-the-counter and illegal ones. And sometimes there's no obvious trigger at all."

"But don't most people with asthma have an inhaler?"

"They're supposed to. Quick-relief inhalers will help relax the spasms and reopen the airways."

"So she must not have had her inhaler with her."

"Or maybe she couldn't get to it fast enough, or perhaps it was out of medicine. There are lots of possibilities."

"So her death might have been prevented."

"If it was an asthma attack, then yes, with the right treatment administered as quickly as possible, her death might have been prevented."

Carlotta frowned. "If?"

Coop shifted in his seat, then glanced in the rearview mirror. "Let's all be alert. I won't relax until we're back in Atlanta."

"This has been a wild trip," Wesley offered.

Coop glanced over at Carlotta and murmured, "You can say that again."

She warmed at his reference to their near miss in the hotel room, and felt a pang of guilt for deceiving him about the

Daytona stopover. "I really do appreciate you inviting me to come along."

"Glad you were at least able to get some business done," he said quietly, so Wesley wouldn't hear.

"Business *and* pleasure," she said.

"You don't have to humor me."

"I'm not."

He opened his mouth to say something, but Wesley's head suddenly appeared between them. "When are we going to stop and eat lunch?"

Coop pushed up his glasses and pinched the bridge of his nose as if in pain. "This trip can't be over soon enough."

It was a couple of hours before Coop gave in to Wesley's wheedling and pulled off on an exit ramp to find a restaurant. Coop picked a table next to a window where the van was visible. They placed an order, then Wesley excused himself to go to the men's room.

"He's probably stealing a smoke," Carlotta said.

"You think so?"

"It's what I want to do," she said with a laugh.

"So you both smoke, but are trying to keep it from one another?"

"Apparently."

"To be so close, you and Wesley aren't very honest with each other."

"I think that's our secret to staying close."

"Why didn't you want to tell him about your father leaving you the note? Or that his fingerprints were found in Daytona?"

She sighed. "You've been around Wesley long enough to know that he doesn't exercise the best judgment."

"Yeah, I noticed."

"He thinks our dad is completely innocent of everything he's accused of. He has this fantasy that one day our parents are going to come home and we'll all be one big, happy family again. I just don't want him to get his hopes up."

"He's not a kid anymore, Carlotta. You can't protect him from disappointment."

"I know. But now he's old enough to react recklessly and get himself in real adult trouble. If I'd told him about the hotel robbery, he would've crashed in there and complicated things."

"*Or* he would've helped you," Coop said. "You said that Jack underestimated your father. I think sometimes you underestimate Wesley. He's smart. And he has as much at stake here as you do."

Carlotta opened her mouth, but she didn't know how to respond.

The waiter delivered their drinks and Wes reappeared. She studied her brother as he sat down. He was looking a little gray—maybe the smoking wasn't agreeing with him. Sometimes he seemed so mature, but other times, he was all teenager. Still, he wasn't a malicious person. Even when he did bad things, it was usually with good intentions.

Or was that the mother in her taking up for him again?

"So is being out of town for a couple of days going to make your problem with The Carver go away?" she asked him.

"I hope so," Wesley said, busying himself with a bendy straw.

She sent a look to Coop that said, *See what I mean?*

"Don't you start your community service tomorrow?" Coop asked.

"Yep."

"What exactly will you be doing?" he pressed.

"Helping the city beef up its database security to keep out hackers like me."

"Do you think maybe you'd like to study computers in college someday?"

Wesley frowned. "Are you a career counselor now?"

"Wesley!" Carlotta admonished.

Coop shook his head and gave a little laugh. "I just told your sister that she treats you like a kid, but the more I'm around you, the more I understand why she does."

The waiter brought their food on a big tray and passed out plates of burgers and fries. When he left, Wesley looked at Coop with remorse. "I'm sorry, man. I'm in a bad mood because my arm is hurting again."

"Fair enough. Are you still taking those antibiotics?"

"Yeah."

"Promise me you'll see a doctor if your arm isn't better by tomorrow."

"Okay."

Carlotta ate her burger, looking back and forth between the men as they talked about music and movies, marveling over how Wesley responded to Coop. How many times had she wished for a man's stronger presence to back her up when she was doling out discipline while Wesley was grow-ing up? She wondered if Coop wanted a family someday. He would be a great father, she acknowledged. The kind of father any kid would want to have.

He glanced her way and caught her staring. She looked down and concentrated on removing the onion from her bun. Her gaze strayed to a large man outside in the parking lot. Something about him seemed familiar…

While she sipped her soda, the man walked up to Coop's van and, in a flash, inserted a slim-jim tool into the window seam and popped open the door. It was the guy from the morgue with the Ferragamo shoes, the one who'd driven the SUV.

"Coop!" she yelled, pointing.

He looked up to see what was happening. "Stay here." He sprinted out of the restaurant, but he had a good dis-tance to cover.

"We need to call the police," Carlotta said, pulling out her cell phone, but Wesley stopped her.

"If the police come, word will get out about our cargo."

He was right—it was Coop's call to make. Her heart hammered against her breastbone. She expected to see the van pull away at any second and disappear, but the thief seemed to be having trouble with the wiring. When Coop reached the van, he dragged the guy out. Carlotta watched in dismay while they exchanged punches. Coop had a height advantage, but the guy was bulky.

Everyone in the restaurant had gathered to look out the window. A dark car pulled up and honked. The would-be thief pushed Coop down, then jumped into the car, and it sped away.

"I'm calling the police," a restaurant employee said.

"Don't let them," Carlotta told Wesley, then ran outside.

Coop was picking himself up when she reached him. "Are you okay? Your eye is bleeding!"

He winced and touched the torn skin on his brow. "It's superficial. I'm fine. Let's get Wesley and get going."

"But what if they come back? What if they follow us and try to steal the van again?"

He put his arm on her elbow to shepherd her inside, scanning the parking lot the whole time. "They can't steal it. I installed a kill switch." He fished in his pocket and held up a strange-looking key. "The engine won't start unless this is in place."

She shuddered. "This is just plain creepy. They won't leave the poor girl alone."

The two of them went back into the restaurant, and Coop assured the manager that calling the police was unnecessary. He paid their bill and gestured to Wesley. "Wrap up your burger and let's go."

Wesley didn't ask any questions—he looked as shaken as Carlotta felt. When they left the restaurant, Coop scanned the area again before they climbed into the van.

"Did you see the plates of the car the guy got into?" Carlotta asked.

"There weren't any plates. Wes, get out the atlas behind my seat."

"Why?"

"Find us an alternate route home, off the interstates as much as possible."

"Won't that take longer?" he asked.

"Just do it," Coop said, glancing in the rearview mirror.

Wesley bent over the atlas. "Looks like it'll be an hour or so before we can leave the interstate."

"Okay, you navigate." Coop looked over at Carlotta. "Are you okay?"

She nodded, then opened the glove compartment to remove a first aid kit she'd seen there. From the supplies, she selected an antiseptic wipe in a foil packet. Twisting in her seat, she cleaned the cut over Coop's eye. He flinched, but let her remove the blood and apply an adhesive bandage.

"I should be so lucky to get punched every day," he said lightly.

"You're lucky he didn't break your glasses...or worse." She made a rueful noise. "You could've been killed back there. What if he'd had a gun?"

"I'm bulletproof," he said with a wink.

"I'm serious, Coop."

He sobered. "I'm sorry you're scared. Believe me, I never would've asked you to come along if I thought it would be dangerous."

"Do you have a gun, Coop?" Wesley asked, his eyes wide.

"I'm not allowed to own one," he said matter-of-factly.

Another intriguing hint about his background, Carlotta mused. "We'll be home soon," she said. "Kiki Deerling is lucky to have you looking out for her."

For more than an hour they rode along in relative silence,

listening to music and the frequent news updates about Kiki's death on the radio. The media seemed to be focusing on the fact that she'd been partying with her ex-boyfriend, Matt Pearson, the night she died. Pearson was an alleged heavy drug user, reputed to host heroin parties and to carry drugs on him nearly all the time.

"Could you tell *anything* when you looked at the body?" Carlotta asked Coop.

"I only saw her face," he answered. He kept glancing in the rearview mirror, his expression taut.

"Do you see the car?" she asked, turning around.

Wesley turned around, too.

"No," Coop said, but he still seemed uneasy.

Carlotta saw a sign for a rest area and shifted in her seat. "I'm sorry, but I can't wait much longer to go to the bathroom."

He smiled. "I wasn't going to hold you captive. I need to make a phone call, anyway, and I'd rather not do it while I'm driving."

He put on his signal and changed lanes, taking the off-ramp for the rest area. After he parked the van, Carlotta climbed down, happy to stretch her legs.

"I'll hurry," she said.

"We have a few minutes," Coop told her, pulling out his cell phone. "I hope the vending area has coffee."

"I'll check," she offered.

He nodded gratefully, then frowned at his phone. "I'm going to walk around and see if I can get a better signal."

"You two do what you need to do," Wesley said. "I'll stay with the van."

"If anything happens," Coop said, "don't be a hero."

"Don't worry," he said wryly.

At least her brother's arm didn't seem to be hurting anymore, Carlotta mused as she stood in line in the ladies' room. He was certainly in a better mood. Of course, all of them were in a strange space after the day they'd had.

When she left the bathroom, she followed a walkway up a slight incline to the detached concrete hut marked Vending.

Thwarting body snatchers not once, but twice… Could things get any more bizarre today?

She was relieved to see a coffee machine, looking forward to a shot of caffeine herself. She fed the machine quarters and stood watching the brown liquid dispense into a paper cup. The second cup was filling when a man came up next to her.

She gestured to the machine. "I'm almost finished."

"Take your time," he said.

But that voice…that voice…

Carlotta jerked her head around and stared up at the tall man wearing a battered fishing hat and a full beard with sunglasses.

"Don't be so obvious, sweetheart. You'll blow my cover."

Her stomach twisted, her vision tunneled, her heart stopped. Her throat convulsed with the attempt to speak, and finally one word emerged.

"Dad?"

18

Carlotta stared at the scraggly man standing next to her, searching for the debonair, handsome father who'd abandoned her over ten years ago. But if not for the voice, she wouldn't have recognized him. She took a step backward and the cup of coffee she held slipped out of her hand, bouncing on the ground and splashing her slacks.

"Easy," her father said with a smile. "Don't do anything that will draw attention."

"What…what are you doing here?" she managed to ask. "Have you been following us?"

"Yes. And waiting for an opportunity like this. God, I've missed you so."

She longed to throw her arms around him, but he also frightened her. She didn't really know this man anymore. "How did you know where we were? Do you live around here? How's our mother?"

He removed the second full cup of coffee from the

machine and slowly fed in more coins with those unmistakable large hands. Hands that had tossed her in the air when
she'd been little. Hands that held her bike when she learned
to ride. Hands that allegedly had stolen hundreds of thou-
sands of dollars from trusting investors.

"I know you have a lot of questions, sweetheart. Let's just
say that I've been keeping tabs on you and Wes. You've done
well, and you're a lovely woman. I'm so proud of you."

She bit her lip to stem sudden tears as anger flared in her
chest. "You've been keeping tabs on us? You broke the heart
of a nine-year-old." She swallowed. "Mine, too. Why?
Where have you been all this time?"

"I'm so sorry that you and Wesley had to suffer. I never
meant to be gone this long. I've been gathering evidence to
prove my innocence."

"For ten years?"

His mouth twitched downward. "Your mother has been
sick on and off."

Her chin went up. "Sick or drunk?"

"Her alcoholism is a disease, Carlotta."

It was strange how she could feel sympathy for Coop in
his struggle with alcohol, but not for her own mother. She
looked over her shoulder and down the hill, to where Wesley
stood next to the van. "Don't you want to speak to your
son?"

"Of course I do. But let's keep this between us for now."
He handed her the cup of coffee he held, and removed the
full cup sitting in the machine for a quick drink. "I need to
lie low for a while, but I'll contact you again soon."

"How? Will you call?"

"No. The police still have a tap on the phone at the town house," he said. "They didn't remove it after that ridiculous funeral they put you through."

"I have a cell phone."

"I have the number."

"A new one."

"I know. Don't worry, I'll find you. Just stay close to Peter."

"Please…don't involve Peter."

"But he's in a position at the firm to help me. I need him. He's the only person there I can trust. When the time comes, I'm going to need your help, too, sweetheart. Then we'll all be together again."

Emotions pelted her. She wanted to scream, wanted to cry, wanted to laugh. Wanted to call Jack and tell him where he could find his most-wanted man.

"How about a hug?" she whispered.

But before her father could move, the sound of screeching brakes tore through the air. She looked down to see a green van lurch to a halt behind Coop's white one. Two men scrambled out and one of them ran to the back of the van that held Kiki's body. When the door wouldn't open, he strode over to Wesley and grabbed him by the shirt. Carlotta's throat clogged with fear. At this distance she couldn't be sure, but the thug looked like the tall, bald man who had posed as Dr. Talon at the morgue. Wesley held up his hands and shook his head.

A shot rang out and the men hunkered down, surprised.

Carlotta looked around to see Coop running toward the potential body thieves, holding a pistol straight up in the air.

The man still standing next to the green van reached inside the door and, to her horror, withdrew a shotgun. "Wesley, get down!" she screamed. Screams rang out all over the rest area.

The sound of a siren pierced the air. She looked back to see a dark car with a red flashing light on top racing toward them. Both of the unknown men lunged into their vehicle and took off, blowing through the rest area at breathless speeds before screeching onto the interstate. The dark police sedan slid in sideways and stopped, siren still blaring. The driver got out, a radio in his hand, communicating to someone what had just transpired.

Jack.

Carlotta had taken two steps forward before she remembered her father. She wheeled around...but he was gone. She pivoted, looking in every direction, but it was as if he'd vanished into thin air.

Again.

With her mind and heart both racing, she ran down the incline to Coop's van. Jack was there, talking to Coop, whose pistol had mysteriously disappeared. Wesley was shaking and had vomit on his T-shirt.

Jack and Coop both turned toward her. "Are you okay?" they asked in unison.

"I'm fine." In truth, she was a jittery mess. "Wesley, are you hurt?"

He shook his head, but was pacing off the scare.

"Jack, what are you doing here?" she asked.

"I called him to send a police escort to meet us," Coop said.

"But since I was only a couple of miles away, I volunteered," Jack said.

"We were still on the phone when the green van pulled in."

"Seems like you're always where you need to be," she murmured for Jack's ears only.

"Just doing my job."

She glanced over Jack's shoulder, wondering where her father had gone, if he was watching them. "Coop, one of the men looked like that guy at the morgue. Was it?"

"Yeah." He turned to Jack. "White, tall, bald. He was at Boca posing as a physician, trying to view the body."

Jack scratched his temple. "Okay, so one of the guys fired a pistol in the air, and the other one had a shotgun."

She exchanged a glance with Coop, who put his hands on his hips. "That's not what I told you, Jack," he stated.

"But that's how it's going to read in the report," Jack said pointedly, then gestured to Carlotta and Wesley. "I'm sure the two of you will corroborate that one of the perps fired into the air."

"Right," Carlotta said, looking at Wesley and nodding until he did the same. She was surprised but pleased that Jack was bending the rules to protect Coop, who by his own admission wasn't supposed to own a handgun.

"Are these the same yahoos who tried to steal the van at the restaurant?" Jack asked.

"I don't think so," Coop said. "I didn't see who picked

up the hefty guy when he got away from the restaurant, but I got a look at the driver of this van. It wasn't the hefty guy."

"So we have a hefty guy, and a tall, bald guy, who could be working together, or not."

Coop quirked his mouth, then nodded.

"I put out an APB on the van, but without a plate number, I'm not holding out much hope that it'll turn up."

"Jack, can you omit the Deerling woman's name in these reports?" Coop asked.

He nodded. "I'll handle it." Then he turned to Wesley. "Are you sure you don't remember anything else?"

Wesley shook his head. He still looked ill. When Carlotta thought about how close he'd come to getting shot, she was terrified all over again. She wanted to console her brother, but frankly, she was afraid if she looked at him, she'd blurt out that she'd just seen Randolph. She had to turn her back to collect herself, and scanned the area once again to see if their father might still be there.

He wasn't.

"Hey," Jack said, walking around to face her. "Don't worry—those guys aren't coming back."

She smiled and nodded.

"Is something else bothering you? You look like you've seen a ghost."

She willed him to see the truth in her eyes so she wouldn't have to tell him that this might be the closest he'd ever get to her father. It made her furious that Randolph simply expected her to cover for him. It made her even more furious that she was willing. Her eyes watered.

"Hey, hey," Jack said, squeezing her shoulder. "You know I can't take the waterworks."

"Sorry." She blinked away the moisture. "It's been a roller coaster of a weekend, that's all."

"You felt as if you were getting close to your father. You must be disappointed."

She smiled weakly. "Yeah, that's it."

"By the way," he whispered. "You neglected to mention that your brother accompanied you and Coop on this trip."

"Did I?"

"Yes, you did." He grinned. "It certainly puts a different spin on your getaway weekend. At least for me."

She frowned up at him, but before she could respond, the passenger door of his sedan opened and Liz Fischer's blond head emerged. "Jack, is it safe to come out?"

"Yeah," he called, but Carlotta felt him tense.

Liz walked up and gave her the once-over. Carlotta knew she looked a fright in her coffee-stained slacks, sagging ponytail and grubby fiberglass cast. Liz, on the other hand, looked impeccable in a tan linen suit and Gucci loafers.

"Carlotta, I see you're still recovering from your infamous tumble at the Fox Theater."

"Yes. Of course, it would've been much worse if I hadn't fallen right into Jack's arms."

Liz pursed her lips. "How is it that you find yourself in the most ridiculous predicaments?"

"I'm my father's daughter," she said sweetly. And wondered if her father was witnessing this little exchange between his daughter and his former mistress.

Jack cleared his throat.

"I think I'll go over and talk to my client," Liz said, nodding toward Wesley.

As the bony woman walked away, Carlotta got a whiff of her strong perfume and winced. While she was trying to remember where she'd smelled it before, she watched Liz's body language with Wesley—wiping his mouth with a handkerchief, leaning into him, looking concerned as he changed T-shirts...looking *interested*. And suddenly Carlotta realized where Wesley had been all those nights he'd come rolling in, stinking of a woman. He'd been stinking of Liz.

Carlotta choked on her anger. It wasn't enough that Liz had been having an affair with Randolph? Did she have to get her claws in Wesley, too?

She spun toward Jack, who was watching Liz and Wesley under his lashes and looking mighty uncomfortable. He knew, she realized.

"Can't keep your cat on a leash, Jack?"

He didn't say anything.

Behind her, Coop asked, "Are you ready to go, Carlotta?"

"Am I ever. Wesley!" she called. "Time to leave."

Jack reached for her arm. "Carlotta—"

She ignored him and strode to the van, climbing into the passenger seat. A migraine threatened to invade her entire head, and her arm was throbbing. Coop slid into the driver's seat and looked over.

"You remembered the coffee."

Carlotta glanced down to see she was still holding one cup

of the vending machine coffee. She exhaled. "Yeah. It's probably cold."

"Okay by me. Want to share?"

She nodded gratefully, and took a Percocet from the prescription bottle in her bag. "Are you still taking the body directly to your uncle's funeral home?"

"Yes, but I called him and asked him to have extra security waiting."

"This is unbelievable." She swallowed the pill and chased it with coffee. "Maybe Kiki's death wasn't an accident. Maybe that's why those guys want to steal her body. Maybe they're afraid that all the rumors about drugs will trigger an autopsy."

He took the coffee from her and drank from the other side. "If that's the case, why would two different guys be trying to steal the body?"

"Don't forget the so-called priest. Maybe it's a conspiracy. Maybe they're trying to steal her body so they can freeze-dry it."

He laughed. "That makes as much sense as anything else."

Wesley opened the door and fell into the backseat.

"You okay?" Coop asked, turning around. "Those antibiotics will upset your stomach if you don't take them with food."

"Thanks." Wesley wiped his mouth with his hand. "Man, you scared me to death. I thought you said you didn't have a gun."

"I said I'm not allowed to own one," Coop stated, turning over the ignition. "Jack could've nailed my ass to the wall back there."

"He did the right thing," Carlotta mumbled into the coffee. Confounding man.

"What the hell was Jack doing down here, anyway?" Wesley asked.

For a moment, she panicked. She hadn't thought about the possibility that Liz might spill her guts to Wesley about their father's fingerprints at the hotel. Then she relaxed— apparently the woman hadn't said anything. She felt Coop's gaze on her, urging her to confide in Wesley. But with her father's voice and image so fresh in her mind, she wasn't ready to talk about it. Not when she wanted to strangle Wesley for fooling around with Liz.

"It was some case he was working on," she said over her shoulder.

Coop quirked his mouth, but didn't comment. Putting the van in Drive, he pulled away, with Jack's sedan bringing up the rear.

Carlotta glanced in the side mirror, watching the rest area retreat in the distance. She was almost numb, slowly processing what had just transpired. On the heels of the joy of discovering that her father was alive was the certainty that he'd willingly ignored them all these years. She had imagined as much, but the realization was still a bitter pill to swallow.

And driving away, it felt as if she was losing her father all over again.

19

Coop set her suitcase inside the living room door. Wesley walked past them, and a few seconds later, his bedroom door slammed.

"I didn't realize how moody he is," Coop said.

"I guess he has a lot on his mind," she said, then muttered, "Don't we all."

Coop rubbed the back of his neck and sighed. "This wasn't exactly how I'd hoped the weekend would go."

"You went way beyond the call of duty to deliver the body to your uncle's funeral home safe and sound."

"That's not what I meant."

"I know," she murmured, then picked up one of his long-fingered hands. "I think our timing is off."

He curled her hand inside his. "I'm ready and you're not."

She nodded. "I'm not. I just have too many things going on right now." She considered telling him about seeing her father—she was bursting to tell someone—but she didn't want to put Coop in a position of having information about a wanted fugitive.

He stepped forward and kissed her, a long, deep kiss to tide them both over for a while. "Don't forget what I said," he whispered.

"I won't."

At the door he turned back. "When your arm heals, will you still consider a body-moving job now and then?"

"Sure. Stay in touch."

"I will."

"Coop?"

"Yeah?"

She angled her head. "Tell the truth. Do you really think Kiki Deerling died of an asthma attack?"

"It doesn't matter what I think. I'm not the M.E." He touched her nose. "And neither are you. Get some rest. And call me if Wes gets to be too much of a handful." He smiled. "Or call me if you just want to talk."

She nodded, but when the door closed behind him, she murmured, "If only."

Carlotta dragged her suitcase into her bedroom, then ran a bubble bath. Everything hurt. She undressed slowly and sank into the tub up to her neck, laying her arm on the rim to keep her cast dry.

And then the tears came.

She cried over the messed up messy mess of her life, over her parents' failures and her own shortcomings. She bawled over her own indecisiveness when it came to men. She was afraid to choose. She didn't want to make a mistake that would come back to haunt her later, and wreck the lives of others in the process. What did she know about relationships, anyway?

She was better off alone rather than pulling someone into the dysfunctional vortex of her family and having them end up hating her for it.

Like Coop… He seemed eager to love her, and her response to him this weekend, frankly, blew her away. But she was fairly certain she couldn't meet his expectations. He was lonely and needed a project; she was a handy fixer-upper. Perhaps it was his experience with the twelve-step program that made him so accepting, so optimistic. But as tempting as it was to share her burden, she wanted at least one man in her life who didn't have a direct connection to her parents.

Her roll in the hay with Jack had led nowhere. To him, she was still first and foremost the daughter of Randolph "The Bird" Wren. A means to an end. According to her father, the tap hadn't been lifted from their home phone after the fake funeral, as promised—and Jack had to know about that, the rat. Just as he'd known about Liz "Mrs. Robinson" Fischer getting her claws into Carlotta's little brother.

She leaned over, picked up the cordless handset on the floor and punched in Hannah's number. After a couple of rings the phone connected, but there was only silence on the other end.

"I know you don't want to talk," Carlotta said, "but did I ever tell you what a tiny penis Detective Jack Terry has? I

walked in on him in the bathroom when he was doing surveillance from my house. *T-I-N-Y.* What Liz Fischer sees in
him, I don't know. But then I've heard that woman will sleep
with anything pointed. Anyway, just wanted to share. You
can call me back on my cell sometime. Talk soon."

She hung up, feeling marginally better that anyone listening in would happily share the fabricated description of
Jack's johnson and his tartlet, Liz. Then Carlotta immersed
herself in the entertainment magazine that she'd inadvertently taken from the morgue in Boca Raton, which
featured a retrospective article on Kiki Deerling's short life.

The young woman had been raised in Atlanta, with a
background that sounded similar to Carlotta's—the best
neighborhood, the best schools, a professional father, a
socialite mother. At fourteen, though, Kiki had begun
modeling, and at sixteen, had begun dating boy-band superstar and all-around badass Matt Pearson. Soon she was a
fixture on the Hollywood party scene, with clothes design-
ers clamoring to get their duds on her tall, lanky frame.

Then came her own line of clothes, her own perfume and
a record deal. Kiki exuded that blend of wholesome innocence and sexuality that fed into fantasies. And the camera
loved her. She wasn't classically beautiful, but imminently
photogenic and instantly recognizable. She and her pug,
Twizzler, were favorites of the paparazzi, and Kiki courted
an entourage wherever she went. Lately, though, she'd
suffered from overexposure, and her behavior had taken a
turn toward the lurid. Rumors of drug use and sexcapades
flourished, fueled by unflattering photos and videos of Kiki

half-dressed and looking stoned. The public couldn't get enough.

Enter Camp Kiki. The apparent brainchild of a concerned manager, Camp Kiki was nestled in the mountains of north Georgia and specialized in reforming "troubled" disadvantaged teens, leaving many fans with the opinion that Kiki could benefit from a stint at the camp herself. She had put in appearances as a "guest" counselor, making it an attraction for groupies and the more ambitious paparazzi who were willing to hike in and hang out in trees for a bankable photo. But there were success stories, too; many teens had testified that the camp had been a life-changing experience for them.

Carlotta flipped through the pages of photos, admittedly as fascinated by the young girl's celebrity as other people were. And saddened that Kiki's entire life seemed to have been a spectacle for the entertainment of others. Had she loved the spotlight as much as she appeared to? Or had she simply become addicted to the fame?

One photograph in particular, though, stopped Carlotta. In the foreground Kiki was on stage, singing—or, as many claimed, lip-synching—wearing an outfit that resembled a slingshot with sleeves. The background showed an audience caught up in worship for Kiki. One individual was unmistakably recognizable: the redheaded "priest" who'd made an appearance at the morgue in Boca. And the way he was looking at Kiki sent chills up Carlotta's spine. His expression was one of hate, loathing…revulsion.

She flipped back to the beginning of the magazine and

studied all the photos carefully. The man was in two other shots, always in the background, and always staring at Kiki with a twisted look on his face. A stalker? Attempting to get into the morgue to see her one last time? To do something vile to her body? And who were the other two men trying to get their hands on Kiki? Henchmen for the tabloids, trying to heist the corpse for photos? Something even more depraved? Those two men seemed more corporate than the pretend priest, who struck Carlotta as just plain creepy.

She climbed out of the tub and murmured a prayer for the girl's family, who were undoubtedly confused and profoundly sad. It was strange how people in the same gene pool could turn out so differently and yet be bound by a sense of relatedness. The things family members did for each other, to each other and because of each other were truly mind-boggling. And unexplainable.

Why else would Carlotta be starting to make room in her brain for the remote possibility that her father was innocent?

She pulled on her fuzzy chenille robe, denying the rogue thought that had slipped into her head. After ten years of thinking the worst of her dad, how could she allow him to sway her opinion in a surprise ten-minute appearance? How could he still have that much power over her?

Yet he did, she acknowledged miserably. That's why she didn't give up Randolph when she had the chance.

She replayed the conversation in her head for the hundredth time, then retrieved a notebook from her dresser and recorded every detail she could remember. He'd worn a beard, sunglasses, fishing hat and nondescript clothing. He'd said he'd been following them, waiting for an opportunity to talk to her; said he'd been keeping tabs on her and Wesley, that he'd been gathering evidence to prove his innocence. He'd said that her mother had been "sick" on and off, with the implication that she was still drinking heavily. He'd asked her not to tell Wesley about his visit, that he'd be laying low for a while, but would contact her. He knew their phone was tapped; he knew she had a new cell phone. He said that Peter was in a position at the firm to help him.

I'm going to need your help, too, sweetheart.

She closed her eyes and cursed her inability to hate Randolph Wren, a weakness that she couldn't seem to overcome. Like a good daughter, she was prepared to put her life on hold and wait until she heard from him again. Because her life would be on hold until she could put this interminable situation with her father behind her, anyway.

Meanwhile, she needed to make plans to see Peter…and to "stay close" to him, as her father had instructed.

20

Richard McCormick extended a big, fleshy hand. "Welcome to Atlanta Systems Services, Wesley."

Wesley pumped it and swallowed the pain that shot through his arm. "Your department acronym is ASS?"

"Huh?" McCormick frowned, then laughed. "Oh, yeah, I guess so. Come on, I'll show you where you'll be working."

Wesley followed the lumpy guy through a maze of cubicles and bull pens that hummed with machinery. Huge clumps of black and gray cables snaked everywhere—over desks and floors, clipped to walls and across ceilings. A few faces looked up from computer monitors as he passed through, but for the most part, everyone seemed engrossed in whatever they were doing. It was his first experience in an office environment and he was suddenly nervous. He didn't know what to expect.

"Here you go," the man said, gesturing to a workstation connected to three others in a cluster, occupied by two young guys and a girl.

"Everyone, this is Wesley."

"Hey," he said, nodding.

"Hi," they chorused.

"I'm Jeff," a dark-haired guy said. His shirt was missing a button and he looked as if he hadn't slept—or showered—in a couple of days.

"Ravi," offered the other guy who appeared to be of Middle Eastern descent and was wearing latex gloves as he tapped on a keyboard.

"Meg," the girl stated. She wore a black Georgia Tech sweatshirt and zebra-striped glasses, her dishwater-blond hair twisted up into coiled pigtails.

"Help Wes get settled in," Richard said. "He's going to be working on our legacy databases."

The two guys snickered, and when McCormick walked away, Jeff said, "Dude, you just got the shittiest assignment in this cesspool."

"Mainframe work sucks," Ravi said.

"Ignore Dumb and Dumber," Meg said dryly. "This isn't a bad place to work. McCormick even lets us work on school projects when we need to."

"You go to Tech?" Wesley asked, setting his backpack on the empty desk.

"We all do," she said. "We're in a work-study program. What about you?"

"A community service sentence."

She frowned. "Did you get arrested or something?"

"Yeah. For hacking into this place."

"Cool," Jeff said, and Ravi nodded. Meg, on the other hand, looked bored with him already.

Wesley scanned the PC sitting on his desk. "Does this boat anchor even have a math coprocessor?"

"Doesn't matter much," Jeff said. "It's basically just a monitor to give you access to the mainframe."

"No Internet access?"

"Nope. We all use our phones." They held up various models of expensive PDAs, all of which had more memory than the dinosaur of a PC on his desk.

"Don't worry. We'll build you something better," Ravi offered.

"How long will you be around?" Meg asked.

McCormick had decided to divvy up Wesley's one hundred hours of community service into four-hour chunks. "Every morning for about six weeks." He sat in his assigned dusty, up-holstered chair and rubbed his arm. The gashes were starting to heal, but the skin was painfully taut. He was down to two OxyContin pills, and would like to get more from Chance, but one problem nagged at him—the possibility that when he reported in to E. on Wednesday, she would make him provide a urine sample for a drug test. If he failed, E. wouldn't think twice about having him tossed in jail, not after giving him a pass on the aborted drug deal in which she'd intervened.

Although with The Carver still on his ass and Father Thom to pay, too, jail might be the safest place to hang out for a while. Wes really needed to win the pot Wednesday night in the game that Chance had secured for him.

Throwing caution to the wind, he palmed one of the remaining pills and chewed it, washing it down with a bottle of water from his backpack. When he looked up, Meg was staring at him. He gave her his best disarming smile, easier because the OxyContin was already flashing through his system. She looked away.

"Nice tie, man," Jeff said with a laugh. "You don't have to wear one here."

"I have to for my other job."

"What's your other job?" Ravi asked.

"I'm on call to move bodies for the morgue."

"Cool," Jeff said again. "What's the grossest thing you've seen?"

"Motorcyclist versus I-285. He lost."

"Ew," Meg said. "Don't you go to college?"

Wesley scoffed. "I don't need college."

"You're going to move bodies for the rest of your life?" she asked, obviously unimpressed.

"No. I'm a card player. I'm going to the World Series of Poker." At her dubious look, he added, "Someday."

"Sounds like a real career plan," she said before pushing back from her desk and walking away. She had possibly the best ass he'd ever seen in a pair of jeans.

"Forget about her," Jeff warned. "She's way out of your league, man. Smart as shit, rich as hell, and under that sweatshirt, has a body that won't quit." He sighed. "She turned down Harvard *and* Princeton. Her father is some genius geneticist, and she's following in his footsteps."

From the looks on Jeff's and Ravi's faces, it was clear they were obsessed with her.

"If she's rich, why is she working here?"

"I think it makes her feel normal," Jeff said. "You know, part of the working masses."

"I think she's some kind of spy," Ravi said. "Or an alien."

Wesley squinted. "What's with the latex gloves?"

"Germ phobe," Jeff interjected.

"A computer keyboard is more contaminated than a toilet seat," Ravi explained.

"Welcome to the freak show," Jeff said to Wesley. "Let's go see if we can steal you a better machine."

Over the next couple of hours, the four of them pieced together a halfway decent system for Wesley from components they begged, borrowed and stole from all over the department. Jeff and Ravi were instructive and friendly, if a little goofy. Meg was amicable, but standoffish. Wesley was secretly impressed with their knowledge and intrigued by the way they talked about their classes at Georgia Tech—as if they wanted to be there, wanted to fill their heads with as much information as possible.

And he was excited by the prospect of having access to his father's court files.

McCormick pulled him into his office and gave him the broad strokes of the systems the department supported. Legacy systems were fat, old and slow, and ran on behemoth computers of days gone by. They were typically the back-bone systems of any company—payroll, accounts payable, human resources—and in the city's case, courthouse records. And because legacy systems were so large and so important, they were usually the last applications that management wanted to risk moving to a more efficient, but untried, system.

"As you know firsthand," McCormick said, "hackers are becoming more and more sophisticated. We can't expect to secure the databases one hundred percent."

"But you should at least encrypt the data," Wesley replied.

"I can see we're on the same page. It's something we've needed to do for a while, but we never seem to have the time or the funding. Since you were able to breach our security, you're an ideal candidate to help us out in this area." The man cleared his throat. "But since we haven't been able to determine exactly what data you changed, I was hoping that first you'd, um, share that with me."

Wesley swallowed a smile. The man was asking him to confess to things they hadn't been able to detect? Right. No one needed to know that he'd removed all references to three speeding tickets for Chance—at five hundred bucks a pop. And he'd left himself a nice easy trail back into the file, kind of like dropping breadcrumbs, so he could sell his services again sometime. That asshole cop Jack Terry had arrested him and confiscated his equipment, but the man didn't know that Wesley had stored his best computer stuff at Chance's condo and was just laying low until he was off probation.

"I didn't change anything," he said solemnly. "I just wanted to prove that I could get in. I was hanging out with a few other hackers and we got points for breaking into different systems. It wasn't about messing with the data."

McCormick looked relieved. "That's very good news."

He passed a manual across the desk. "Okay, this should get you up to speed on encryption techniques and two different encoders that we have access to. Take a couple of days to read it, then we'll sit down and come up with some general guidelines on how to proceed."

"Okay," Wesley said, a little perplexed that the man would be putting such an important job in his hands. It made him feel oddly...responsible.

"See you in the morning, Wes."

Wesley stood there for a few seconds, then attributed the giddy feeling to the OxyContin. "See you in the morning."

He left the building and noticed what a nice day it was—everything seemed better on the little white pills. He was more in tune to his surroundings; his senses were more keen. He rode his bike to the courthouse and forked over the last of his cash as a payment on his fine—the other part of his sentence. Then he pedaled to Chance's condo.

His friend was high as a kite, in a great mood. "Come on in, man."

The room was smoggy with pot smoke. A half-naked woman lay curled up asleep on the living room rug.

"You want something to eat? I just had a pizza delivered."

Wesley scooped up a slice. "I was hoping to practice a few hands of poker."

"Yeah, sure, just step over her."

Wesley peered at the woman as he maneuvered around her. "Is she okay?"

"Yeah, she's just stoned."

"Who is she?"

"My economics teacher. I'm not going to need for you to take that exam for me, after all."

"Dude, at least cover her up."

"She doesn't know the difference. Hey, you still banging your attorney?"

"Occasionally."

"Sweet. How's your arm?"

"Better."

"Need some more OC?"

Wesley hesitated. "I'd better not. My probation officer sometimes takes a urine sample for drug testing."

Chance laughed. "So what? Man, I can fix you up with a blocker. You just pour it in your sample and it's clean, like that." He tried to snap his fingers but missed.

"Are you sure?"

"Yeah, man, I'm sure. I sell to lots of truck drivers, and those guys have to get their whiz tested all the time."

"I don't have any cash."

"Don't worry about it." Chance pulled out a key ring and unlocked a cabinet drawer, then pulled out a small bag of white pills. "Are you chewing?"

"Yeah. You were right—it's good."

Chance handed him the bag. "Don't chew with alcohol, got it?"

"Thanks."

"Where did you disappear to all weekend?"

"I had a body run to Boca Raton."

"Why Boca?"

"It was to pick up that celebrity chick, Kiki Deerling."

Chance's jaw dropped. "No shit?"

"No shit."

"Did you get a look at her body?"

"Briefly."

"Were her tits real?"

"I don't know, man. All I saw was her face, and it was bad."

"Bummer. She looked like a nice piece of ass. Speaking of nice, why don't you put in a good word for me with that chain-gang woman your sister hangs out with?"

"Hannah?"

"Yeah, I really dig her."

"She'll dig you, too—a grave. Steer clear, man."

"Get me a date with her and you can have another bag of OC."

Wesley hesitated, but the inducement of having yet another bag of white pills at his disposal was disturbingly appealing. "I'll see what I can do."

"Hannah, this is Carlotta. Did I ever tell you that when Detective Jack Terry was here, he told me that he gets a manicure regularly? I know your hands are always dry from washing them so often with your catering job, so I got the name of the cuticle cream he uses. Call me on my cell if you want to chat."

Carlotta put the cordless phone back into its cradle and chuckled, wondering how long it would take for the bits of made-up personal info to trickle down to Jack. Maybe it was petty, but it was the only diversion she had at the moment.

"Breaking news in the death of celebrity Kiki Deerling," the television announcer said.

Carlotta moved closer and turned up the volume.

"The medical examiner in the Boca Raton district has issued his findings. Dr. Shore's statement read that, quote, 'After consulting with the attending physician at the hospital where Ms. Deerling was treated, and after performing a visual examination of the body, my conclusion is that the cause of death is due to complications from an asthmatic incident,' unquote. There was no mention of illegal substances. From the M.E.'s report, we are left to believe that Kiki's Deerling's death was simply an unforeseeable tragedy."

"I guess that's that," Carlotta murmured, chiding herself for wanting there to be more drama associated with the starlet's demise. The ex-boyfriend was officially off the hook, although she suspected that rumors would always connect him to the scandal, that some people would accuse the family of a cover-up to hide Kiki's drug use and say that Matt Pearson had benefited from the conspiracy.

Footage rolled of the squeaky-clean decoy van leaving the morgue entrance, the pink bow on the antenna fluttering in the wind. The caption read "Deerling's body leaves Boca Raton morgue."

She smiled. At least most of the people had been fooled.

"Meanwhile, we've learned that a memorial service for Kiki will take place in Atlanta Wednesday afternoon at the Motherwell Funeral Home in Buckhead. The service is private—only for the family and close friends of Kiki—but the public is welcome to gather outside in a parking lot. There's a rumor that Kiki Deerling's ex-boyfriend Matt Pearson will sing a song at the service, but his publicist, who was also Kiki's publicist, has not yet confirmed it. Afterward, the body will be interred at the Deerling family cemetery plot in Atlanta."

Carlotta wondered what Kiki's sister thought of Matt Pearson performing at her sister's funeral. Maybe Kiki's publicist had convinced the sister it was in everyone's best interests to play nice.

And what a blow to the publicist, to lose a cash cow like Kiki Deerling. Hollywood movers and shakers were probably already convening all over town to establish the next "it" girl who would assume Kiki's role as partyer extraordinaire and arm candy to the rich and dangerous. Chances were good that the spoils would go to Kiki's on-again, off-again BFF, Naomi Kane. Naomi didn't have sparkle, but maybe it just looked that way because she was always in Kiki's shadow. Carlotta remembered that the girl had gotten good reviews for her performance in an independent film, but her acting career had never taken off. She and Kiki were supposedly always squabbling about something trivial, but Carlotta suspected most of it was simply fodder for the publicity mill. And for that matter, their friendship itself might have been one of those choreographed partnerships dreamed up on an agent's dry-eraser board.

Carlotta clicked off the TV. "You have enough drama of your own," she reminded herself aloud.

She showered and dressed carefully, dreading her errand and allowing her mind to wander. She hoped Wesley did well at his community service job—deep down she wished it would make him start thinking about a career. He was so damn smart. It was a shame he had so little ambition.

She sighed. Of course, in his mind, he had all kinds of ambition—to win the World Series of Poker, for example.

She surveyed her outfit of swingy white skirt and royalblue Kay Unger long-sleeved tunic to help mask her arm cast. The pair of Tory Burch silver ballerina flats that she coveted would be a perfect complement, but she had resisted the urge to splurge.

Not that she'd had much of a choice, with her Neiman's card maxed out. And after Wesley had dared her to cut up all of her credit cards a couple of weeks ago, she was left with one paltry Visa and one measly Mastercard, neither of which could withstand the force of a shopping trip to Target, much less the mall.

The Fendi patent leather rainbow flats would have to suffice.

She left her hair loose, then chose a beige Valentino straw-and-leather bag to add polish to her summery outfit. It was last year's bag, but Peter probably wouldn't notice—although the women he worked with would.

She walked to the Lindbergh MARTA station and rode the train one stop north to the financial district in Buckhead. From there it was a short walk to Mashburn & Tully Investments, formerly Mashburn, Tully & Wren. Their offices were housed in the Pinnacle Building, an iconic structure with an awning of curved glass sloping over the topmost floors, two of which housed Mashburn & Tully.

As she rode up the elevator, Carlotta questioned once again whether she should've called Peter first. But she'd been afraid that when she said she needed to talk to him, he would ask her out for a romantic dinner, or worse, invite her to come to his house. And she wasn't ready for that yet, not with the engagement ring he'd had customized for her hanging over her head.

She wished for the thousandth time that she could separate her relationship with Peter from her father's impossible situation. But the two threads kept crossing and doubling back on each other.

She stepped off the elevator and noted the subtle changes since she'd last been here. When she was a teenager and her father had serviced accounts of celebrity athletes and other prominent people, he would sometimes allow Carlotta to bring her autograph book and politely ask for signatures. Her father had been an important man in his own right, successful and gifted when it came to making investments, well-liked and respected. Everyone the media had interviewed—coworkers and clients—had seemed incredulous when he was accused of fraud.

Aside from her father's name having been removed from the glass doors, the corporate color scheme had changed from browns to blues. A receptionist just inside pressed an intercom button and asked if he could help her.

"Carlotta Wren to see Peter Ashford."

"Is Mr. Ashford expecting you?"

"No."

"Just a moment, please." The man picked up the phone, and after a few seconds a clicking noise sounded. "Come in, Ms. Wren."

She pushed open the heavy glass door and walked inside. The place reeked of money, giving the impression that a machine in the back room churned out hundred-dollar bills.

"Mr. Ashford is coming out to get you himself." The

receptionist's tone was part curious, part impressed. "Nice bag," he added.

"Thank you," she said self-consciously, until she realized he was being sincere. "I'm sorry, I didn't get your name."

He smiled, revealing teeth so perfect that they made her aware of the gap between her own front teeth. "I'm Quentin Gallagher. And I couldn't help noticing that your last name is Wren. Are you related to Randolph Wren?"

"He was—is—my father," she said, steeling herself for a rebuke.

Quentin leaned forward and snapped his fingers. "I knew you looked familiar—you're the woman who fell from the balcony of the Fox, aren't you?"

She tapped her cast. "The one and only. But for the record, I was thrown."

"Fascinating."

At the sound of footsteps, she turned. Peter's smile was so wide, she instantly felt guilty for not wanting to come. He looked striking and crisp in a gray pinstripe suit, white shirt and yellow tie—the best that money could buy. "Hi."

"Hi," he said, picking up her hand. "What a wonderful surprise."

"I was in the area and was hoping you were free for lunch."

He grinned. "I can move some things around. Give me five minutes?"

She nodded and watched him stride away.

Quentin made a noise in his throat. "I haven't seen that man so happy in…never."

"Peter's been through a lot. I knew his wife."

"Yes, such a shame." Then his eyes twinkled. "But you seem to put a spring in his step."

"He and I are old friends," she murmured. She moved aside as employees began to leave in clumps for their lunch break, then turned her head at a familiar voice.

Walt Tully, her father's former partner and her godfather, and Brody Jones, chief legal counsel for the firm, were walking toward the door. Walt saw her and did a double take.

"Hello, Walt."

He seemed flustered. "Carlotta, dear. What brings you here?"

"Peter and I are having lunch."

A little frown appeared between his eyes. "Brody, this is Randolph's daughter, Carlotta."

The other man seemed dubious. "Well, this is a little awkward. I attended your memorial service, young lady."

"A big misunderstanding, thank goodness." She smiled. "Still, it was good of you to come."

"We were all very happy to hear that you were okay," Walt said, although surely even he could hear the note of insincerity in his voice?

Not that she thought Walt wanted her dead. He merely wanted her out of his line of vision. Every time he saw her, he was probably thinking the same thing she was thinking—that after her father had walked out, Walt hadn't done right by his godchildren, hadn't cared enough to send them twenty bucks or even call to check on them.

"How's Tracey?" she asked.

Tracey Tully Lowenstein. Walt's daughter, who had gone to private school with her, had had made sure Carlotta was ostracized after Randolph had been fired from Mashburn, Tully & Wren.

"She's fine. She married a doctor, you know."

"Oh, yes. Tracey reminds me every time she sees me."

"Yes…well, we'd better be going. It was nice to see you again."

Brody Jones nodded, and she returned their friendly gestures. After they walked through the door, though, Quentin shuddered. "Brrr, it just got chilly in here."

"Old wounds," she said, then brightened when Peter reappeared. "Excuse me. It was nice to meet you."

"Best part of my day so far," Quentin said with a salute. "Come back sometime."

"I'm yours for a full hour," Peter said, then lowered his mouth to her ear. "And for as long as you want me."

She laughed, catching his good mood. "Where shall we eat?"

"There's a nice place just around the corner—great sushi."

"Sounds perfect."

They chatted about the weather and his trip to Manhattan until they were seated at a table for two inside.

"You got some sun," Peter said, opening his menu. "It suits you."

"Thanks. Although when I get this cast removed, I'm going to have one white arm and one brown one." She opened her menu with a clammy hand. She was antsy to unburden herself.

"See something you like?"

She closed her menu and wiped her palms on her napkin. "Whatever you like, I'm sure I will, too. But maybe we could go ahead and order?"

"Are you in a hurry?"

"I need to talk to you."

He flagged the waitress and asked for drinks and a couple of rolls of sushi, then turned back to Carlotta with a small smile. "I had a feeling this wasn't just a social call."

"No, it is," she said, reaching out to touch his hand. "I just wanted to tell you that…I saw my father."

His eyes widened. "You saw Randolph? Where? When?"

"While I was in Florida. I went with Coop and Wesley on a job, but what I couldn't tell you on the phone was that my father's fingerprints were found at the scene of a hotel robbery in Daytona. I went down so I could see for myself if he was there, maybe working at the hotel."

"What did you find?"

"No sign of him or my mother."

"Do the police think he committed the robbery?"

"They don't know. Jack is still investigating."

His jaw hardened. "Jack Terry?"

"Yes. The D.A. assigned him to my father's case. I don't like it, either, but at least he's keeping me in the loop."

"So when did you see your father?"

"On the way back, we stopped at a rest area. I was getting coffee out of a vending machine, and my father just walked up and started talking to me."

"Just like that?"

"Yeah. I didn't recognize him. He was wearing sunglasses

and had a beard. He said he'd been following us and waiting for an opportunity to talk to me alone."

"But you're sure it was him?"

"Yes."

"Did he say where he's been, what he's been doing?"

She told him all the details she could remember, including what Randolph had said about gathering evidence to clear his name. "He said he was going to lie low for a while, but that I would hear from him again."

"But how did he know where you would be?"

"I don't know. He just said that he's keeping tabs on us."

She left out the part about Randolph saying that Peter was in the best position at the firm to help him, and would do it because of her. "He says that our home phone is still tapped from when the police were doing surveillance, so if you call me at home, please don't mention this."

"No one else knows you talked to him?"

She shook her head. "Not even Wesley. Dad wants it that way, and I agree."

Peter smiled. "I'm happy you confided in me."

"I'm so sorry that Dad involved you by calling you at the office that one time. I know it put you in an awkward position. I don't want you to lose your job." *Because my father needs you at the firm to help him clear his name.*

"Don't worry about me," Peter said. "I'm worried about you, about what this uncertainty with your father is doing to you…and to Wesley."

She closed her eyes briefly. "Wesley showed me his arm. He told me what you did for him."

Peter looked panicked. "He did?"

"Yes." Humiliation washed over her, followed by gratitude. "Thank you for picking him up from that awful place and cleaning his wounds before bringing him home. He must have looked horrible."

Peter relaxed and nodded. "He did. And you're welcome."

"He keeps getting into trouble with these loan shark characters. I'm worried half to death when he's not at home." She sighed. "I keep hoping he'll grow up. But not having parents around has affected him more deeply than it's affected me."

"I'm just glad Wesley felt he could turn to me for help." Carlotta smiled. "Me, too."

The waitress brought their sushi, and while Carlotta ate, she studied Peter. He was the perfect specimen—handsome, wealthy, with a pedigree. He had certainly grown into the man she had envisioned he'd be. Even though he had married Angela, and their marriage had deteriorated before her untimely death, he had still followed the road that he and Carlotta had mapped out for themselves when they were engaged. It was her path that had been detoured.

They said goodbye in front of the café. Peter kissed her on the mouth—a surprisingly nice kiss that made her stare after him as he walked away. They had once been electric together and she couldn't have imagined her life without him. When he'd left, she'd trained her heart to stop thinking about him. But maybe with a little reconditioning...

No. She had one man to get out of her system—her father—before she could let another man—any man—in.

She took the long way back to the train station, enjoying the beautiful summer day. Unwittingly, her thoughts turned to Kiki Deerling and how she would never again enjoy the sun on her face.

The return trip took her past the Buckhead branch of the public library. She hadn't been to the library since Wesley was little, but her library card was one of the few cards in her wallet she hadn't cut up.

When Carlotta walked inside, a graying black woman, plump and pleasing, smiled at her from behind one of several occupied desks. The lanyard she wore read Lorraine. "May I help you?"

"I hope so. I'm looking for books on strangulation and postmortem bruising."

Lorraine didn't miss a beat. "Right this way."

22

The parking lot outside Motherwell Funeral Home was a three-ring circus, packed with television crews, fans with signs and mourners with candles—which necessitated a fire truck to be sitting nearby. The mound of fresh flower bouquets had grown into a small mountain, wilting under the scorching rays of the sun. Bursts of lyrics ranging from "Amazing Grace" to Kiki's one and only hit, "Running Too Fast," swelled and faded as different factions of the crowd maneuvered for visibility and control. There were countless look-alikes, including a group of drag queens, many with pugs on leashes. The pugs were not particularly friendly, which necessitated an ASPCA van to be sitting nearby. Motivated vendors (without permits) sold Kiki T-shirts, dolls and hairpieces spread out on blankets that could be quickly folded up and carried to another corner if the police came around.

But the police had their hands full trying to enforce the

temporary perimeter that had been installed. The waist-high railed sections provided little resistance to the boisterous mob.

The "private" memorial service in the chapel of the funeral home had grown to include a few hundred of Kiki's closest friends, and was being televised live on at least two cable entertainment channels. The crowded walkway leading into the funeral home looked like a Who's Who in Hollywood under the Age of 25. The paparazzi were having a field day.

Naomi Kane, Kiki's closest gal-pal, arrived with her own entourage, looking tearful and fluttery. But since she stopped to give a comment in front of every camera, Carlotta wondered how much of the girl's grief came from Kiki's demise and how much came from the seemingly imminent demise of her own career without Kiki to front her.

Kiki's ex-boyfriend, Matt Pearson, arrived with members of his former boy band in tow and the crowd went berserk. Although Matt was dressed in black and seemed somber as he approached the entrance of the funeral home, most of the guests appeared positively perky and wore outfits that were more suitable for a rock concert than a funeral.

Carlotta had opted for black slacks, a short-sleeved off-white jacket, and a turquoise Prada cross-body bag just large enough to hold her wallet, cell phone, a pair of binoculars and a protein bar, in case it turned into an all day affair. The humidity was high and the sun relentless. She fanned herself with a "Kiki Is With Jesus, And You Can Be Too" flyer that someone had given her. Behind big white sunglasses, she surveyed the pandemonium, awestruck at the spectacle and feeling more than a little sordid for participating.

She'd always been in love with the celebrity lifestyle, adored watching glamorous people on TV wearing glamorous clothes and doing glamorous things. It was an escape from her own life, especially after her parents had left. But she had to admit that being this close to the action took some of the shine off the fantasy. The made-up actors and actresses parading on the walkway looked garish under the glare of the sun, their actions choreographed. Most of them were using Kiki Deerling's death as an opportunity to boost their own personal profile, knowing that the clips and sound-bite interviews would be broadcast all over the world. The paparazzi, the TV shows, the Web sites, the celebrity guests—all of them would profit from the death of the young woman. Admittedly, Kiki herself shared some of the blame because she had so aggressively courted the press when she was alive. In fact, some might say that she'd be the first person who would want her funeral to be sensationalized. But it still didn't seem appropriate.

"I thought that was you."

Carlotta turned around to see Coop standing outside the mock fence, handsome in a slate-blue suit, white shirt and navy tie.

Her heart lifted. She'd missed him in the three days since their road trip, but had tried not to think about him too much. "How did you spot me in this swarm?"

"You're hard to miss," he said with a wink, then nodded toward a group of girls wearing pink T-shirts that spelled out

"We lve you, Kiki." (The O must have been detained in traffic.) "And you don't exactly fit in with the rest of the crowd."

She felt sheepish. "It's silly, I guess, but after everything that happened, I feel close to her somehow."

"I can understand that. Do you want to come inside? I can smuggle you in the back."

"Are you sure it's okay?"

"There's no room in the chapel, but you can sit in our upstairs lounge. There's a speaker if you'd like to listen to the service."

Carlotta smiled. "That sounds nice."

She elbowed her way through the crowd to the nearest opening in the fence. Coop showed his identification to a cop at the edge of the parking lot, and he let them pass.

"Motherwell's is going to be famous after this," she said.

"No offense, but I think my uncle would be happier if we didn't have a funeral like this again anytime soon. The security alone has been a nightmare."

"Have there been more incidents?"

"No, thank goodness."

"Were you the one who, um, took care of the body?" she asked nonchalantly.

He pursed his mouth. "What are you getting at?"

She shrugged. "I just wondered if you noticed anything… strange."

"For instance?"

She shrugged again. "A fracture of the hyoid bone or thyroid cartilage, perhaps?"

His eyebrows shot up. "A little nighttime reading on forensic pathology?"

"I was curious, so I looked up a few things. I'm trying to expand my mind."

"Okay. Well, you're right that a fracture of the hyoid is an indication that a person was strangled."

"So was Kiki's fractured?"

"What makes you think I checked?"

"Because I saw your face when you looked at her at the morgue. You don't agree with the M.E.'s findings."

"I don't agree with his methods," he corrected. "His findings might be completely accurate."

"Or not."

Coop sighed, then looked at her sideways. "I checked. There was no fracture."

Her shoulders fell.

"You seem disappointed," he said, sounding amused.

"No, it's not that. I just thought if her death wasn't an accident, she deserves justice."

"I agree," Coop said.

"But it sounds as if her death was an accident, just as the M.E. ruled."

"Could be." Coop pulled out a set of keys to unlock a back entrance. "On the other hand, a fractured hyoid is less common in children and young adults during strangulation because the bone hasn't yet calcified."

She walked inside and waited until he'd locked the door behind them. "You're saying that she still could've been strangled."

"There are a couple of dozen possible causes of death, including a severe asthma attack, just as the M.E. ruled."

"I saw you look at her eyes. Was there petechial conjunctive hemorrhaging?"

He squinted. "Have you been watching *CSI?*"

"You're being evasive."

He pressed his lips together, then said, "Broken blood vessels in the eyes is an indication of asphyxia, which doesn't necessarily mean the person was strangled."

"I know. She could have been smothered, or choked to death. But did you notice the circle imprint below her neck? As if she was wearing a necklace and it was pressed into her skin when someone wrapped their hands around her neck."

"Or the EMTs did it when they tried to resuscitate her. Or maybe the impression wasn't a necklace at all, but the end of an instrument they were using to revive her." Coop smiled. "Look, I think it's admirable that you want to help this young woman, Carlotta, but unless we have proof that she was murdered, there's nothing we can do."

"Can't you get Dr. Abrams to do an autopsy?"

He shook his head. "She didn't die in his jurisdiction and only the D.A. or the family can request an autopsy. Since her family objected in the first place, that's not likely to happen. And since there's no reason to suspect her death was anything other than an asthma attack, the D.A.'s office won't get involved."

"What about the fact that someone—three different men, in fact—were trying to claim her body, not to mention the attempts to actually steal it?"

Coop held up his hands. "Freaks, perverts, cults, paparazzi—take your pick."

She followed him into the lobby, where guests were still arriving in all their contrived finery. A door to a rear lounge opened and the family emerged. Carlotta recognized Kiki's parents from TV and newspapers. The Deerlings had been well known in Atlanta even before their daughter had become a celebrity. They looked drawn and devastated. Carlotta's heart twisted for them. Kiki's older sister, Kayla, was by their side, looking just as distraught. Her boyfriend, Jamie Reardon, a local land developer, seemed to be supporting her weight.

The lobby quieted as the family made their way into the chapel, and Coop leaned down. "I need to go. The stairs to the second-floor lounge are through that door. Help yourself to a beverage from the refrigerator. With transporting the body to the cemetery, I probably won't see you afterward."

"I'll let myself out. See you soon."

He smiled. "I hope."

Carlotta slipped through a door at the other end of the lobby and climbed the stairs to the second floor. Off the landing were three doors, marked Office, Storage, Lounge. She pushed open the door to the lounge to find a room with upholstered sofas and easy chairs, a small television, plus table and chairs and a kitchenette. A speaker was mounted on the wall and underneath was a sign that read Chapel, along with an on-off switch. Carlotta snapped it on. A hymn was being played on the piano. An older man's voice sounded, announcing that the service would begin. Carlotta remembered hearing that the family's minister would be conducting the service. He said a prayer, then introduced Matt Pearson to sing a song.

A hush fell over the chapel. Carlotta found herself holding her breath, too.

"I wrote this song for Kiki after I first met her," he said, ending with a choking sob. He'd obviously lost his composure, and Carlotta hoped the young man was sincere. Sniffling noises sounded, then he gulped a deep breath and piano music began to play. She recognized the melody from the radio, a ballad that had been popular a few years ago. His voice was sweet and mellow as he sang of young love that would last for all time.

A pang struck her chest at the poignancy of it. Young love could be so powerful, as she well remembered with Peter. But it could be so optimistic and misguided, too, to think that love was enough to get two people through anything.

"Love isn't enough," she murmured aloud, "because life intervenes. Logistics get sticky, and people change."

Her arm was aching again. She hadn't thought to bring her Percocet, but on the kitchenette counter were scattered packets of over-the-counter painkillers and smelling salts—necessities for a funeral home, she realized. She picked up a packet of ibuprofen and removed a bottle of water from the refrigerator. After swallowing the tablets, she wandered to the window that overlooked the parking lot.

If possible, the crowd had swollen in size, a heaving mass of moving color, with countless satellite dishes and pole microphones jutting into the sky. Carlotta set down the water, withdrew the binoculars from her purse, and scanned the mob that represented the incredibly diverse appeal of Kiki Deerling. All shapes and sizes, all races, male and female, young and old.

Redheaded.

She stopped and focused on the figure standing separate from the people around him, arms crossed awkwardly. He was openly crying, his face twisted in anguish. Without the priest's collar, he looked different, but she was sure it was the same man who'd approached her at the morgue, the same man in the crowd in the magazine pictures.

Carlotta left the room at a trot. She descended the stairs as quietly as possible, conscious of how noise might travel in a silent building. At the double-door entrance stood two security guards.

"I need to get some air," she said, and they stepped aside, obviously less concerned about who left the building than who tried to get in.

When the door opened, cameras clicked furiously until their owners realized she wasn't a known entity.

"Who are you?" photographers shouted.

"Did you know Kiki?"

"Are you a member of the family?"

"Who are you wearing? Dior? Versace?"

She paused at that one, because she'd always dreamed of being asked *who* she was wearing. But out of the corner of her eye, she spotted the redheaded man—at the same time he spotted her. His jaw dropped, then he spun on his heel and sprinted in the opposite direction. Carlotta ran after him, but was slowed by the crowd, her stiff arm and the fact that her Marc Jacob platform sandals weren't meant for aerobic exercise.

At the edge of the property she stopped to catch her breath and look around, but the man was nowhere in sight.

Minus ten points.

23

"You made the payment on your court fine, Mr. McCormick is happy with your work and you've been staying out of trouble." E. looked up from Wesley's file and smiled. "Very good."

Wesley nodded. "Are we finished? I have somewhere I need to be."

She eyed him thoughtfully, then closed the folder. "Okay, yes, we're finished."

He exhaled and stood.

"Just fill this before you leave," she said, handing him a cup with a paper lid. "See you next week."

He hesitated, then took the cup and left her office. Standing in the hall, he broke into a cold sweat, then made himself walk to the restroom, where an officer was standing guard. When the man saw the cup, he opened the door and followed Wesley inside. Wesley went to the urinal and unzipped his pants. The guard looked over Wesley's shoulder long enough to see him pull out his johnson, then turned away.

Wesley took his time whizzing in the cup. With some deft handwork, he managed to simultaneously empty the contents of both vials that Chance had given him into the container. He capped it with the paper lid and passed it off, then put everything back where it belonged, zipped and washed his shaking hands.

He tried not to stare at the urine sample while he dried his hands on a paper towel—he was afraid it would turn blue right in front of their eyes. It didn't, though, and the officer didn't seem to suspect anything. So Wesley nodded, like always, swung his backpack to his shoulder, then strolled down the hall and out the building. He'd know soon enough if he failed the drug test.

He rode to Chance's, and when his friend opened the door, he gave him a high five.

"Ready to win tonight, my man?"

"Yeah," Wesley said, cracking his knuckles. "I'm feeling it."

Chance was fully dressed for a change, with homemade porn on the TV, but no drug runners and no naked women lying around. When it came to money, Chance was usually all business. His sobriety alone told Wesley how much he wanted half of that twenty-grand winning pot tonight.

To warm up, Wesley played Poker Smash until it was time to leave for the card game. It was being held in a midtown nightclub that had closed down in preparation for the wrecking ball in a few weeks' time.

When they walked inside the vacant, gutted building, a man named Grimes welcomed them and counted the five-thousand-dollar chair fee that Chance handed over in hundreds, as requested. Another guy patted them down. When all was in order, Wesley and Chance were led through another door. Several sets of tables and chairs were arranged on what had once been a dance floor. Many players were already seated, the cigarette smoke trailing thick into the air. Wesley noticed a couple of familiar faces from previous games. When a case of nerves threatened to take hold, he chomped an OxyContin and relaxed. Within seconds, a feeling of euphoria began to descend. Everything seemed rosy and his confidence level soared.

The games of Texas Hold 'Em poker began, and Wesley was hot from the start. It took a couple of hours, but one by one he eliminated every player at his table to win a spot at the final table. He was already guaranteed the entry fee back. Anything else he won he would split with Chance, fifty-fifty. After a short break, the final five players took their seats. Under the table, Wesley's leg began to bounce, a spontaneous and unwelcome tic. He crossed his ankles and lit a cigarette in an attempt to get it under control.

For the first few hands, his two pocket cards were crap. He folded early, not yet ready to bluff. But when Chance threw him a look of exasperation, Wesley decided if he was going to lose, he would do it with style.

In the next round he was dealt the two of clubs and the eight of diamonds for his pocket cards—a truly shitty hand. He bet high, hoping to scare the others into thinking he had something. Two folded, leaving him and two other guys playing the hand—a fat, squishy character with moles on his eyelids, and a clean-cut fellow who chewed gum like a girl. But Wesley liked gum chewers. They had more tells than a four-year-old. He put Squishy-Moley with at least one face card, and Chewy with a low pair.

The first three community cards, the flop, were dealt faceup: the three of clubs, the four of clubs, and the eight of spades. The next two community cards, the turn card and the river card, were dealt facedown. With a possible straight flush going and now a pair with the flop cards, Wesley slow-bid the hand until everyone had raised twice.

The dealer flipped the turn card, a six of diamonds. Chewy folded. Squishy-Moley raised. Still working a straight, Wesley called the bet. The river card was the eight of hearts, giving Wesley three of a kind. Not bad, but the other guy could have the straight. Squishy-Moley hesitated, then raised. Wesley called and raised. Squishy called, then revealed his pocket cards—a pair of fours. With the community cards, he had three fours. Wesley won the hand with his three eights, and set the tone for the next two hours of play. One by one, the players fell, leaving Wesley and Squishy-Moley to square off.

Chance was so excited he could barely watch. Wesley's leg was jumping badly now, so he asked for a bathroom break and chewed another pill. By the time he emerged, his leg was still and he was feeling good again. This was the kind of local exposure he needed to build his reputation as a solid card player and make his way to a big regional game, leading up to a tournament sanctioned by the World Series of Poker.

He lowered himself into the chair and nodded at Squishy-Moley, whose real name, he discovered, was Andy. Andy had that hangdog jowly look that was hard to read—his eyes were hooded and he rarely glanced up from his cards. But that was a tell, too, because it meant he usually bet on the basis of his own hand rather than trying to figure out what the other guy was holding.

They played a few rounds, passing chips back and forth across the table. Then slowly, Wesley began to get the upper hand. And at last, he got gorgeous pocket cards: a pair of aces, clubs and hearts. Still, he bet conservatively, because he'd seen plenty of ace pairs beaten with a low three of a kind. Andy didn't seem overly excited about his pocket cards, either.

The flop was the queen of hearts, the seven of hearts and the four of clubs. The best Andy could have at this point was three of a kind, but Andy was probably thinking the same thing about Wesley's hand, and he was wrong. Wesley raised twice. The turn card was another queen, which stung. If Andy held queens, he was looking at four of a kind, and three of a kind was still a winner over Wesley's pair of aces. The river card was a ten of hearts, which didn't help. Wesley kept raising, though, and just when he thought Andy would fold, the guy pushed his chips to the center of the table.

"All in."

Wesley hesitated. He didn't want to be one of those chumps who bet the farm and lost it on a pair of aces—that was a beginner's mistake. If he folded, he still had time to make it up, and he'd been getting good cards all night.

On the other hand, this could be the end of his streak, the last decent pocket cards he'd get all night. And he didn't want to be the chump who folded with a pair of aces to a guy who held squat. Thirty seconds went by, then a minute. Under the table his knee started jumping again, and to his embarrassment, sweat dripped off the end of his nose onto the table.

The dealer cleared his throat, a warning to place a bet or fold by default.

"Call," Wesley said, pushing the better portion of his chips in to match the other man's bet. "What d'ya have?"

His opponent rolled his eyes upward and Wesley felt a flash of panic. Then Andy sighed and tossed down his cards. A three and a nine—garbage.

Chance came off his chair, whooping with joy. Applause broke out and players pumped Wesley's hand in congratulations. His arm hurt like hell, but he didn't mind. Grimes carried the till to Wesley's table and started counting out the twenty grand in bundles of hundreds. Between the Oxy and the win, Wesley felt as if he were floating. With his half of the pot he could get The Carver and Father Thom off his back for a while, and give Carlotta some money for bills. This time he wasn't going to blow the cash like he had before.

For once, he'd be a hero.

A commotion sounded at the door. "Everybody, hands in the air!"

Wesley jerked his head around to see three hooded men standing in a semicircle, handguns extended. One guy shot into the ceiling, sending drywall raining down. "I said hands in the air!"

Wesley obeyed, as did everyone else in the room. While two of the men kept their guns trained on everyone, the third guy walked up to Wes's table and stuffed the cash into a duffel bag. Twenty guys had paid five grand apiece—not a bad take for a few minutes' work. Wesley set his jaw to keep from crying at the sight of his prize money disappearing. He'd been *so* damn close.

While the masked man crammed the money in the bag, he looked up at Wesley with mockery in his eyes, then zipped the duffel closed and backed out of the room.

The other two gunmen waited a few seconds, then backed out, too. Their pounding footsteps echoed in the empty building, then the front door slammed.

Nobody moved for a few seconds. And nobody dared call the police because the impromptu card house was completely illegal. It was exactly what the gunmen had been counting on. Grimes threw a few chairs and cursed a blue streak, but they'd all been had. It wasn't the first time a card club had been robbed. They were lucky everyone's wallets hadn't been stolen, as well.

Worse, Wesley thought there was something familiar about the hooded gunman who'd handled the money. The way he stood, the bulk of his shoulders…the mockery in his eyes as he'd singled out Wesley.

It was Leonard, he was almost positive. E.'s boyfriend, Chance's drug runner. The man had been listening when Chance had told Wesley about the card game. And Wesley wouldn't put anything past the guy.

Anger burned a hole in Wesley's stomach. Leonard had everything that Wesley wanted—including E.—for now. But Wesley would find a way to even the score.

24

"Hannah, hi, it's Carlotta. I just called to check in." She laughed gaily into the receiver. "Oh, I've got the funniest thing to tell you. Did you know that when Detective Jack Terry was here, I caught him watching the *Gilmore Girls?* I kid you not. The man isn't nearly as macho as he likes to pretend. Call me on my cell when you want to catch up."

Carlotta put down the phone and sighed. *Or make up.* She knew Hannah was upset over her taking the road trip with Coop, but Carlotta hadn't thought her friend would hold it against her for this long. She'd always assumed Hannah's comments about Coop were just indiscriminate flirting. But maybe Hannah really cared about him.

Carlotta picked herself up from the bedroom floor. If her friend was in love with Coop, all the more reason for Carlotta not to get involved with him. He deserved someone who could give her entire heart.

In Hannah's case, if she really loved a man, she'd

probably be willing to cut out and hand over any body part he wanted.

Carlotta left her bedroom, conscious of the quiet hush in the house. It was nice for Wesley to have someplace to be every morning, she conceded, and he seemed content with his community service job. Every day he brought home a stack of manuals about things that would make her head explode. But without him bustling around the kitchen and playing his music at deafening levels, she felt restless in the house alone, bored and claustrophobic.

And since Kiki Deerling's memorial service the previous day, she'd been nursing a feeling of discontent. Granted, her disappointment was probably rooted in the "lifting of the veil" on the fantasy of celebritydom that the whole experience had produced. But this lingering sense of grief seemed more…pervasive.

She glanced down the hall to the closed door of her parents' room and sighed. And then, of course, there were her parents.

Always, her parents.

Giving in to the pull, she went to the door and twisted the knob. The door had swollen in the heat, so she had to give it a shove with her good shoulder. When it creaked open she slid back in time ten years—as she always did.

Their bedroom was much the same as Randolph and Valerie had left it, only without some of the photographs and other personal items the police had taken after the pair had gone missing. The matching furniture—bed, dresser, wardrobe and two chests—that had sat in one corner of their enormous bedroom in the house they'd lost, overwhelmed this modest-size master bedroom. The oversize pieces made it feel as if the walls were closing in.

Her mother had hated living here. She'd hated the small rooms in the cramped town house on the unimpressive street in the inconsequential neighborhood. She'd missed lunch at the club and afternoons at the spa, personal shoppers and domestic help. Valerie had rarely talked about her childhood, because her parents had died when she was young, but Carlotta had the impression that her mother had grown up very poor. Perhaps that was the reason she'd affixed herself to Randolph Wren and the luxurious lifestyle he had provided, why she had chosen to go with him on the lam rather than stay behind with her children and struggle to make ends meet.

Carlotta couldn't say her parents had been in love. What they'd had was so much more unhealthy. It was an obsession for each other that was almost immature in its intensity, a possessive, jealous bond that left no room for anything or anyone else…at least not to her mother's knowledge.

The air in the room was stale, but still reeked of them both, if that was possible. The box of cigars on her father's nightstand had long since dried out, but the scent of tobacco lingered. Her mother's perfumes had turned to mostly alcohol, yellowing the glass of the fancy bottles. Her father's ties still hung over his valet stand. Her mother's flowered silk robe was draped over the back of the chair in front of her dressing table. A layer of dust made everything fuzzy and slightly out of focus, like an old photo. Wesley had come in occasionally over the years and dusted, but Carlotta had always refused. She'd spent less than twenty minutes in this room since her parents had left.

Now she went to their bathroom and removed a folded washcloth from the closet, wetting it with water from the faucet that ran rusty before it ran clear. Then she backtracked and began cleaning everything. One by one, she picked up items and carefully removed the dust and built-up grime. The job somehow seemed more purposeful now that she knew they were both still alive. She picked up a photo of her parents that had been taken at some gala event. Her father was in a tux, her mother in a long white, sequined gown. They looked glorious together, tanned and fit, smiling.

But her mother's eyes looked glassy, the telltale sign of a well-functioning alcoholic. Valerie had always been fond of happy hour. But after they'd lost the Buckhead house, her Bloody Mary breakfast extended to a two-martini lunch, which stretched into an afternoon nip that morphed into the cocktail hour which held her over until after-dinner drinks and wrapped up with a nightcap.

Randolph had indicated that her mother was still drinking "on and off." Had Valerie tried rehab? Entered a twelve-step program? If so, she hadn't yet gotten to the part about seeking forgiveness from those you've wronged. Carlotta lifted her mother's robe to her face and inhaled the scent of dust and age and the merest hint of ylang-ylang. Tears filled her eyes, but as always, she was hard-pressed to attach any one emotion to her parents—anger, fear, frustration, love, hate, betrayal. She still felt all those things.

But she was so profoundly grateful that they were still alive.

By the time she finished cleaning the room, she felt better…and hungry. For lunch she heated a can of soup, grabbed some mini carrot sticks from the veggie drawer, and sat down in front of the TV to relax while she ate. She channel surfed, stopping on an all-news network showing the crypt in which Kiki Deerling's body had been placed, in her family's cemetery plot.

The white stone structure sat on a raised platform, ornately carved with birds and flowers, surrounded by a tall, black, wrought-iron fence. Fresh flowers lined the fence in tribute. Carlotta understood that crypts were a comfort to family members who couldn't bear the thought of putting their loved one in the ground, and in this case, it was grander and safer than a simple headstone, considering how many and what type of people would likely visit the grave site.

"Kiki Deerling's ex-boyfriend, Matt Pearson, is said to be taking the starlet's death particularly hard," the news announcer said. "Close friends say he is devastated, which seemed evident when Pearson broke down yesterday while singing at Deerling's funeral."

Film of the funeral rolled, showing the young man stopping to compose himself before continuing, the image then switching to that of a white multistory building.

"Word is that Matt Pearson is holed up in this Buckhead hotel, grieving for Deerling. An unconfirmed report has Pearson on suicide watch. Even though a medical examiner ruled that Deerling's death was caused by a severe asthma attack, rumors persist that the night she died, she was partying hard with Pearson, who has a history of substance abuse."

Carlotta frowned, her mind churning as she changed the channel. Kiki Deerling was still everywhere. The local talk show *Atlanta & Company* was replaying the interview that Carlotta and Hannah had been watching live when Kiki promoted her camp for troubled teens. Carlotta studied the young woman's throat. Because of the leopard-print scarf wrapped around her neck, Carlotta couldn't tell if Kiki was wearing a necklace. At the end of the interview, Carlotta spotted a flash of gold, but it was still unidentifiable.

"This was Kiki Deerling's last known interview," host Holly Firfer said, then shook her head at her cohost. "I still can't believe she's gone. Just a few days ago, she was sitting on this set talking to me, happy and laughing."

Carlotta pursed her mouth and glanced at the clock. She could make it down to the affiliate studio before the show ended. Why not talk to one of the last people who'd talked to Kiki?

The cohost of *Atlanta & Company* was unmistakable in the lobby of the TV station; blond and bubbly, she walked with the same energy that came across on-screen. Carlotta watched as the receptionist stopped her and pointed in Carlotta's direction. Carlotta stood and smiled as the woman approached.

"Hello, I'm Holly Firfer."

"I'm Carlotta Wren, a big fan of your show."

"Thank you."

"And...I was wondering if I could have five minutes of your time."

"What's this about?" Holly asked.

Carlotta hesitated. "This is a little awkward, but I'm investigating the death of Kiki Deerling. I know you were one of the last people to talk with her. I wondered if you could tell me if she was wearing a necklace when you interviewed her."

Holly looked dubious. "You're a police officer?"

"No. I work for the morgue. I believe the proper term is 'body hauler.' I went to Boca Raton to pick up her remains and brought them back to Atlanta." Carlotta showed her the morgue ID she used when she worked with Coop.

The blonde winced, but nodded. "What's this about a necklace?"

"We're trying to verify that all of Ms. Deerling's personal effects are accounted for. It's been brought to our attention that she might have been wearing a necklace when she died. Since you talked to her only a few hours earlier that day, I wondered if you remembered seeing one."

"I don't know."

"Please try to remember. It's not apparent on camera. She was wearing a leopard-print scarf around her neck."

Holly's eyes widened. "Wait a minute. She *was* wearing a pendant. I remember her toying with it before we went on air."

Carlotta's heart rate increased. "Can you tell me what it looked like?"

"It was a circle of diamonds. I remember she had her finger through it, sliding it back and forth on a short chain."

"Do you remember how big it was?"

Holly made a circle with her finger and thumb to indicate the pendant had been about an inch in diameter—the same size as the reddish circular imprint on Kiki's collarbone.

"Thank you. That helps a lot."

"It's such a tragedy," Holly said. "She was so young. I couldn't say this on air, but the worst thing is that after the interview, I overheard Kiki and her publicist arguing about her inhaler."

"Arguing how?"

"Her publicist asked if she had her inhaler with her. Kiki said yes, then remarked that the woman was only concerned because she had the most to lose if something happened. In hindsight, it's kind of eerie."

Carlotta nodded. "Just one more thing. Was there a crowd here when Kiki did the interview?"

"Yeah, fans gathered in front of the building. But Kiki was nice about it. She even stopped to sign autographs."

Carlotta pulled out a photograph she'd clipped from the entertainment magazine that best showed the face of the redheaded man. "Do you remember seeing him?"

Holly studied the photo, then nodded. "Yeah, he was here. But he was apart from the crowd. I wondered if maybe he was on Kiki's security detail."

"Thank you," Carlotta said. "You've been very helpful."

"I'm glad," Holly said with a smile and a wave. "I hope you find the necklace."

"Me, too," Carlotta murmured as the woman walked away. She pulled out her cell phone and dialed Coop's number.

"Coop here."

"Coop, it's Carlotta."

"I came up to check on you yesterday before the service ended, but you'd disappeared."

"Remember the redheaded guy pretending to be a priest? I saw him in the crowd outside."

A sigh sounded over the phone. "I take it you confronted him?"

"I tried, but he got away. Coop, I found out that Kiki *was* wearing a pendant the day she died, one that matches the impression I saw below her neck."

"How did you find that out? No, wait. I don't want to know. Besides, it still doesn't prove anything."

"Can you call the medical examiner in Boca and find out if there was a pendant in her personal effects?"

His hesitation told her he didn't want to.

"Please, Coop?"

"Only if you promise me that if there was no pendant in her personal effects, you'll let this go."

Carlotta crossed her fingers behind her back. "I promise."

25

"Hey, Wes—"

Wesley startled in his chair and hit a button on his keyboard to replace his current screen. He turned in his chair, frowning at Meg. "What?"

She made a face. "You're awfully jumpy. And secretive. What are you working on?"

"Reports on the databases I'm encrypting. McCormick said to be careful with the data."

"Is that why you got your own dedicated printer?" Meg asked, gesturing to the newly added machine.

"Yeah."

"And shredder?"

"Yeah."

She walked to her own workstation and sat down. Wesley turned back to his computer, perturbed at the interruption.

"You on something?" she asked.

He jerked his head around. "What?"

"You heard me."

"No, I'm not *on* something."

She shrugged. "You've got the look."

Wesley raised his eyebrows. "What look is that?"

"Jittery, moody, irritable. And you never eat."

"I'm just a skinny dude."

"I noticed," she said dryly. "And smart. You should get your bony ass in school."

He sat back, both irritated and intrigued. "And do what? Become a doctor?"

"Why not?"

"That's not me," he said, looking back to his screen.

"Why? What do your parents do for a living?"

He looked up. "None of your business."

She blanched. "Sorry. Didn't mean to hit a nerve."

Wesley felt contrite. "Just drop it, okay?"

"Yeah, sure. Listen, the guys and I are going to get a sandwich around the corner for lunch. You wanna come?"

He was tempted—Meg was hot. Today she had traded her GA Tech sweatshirt for a Curious George tee that hugged her in a way that explained why George's curiosity had been aroused. But she also had that crazy-cool demeanor that screamed privilege. Her parents were brilliant scholars. She probably lived in a mansion, dined with great thinkers all over the world. He'd never measure up.

"No, thanks," he said. "I have to be somewhere."

"Okay, see you tomorrow."

He watched her walk away, feeling depressed and for

good reason. He was still smarting over his prize money being stolen right out from under him. He needed cash, so he was going to have to lean on Coop to get him more body-moving jobs. And he hadn't yet been able to locate the grand jury transcript from his father's hearing in the courthouse records database. He needed more information—a trial number, specific dates—to build the search keys. Information that was in his father's file at Liz's home office.

He packed up his workstation and punched in the attorney's number as he left the building.

"This is Liz Fischer," she answered.

"Liz, it's Wes."

"Well, this is a nice surprise."

"Are you busy for lunch?"

Her rich, cool laugh floated over the line. "What did you have in mind?"

"I can meet you at your place in fifteen minutes."

"See you then."

He rode his bicycle hard and fast to get to Liz's house, but it helped to burn off some excess anger…and the last of the OxyContin he'd taken earlier, so he could pop a new one before popping Liz.

She was waiting for him in the living area of the guesthouse, dressed in a narrow skirt and a sleeveless blouse that was already unbuttoned, revealing a lacy black bra.

"Hi," she said in greeting.

His dick stood straight up. "Hi."

"Want a beer?"

"Just iced tea for me," he said, remembering Chance's

warning about not mixing the Oxy with alcohol. "Care if I take a shower?"

"Go ahead," she said, then glanced at her watch. "But you'd better hurry."

He went down the hallway to the john and turned on the shower head, then crept across the hall to her office. With one ear to the door, he slid open a file drawer and located the fat, familiar folder with his father's name on it. He'd slowly been reading through it when he could sneak the time between balling Liz.

He opened the file and scanned the first few documents, looking for a trial number, the dates he needed.

"Wesley!" she called from the other room. "Hurry!"

He grimaced, then closed the file. He started to put it back, but changed his mind. Holding it behind him, he crept back to the hallway. After a quick check to make sure Liz wasn't looking, he tiptoed into the bathroom and shoved the folder into his backpack. He'd read it at home, take his time, make copies of things he needed, then put it back the next time he came over.

Liz would never miss it. She probably hadn't thought about his father in years.

He washed his hair and soaped up his boys in record time. The cuts on his arm still hurt like hell, but the water softened the tight skin a little.

Just before he left the bathroom, he popped a white pill in his mouth and chewed it. He was starting to get used to the bitterness of it, starting to like it, even, because he knew what came afterward—the feeling of being lifted and carried along on the most feathery cloud imaginable. Everything looked better, smelled better, sounded better.

The world improved.

He padded back to the living room, naked. His hard-on was so stiff, it hurt to walk. Liz stared at his cock and smiled. "I love how you have no pretenses."

Wesley wondered what she'd think if she knew he'd started sleeping with her to get to his father's files.

But then again, the sex was pretty damn good—a nice bonus.

Then Liz saw his arm. "What happened to you?" She jumped up to inspect it.

"It's no big deal."

"Someone did this to you. Who?"

"No one you want to know," he assured her, moving her hand from his arm to his erection.

"This has something to do with you calling me the other night, doesn't it? Is that why you needed the money? To keep someone from doing this?"

"Uh, no, he did this anyway. The cash was to keep him from cutting out my liver."

She gasped. "I'm so sorry I couldn't get involved, Wesley. What did you do?"

"I worked it out. Don't worry about it."

She kissed him, hard. And rubbed his dick like it was some kind of magic lamp. The woman had always been a good lay, but suddenly, she was an animal. Maybe it was knowing he'd come close to being filleted like a fish that had her jazzed, or maybe it was the sight of his roughed up body. Whatever, he just lay back and went with it.

She ripped off her own clothes, snapped a condom on his wood, then impaled herself on him and rode him like a pogo stick. He helped her along as best as he could—the porn at Chance's was nothing if not educational—although he felt more like a prop than anything else. She felt so damn good sliding up and down on him, her boobs bouncing. Man, she was smoking hot. And her ass… Damn, what a sweet handful.

Maybe it was the heat of the moment, maybe it was the drug, but for some reason, he slapped her bottom. Hard. It echoed loud in his ears, and his hand stung like fire. Liz's eyes widened and she paused. Wesley swallowed, steeling himself against her wrath. She'd probably throw him out on his dick for daring to…well, *spank* her.

"I'm sorry," he blurted.

"Harder," she moaned, then started rocking on him as if he had chair runners.

He wet his lips, then tapped her ass lightly, in case he'd misunderstood.

"Harder," she insisted.

He obliged, and she urged him on. The spanking spurred them both to crashing orgasms, then they fell back, exhausted.

"That was amazing," Liz said, looking over her shoulder to rub her red cheeks. "I wish I had time for more." She lay down and lit a cigarette for them to share, like always. She drew off it, then passed it to him. He was almost too weak to pucker.

"Wesley, Jack doesn't know about us, does he?"

Wesley made a disdainful noise. "No. Why would he?"

"The night you were in trouble, he called me to see if I knew where you were."

"So? You're my attorney."

Liz pulled on the cigarette, then exhaled. "I guess so. I don't know, there was just something about the tone of his voice."

"You balling the cop, too?"

She frowned. "That's none of your business. Jack and I have known each other a long time."

"Am I better in the sack?"

She shook the cigarette at him and pushed herself to her feet. "Don't go there, Wesley. Let's just have fun, okay?"

"Why were you with him in Florida?"

She looked up, then averted her gaze. "It was a case that involves one of my clients. Jack asked me to go as a second set of eyes, that's all."

"Why aren't you married, Liz?"

She paused from fastening her bra, then continued dressing. "I don't know."

"Never met the right guy?"

She gave a quiet little laugh. "Actually, I did meet the right guy once. But he wasn't available. Get dressed. I have to get back to work. How's your community service going, by the way?"

"Fine. My boss likes me okay."

"Your father would be proud of you," she said, looking wistful.

Wesley sat up and considered telling her that his father had come to see Carlotta at the funeral home, in disguise. But he was afraid she'd tell Jack Terry, and that would ruin everything.

Wes backtracked to the bathroom to clean up, then stared down at the split condom in alarm. Hell, that couldn't be good. But Liz was probably on birth control. A career woman like her wouldn't take chances.

He dressed quickly, then grabbed his backpack, comforted by the extra weight it contained. Liz was right. His father *would* be proud of him.

Especially once he found a way to help Randolph prove his innocence.

26

"Hannah, hi, it's Carlotta. I remembered something else I found out about Detective Jack Terry when he was here doing surveillance. Two words—*pec implants*. He told me all about it. I'm just glad he didn't offer to show them to me." She shuddered dramatically. "Call me back on my cell. I'm going on a stakeout at a cemetery and thought you might like to join me."

Carlotta hung up the phone and sighed. If dangling a cemetery job in front of Hannah didn't work, she didn't know what else to do.

Her cell phone trilled. When Hannah's number came up on the caller ID screen, she whooped and connected the call. "Hi!"

"I'm listening," Hannah said.

"I need to do some surveillance at a cemetery. Want to come?"

"When?"

"How about now?"

"I'm sitting in your driveway."

Carlotta went to the living room window and, sure enough, Hannah's van sat there. Carlotta smiled and waved.

Hannah gave her a curt wave back—with her middle finger.

"Let me grab my purse," Carlotta sang, then clicked the phone shut.

Outside, she opened the van door and pulled herself up into the passenger seat, then slammed the door. "Hi!"

Hannah glared at her.

Carlotta sighed. "I didn't sleep with Coop."

She pursed her mouth into a little black knot. "But you wanted to."

"But I didn't."

Hannah continued to pout, jutting out her chin. Finally, she growled, "Damn it, I thought I'd at least get some juicy details. You know, find out if he's circumcised."

"You'll have to find out on your own." Then maybe her friend could tell *her* the juicy details.

"And why have you been leaving those bizarre messages about Jack Terry?"

"Because the brute hasn't lifted the tap on my phone yet."

"Oh. Good one. How did you know?"

"Know what?"

"That the tap hasn't been lifted."

My long lost father told me. "Um…you can tell. There's a clicking…thing."

"So what's up with the cemetery watch?"

"We're going to Kiki Deerling's grave."

"And why would we want to do that?"

Carlotta pointed to the right. "Just drive, and I'll fill you in." She told Hannah about the road trip, leaving out the details about the hotel robbery and her parents and her own near-nakedness with Coop.

When she got to the part about the attempts to steal Kiki's body, Hannah smacked the steering wheel. "You get to have all the fun!"

"Believe me, it wasn't that fun when it was happening."

"So you think this girl didn't die of an asthma attack like the M.E. said?"

"I don't know. Her injuries are curious, that's all. And the attempts to steal the body could have been to cover up something."

"What does Coop think?"

"He thinks I'm bored."

"Aren't you?"

"Out of my mind. But since I don't have anything else to do, why not follow up on some of these leads?"

"What makes you think we're going to see this mysterious redheaded guy at the grave site?"

"Because he's obsessed with Kiki."

"So you think he killed her?"

"Maybe. Some killers like to hang around, revisit their victims."

Hannah raised her eyebrows.

"I read that in a book at the library."

"Christ, you are bored."

They arrived at the cemetery to find several cars in the parking lot. Hannah drove around until they found a spot where Carlotta could see the crypt through her binoculars. Clumps of people stood around it.

"Gee, do you think it stands out enough?" Hannah asked dryly. "That thing looks like it could glow in the dark."

"Makes our job easier," Carlotta murmured.

"Do you see our guy?"

"No. There's a security guard, and people taking pictures and laying flowers against the fence."

"What makes you think he'll be here today?"

"Because today's her birthday."

"I thought she died on her birthday."

"No, she started celebrating early. Kiki would've turned twenty-one today."

"Kiki? You're calling this girl by her first name, as if you knew her."

Carlotta lowered the binoculars and looked at Hannah. "Sometimes I feel like I do know her."

"Okay, you're creeping me out, and that's hard to do. But you're right. If this guy is obsessed, he'd want to visit the grave today. Still, we could've just missed him. Maybe he's already gone back to the rock he crawled out from under."

"Maybe," Carlotta admitted. "Do you have something better to do?"

"Hell, no. Want some pasta salad?"

"Sure." She took another look through the binoculars. Being on a stakeout with Hannah had its perks—her friend always had gourmet leftovers in her refrigerated van.

Five hours later, they'd eaten their way through a bowl of pasta salad, a plate of ham wheels, a tub of crab dip and a third of a white-chocolate cheesecake.

"I'm think I'm going to be sick," Hannah muttered.

"Hang on," Carlotta said, her binoculars riveted on the crypt. "I think this is our guy." She adjusted the focus until the man's face came in clearer as he approached the grave. The security guard was gone and all the fans had left. The man must have been watching from somewhere, waiting until he could be alone. "Yeah, it's him." She opened her door and jumped down.

"What are you going to do?"

"*We* are going to talk to him."

"I don't know. My stomach is kind of upset."

"Okay, stay here. But keep an eye out." She handed Hannah the binoculars.

A tall wrought-iron fence surrounded the cemetery. Carlotta made her way to the closest gate and opened it as noiselessly as possible. Then she moved quickly toward the grave site, maneuvering around headstones to stay behind him, taking care not to step on graves, out of respect and out of an old superstition she'd heard that if you stepped on a grave, you would next be in one. Despite the high temperatures, she felt a chill as she walked among the headstones, new and old, large and small, like the people they represented. Burial was such a bizarre human ritual.

The man had wrapped his hands around the bars of the fence that surrounded the white crypt, and was crying. She managed to get within a few yards of him before he turned and saw her. Carlotta froze. Recognition dawned on his face. He took off at a gallop.

"Wait!" she yelled. "I just want to talk to you!"

She'd worn sneakers this time—Liz Claiborne—but the cast slowed her down because she couldn't swing her arm. He also did not subscribe to her superstition about stepping on graves. She tried to keep up with him, yelling for him to stop. When he did, though, it wasn't by choice. Hannah took him down with a flying leap. It must have knocked the wind out of him because he lay in the grass even after Hannah rolled off him and started puking her guts out.

By the time Carlotta ran up, her friend waved her off. "I'm fine. Stay with Opie."

The man was sitting up, holding his chest. "I ought to call the police and have you two arrested for assault," he said, wheezing.

Carlotta stood over him, hands on her hips. "Go ahead. When they get here, we'll ask them about the penalty for stealing a body. It's a felony, you know."

He frowned, rubbing his breastbone. "I wasn't going to steal Kiki's body when I came to the morgue. I just wanted to see her, to see what he did to her."

"See what who did to her? The coroner?"

"No. That a-hole Matt Pearson. He murdered her."

Carlotta felt her eyes bulge. "You saw Matt Pearson kill Kiki Deerling?"

"Yes…no. I saw him slowly killing her, getting her hooked on heroin when they were together. After she broke it off, Kiki was staying clean, but then he showed up for her party."

The man started crying. "I know he killed her, I just know it."

Carlotta sighed and squatted down at eye level with him. "What's your name?"

He sniffed. "Wayne Barber."

"And how are you connected to Kiki? I've seen you in the background in pictures of her."

"I'm…her friend."

Hannah had recovered and wiped her mouth, streaking her black lipstick. "Her stalker friend?"

He looked angry. "I didn't stalk Kiki. I…followed her. And looked out for her. I'm president of her fan club."

Hannah rolled her eyes.

From her pocket, Carlotta pulled the clipped magazine pictures with him in them. "You look pretty angry in these."

"I wasn't angry with Kiki. Matt was with her all those times. I hate him. I know he killed her, the bastard. Gave her too much heroin, and took away the world's most beautiful flower." He started sobbing.

Hannah made the universal "cuckoo" sign, circling her finger next to her ear.

"There were two other men at the morgue trying to claim the body," Carlotta said. "Do you know anything about that?"

"No, I swear."

"Were you following Kiki the night she died?"

He nodded. "I snuck into the party, pretended I was a waiter. It was heaven."

Well, that was hard to condemn, since Carlotta had done

it herself a time or two. "Do you remember if she was wearing a necklace that night?"

The man jammed his fingers in his hair, leaving it at all angles. "Yeah, she was wearing a circle of diamonds. She wore it a lot lately. I thought maybe it was her talisman for staying sober." He heaved a mournful sigh. "Today's her birthday, you know. She would've been twenty-one."

His lost expression tugged on Carlotta's heart. "I know." She used her good arm to help him up and dust off the grass. "Where are you from, Wayne?"

"Here in Atlanta. Kiki and I went to grade school together. I knew back then she was something special."

"You got your own special thing going there, Wayne," Hannah said. "Can we give you a lift somewhere?"

"No, my car is through those trees." He looked at Carlotta. "Who are you? Why do you care about Kiki?"

"My name is Carlotta Wren. I didn't know Kiki. I helped to transport her body back to Atlanta."

"Did you see her body? Was she at peace?"

The bleak look in his eyes showed the depth of his obsession with Kiki, how much he had worshiped her. Carlotta felt compelled to give him some measure of comfort. "Yes, she was at peace."

The man smiled through his tears, as if a great burden had been relieved. "Thank you."

They watched him walk away, and Hannah made a rueful noise. "Now why can't I find a man who'll idolize me like that?"

Carlotta smiled. "Maybe you will someday." She pulled out her cell phone.

"Who are you calling?"

"Coop. Want to talk to him?"

"No," Hannah said primly. "I'm officially playing hard to get."

Carlotta shook her head while the phone rang.

"Coop here."

"Coop, it's Carlotta. Did you find out if the necklace was in Kiki Deerling's personal affects?"

"Hello to you, too."

"Sorry. It's been a long day."

"The M.E. said there was no necklace in her belongings. But it could've come off in all the commotion, either at the club, in the ambulance or at the hospital. Or someone could've stolen it."

"Yeah, like the person who murdered her."

He sighed. "You promised me you'd let this go."

"I just talked to our redheaded priest. He's convinced that Matt Pearson killed her by giving her a heroin overdose."

"Who is this guy?"

"A very devoted fan."

"A fan? You can't be serious."

"Come on, Coop. I suspect you noticed discrepancies about the body that you aren't sharing. Between what you know and what I found out, don't you think we should at least talk to Jack? Maybe the police know something we don't. They might have tracked down that green van already.

Maybe Matt Pearson hired those goons to steal the body to cover up what he did to her."

Carlotta took Coop's silence as a good sign, that he was, in fact, more suspicious about the cause of death than he'd disclosed.

"What could it hurt?" she prodded. "Hannah will drop me off at the police station. I'll meet you there."

He groaned. "I can't wait until you go back to work at Neiman's."

27

"Hi, Brooklyn," Carlotta said to the woman behind the Plexiglass cage in the police station.

She smiled. "How you doing, Carlotta?"

"Great, thanks. Hey, were you able to use that Neiman's clearance coupon I gave you?"

"Girl, take a look." The woman held up her arm to reveal a dazzling diamond tennis bracelet.

Carlotta nodded. "Nice." She gestured to Coop. "This is my friend Dr. Craft. We're here to see Jack. Is he available?"

"Let me check to make sure he's not back there getting a manicure." Brooklyn chuckled, then picked up the phone.

Carlotta smothered a smile and waited while Brook had a terse exchange with Jack. She set down the receiver. "He said to come on back. You know the way. I'll buzz you in."

"Thank you." Carlotta turned to Coop. "Follow me."

He looked uncertain. "Jack isn't going to like this."

"Probably not," she agreed.

They walked through a secured door, then wound their way back to Jack's cubicle. Carlotta remembered well making this trip the day Jack had arrested Wesley for hacking into the city's computer system. Jack had recognized their last name, and immediately figured they were Randolph Wren's kids.

It had not been a stellar beginning.

Jack was standing, minus jacket and tie, his sleeves rolled up, waiting for them. "What's this all about?"

"Kiki Deerling," Carlotta said without preamble. "We have some new evidence in her case."

Jack's eyebrows climbed. "What case?" He looked at Coop. "What has she talked you into?"

Coop pulled on his chin. "Maybe we should all sit."

Jack frowned, but relented. "Let's go to an interview room."

Once they were seated at a table in a small room, Jack gazed at Coop. "I'm listening."

Coop looked toward the door as if he might change his mind, then leaned forward, his forearms on the table. "There were some discrepancies between the body and the M.E.'s report, Jack."

"The M.E. said she died of an asthma attack, right?"

"Yes. And she did have a history of asthma." Coop glanced at Carlotta, then pressed his lips together. "But... there were other injuries that were inconsistent with an attack."

"Such as?"

"Bruising on the neck, broken blood vessels in the eyes,

an absence of the kind of mucus one would expect to find in the nasal cavity and throat, and her chest cavity didn't appear to be swollen."

"Why would it be swollen?"

"During a severe asthma attack, the lungs hyperextend."

"Can that be explained away?"

Coop shifted in his chair. "Yes. If CPR was performed for an extended period of time, the lungs might have deflated."

"And the mucus—wasn't her body cleaned before you picked it up at the morgue?"

"Yes."

"So it could've been there and been washed away?"

"It's possible."

"As for the broken blood vessels, I had an aunt blow a blood vessel in her eye once from coughing."

"That could happen," Coop admitted.

"What about the bruising on the neck? Could she have done it to herself during an attack?"

"It's not likely."

"Is there another explanation?"

"It's possible the EMTs could have caused the bruises when they were trying to treat her."

Jack lifted his hands. "So you've got nothing."

"There was an imprint on her collarbone," Carlotta interjected. "A small circle that matches a diamond pendant she was wearing on the day she died. And the pendant wasn't in her personal effects."

"So?"

"So, someone could have pressed it into her neck when they strangled her, then stolen the necklace afterward."

Jack's head jutted forward. "That's it? You've conjured up some half-baked theory that she was strangled based on a piece of jewelry someone said the girl *might* have been wearing?"

Carlotta frowned. "I located one of the men who showed up at the morgue trying to see the body. He thinks Matt Pearson killed Kiki by giving her heroin."

"Was he in the room when this allegedly happened?"

"No, but he was at the party where she died. And he seems to know a lot about her, um, habits. Maybe you could at least bring him in for questioning."

"What's the guy's name?"

She told him, and gave a description. Jack picked up the phone.

"It's Terry. Run a background check on a Wayne Barber of Atlanta. Caucasian, red hair, blue eyes, age approximately twenty-one. Ring me back in interview three." He hung up the phone, then asked Carlotta, "Did this Barber fellow happen to know anything about the other two kooks trying to steal the body?"

"He said he didn't. Were you able to locate the green van?"

"We're still running a couple of leads, but there's nothing concrete." He looked at Coop. "I assume the body was interred without incident?"

"Yeah, but security was tight."

Jack shook his head. "It's sad that she died, but I don't understand the uproar over this girl. Jesus, I must be getting old." The phone rang and he picked it up. "Any hits?" He listened, pursing his mouth and murmuring "uh-huh" occasionally, then said, "Thanks," and banged down the receiver.

He turned his head toward Carlotta. "Your source is a nut job. He's had numerous run-ins with the law, mostly disorderly conduct and trespassing. He also spent six months in a mental facility for unknown illnesses. Kiki Deerling issued a restraining order against him two months ago."

Carlotta swallowed hard. "Just because he's crazy doesn't mean he's wrong."

Jack looked at Coop. "I expect this kind of cockamamie stuff from her, but not from you."

"Carlotta's just trying to help," Coop said. "She has some valid points."

Jack frowned. "Stop humoring her."

"Hey," Carlotta said, waving her arms, "I'm in the room."

Coop's jaw moved as if he were chewing on his thoughts. "Jack, there do seem to be some lingering questions about this woman's death."

"Not in my mind," the detective stated. "There's still no motive. Why would someone want to kill this girl? She seemed to be making everyone a hell of a lot of money."

"Maybe it wasn't premeditated," Coop said. "There was something else on the body—track marks."

Jack pursed his mouth. "Could you tell if they were new?"

"No."

"Did you bring them to the attention of the Boca M.E.?"

"No. I didn't see them until I was helping to prepare the body for viewing."

"I thought models snorted heroin these days to avoid track marks."

"Smoking or snorting is dangerous for an asthmatic," Coop said.

Jack pinched the bridge of his nose. "I'm confused. Do you think she was strangled, or do you think she was given an overdose of heroin?"

Coop sat back in his chair. "That could only be determined with a full autopsy."

"Didn't the M.E. at least do a tox screen?"

"No."

"What about the hospital where she was taken for treatment? Did they do a tox screen?"

"No reason to. They were operating under the impression that she'd had an asthma attack."

"Can asthma kill a person that quickly?"

Coop nodded. "If death occurs from an attack, it's usually within thirty minutes of the onset."

Jack pulled his hand over his mouth, then shook his head. "Sorry, it's not enough. The D.A. will never order an autopsy based on bits of circumstantial evidence. You haven't told me anything that makes me believe she died any way other than exactly how the M.E. reported." He pushed himself to his feet. "If that's all, I need to get back to work."

Carlotta looked at Coop, pleading with him with her eyes. He shrugged, as if to say "we tried." As they left the interview room, he had his hand on her waist, which Jack seemed to zone in on.

"Carlotta," Jack said. "A word?"

She indicated to Coop that she'd meet him outside, then turned back. "Yes?"

He made sure Coop was out of earshot, then scowled. "*Pec* implants?"

She scowled back. "You told me the tap had been removed from my phone."

He leaned in. "It was supposed to be, but when we got the news that your father's fingerprints were found in Daytona, the decision was made to keep it."

"Made by whom?"

"Me," he said through gritted teeth.

"Asshole," she muttered.

"And trash talk me all you want, but leave Liz out of it."

She narrowed her eyes. "Liz is lucky I haven't kicked her scrawny ass for seducing my brother."

"Wesley's a full-grown man, Carlotta. He can screw whoever he wants."

"Too bad the both of you have the same taste in women."

Jack arched an eyebrow. "When you question my taste, you're throwing yourself under the bus."

"That was a one-time occurrence," she snapped.

"Coop keeping you warm now, is he?"

"Keep Coop out of this. He's a good man."

"Liz isn't a bad person, either, Carlotta. At least I know what to expect from her." Jack gave her a pointed look. "That's probably why your brother likes her, too."

Her mouth fell open, then clamped shut with indignation. "Are you going to stop listening in to my phone calls?"

"Probably not."

"I agreed to the tap as part of a deal with the D.A., which he reneged on, by the way."

"This phone tap is based on a separate incident."

"I don't appreciate being spied on without reason."

"You're acting as if you and your family have something to hide."

Unbidden moisture sprang to her eyes. "What's left to hide, Jack? My family's dirty laundry has been a public spectacle from the beginning." She pivoted on her heel to walk away.

"Hey."

Carlotta swung around, waiting.

His shoulders sagged. "Give me a break. I have to do my job."

"And tormenting me is just a bonus?"

"No, I…" He stopped and squinted. "Wait a minute. How did you know the tap was still on the phone?"

She turned her back on him and kept walking.

28

Wesley opened the lid on the aquarium that housed Einstein, his adult male, black-and-gray axanthic python, and dropped a live white mouse inside. As was his quiet way, Einstein didn't appear to notice, and the mouse didn't seem to know it was in imminent danger of becoming dinner, because it set about exploring the aquarium, its whiskers twitching.

The mouse was probably relaxed because this was its third trip into the aquarium and Einstein had yet to move a muscle. The snake was finicky that way, seeming to eat only when it had to. Wesley spent more money feeding the mice to keep them alive until his snake worked up an appetite, than he did on the mice themselves.

Settling back on his bed, he reached beneath the mattress and withdrew his father's file that he'd taken from Liz's cabinet. It was crammed with lots of forms and legal motions that didn't mean much to him, but he did find the trial number and dates that he needed to search the courthouse databases. What fascinated Wesley most were the handwritten messages his father had scribbled on yellow sticky notes and letterhead from Mashburn, Tully & Wren.

Liz, what can you do about this?

Liz, what do you think?

Liz, check into this.

It was fascinating to see his father's handwriting, to imagine him sitting at his desk, jotting down notes to his attorney. It made the man seem more real, and his concern more immediate, more palpable, as the notes became more abbreviated and the tone more grave.

Liz, take care of this.

Liz, this worries me.

Liz, help me.

The notes were stuck to letters that his father had received to be deposed, notices of foreclosure on the house, summonses to appear in court. There was a letter of dismissal on the company letterhead that bore his own name, signed by Brody Jones, chief legal counsel for the firm. And warnings from the IRS of taxes and penalties due, pending legal action.

Wesley remembered seeing his father sitting at the kitchen table with his head in his hands just a few days before he disappeared. Wes had asked him what was wrong. His dad had smiled and said that he was in a little bit of trouble, but he was figuring out a way to fix things. He had ruffled his son's hair and told him that no matter what happened, to remember that he loved him.

And Wesley had never forgotten.

His cell phone rang. When Liz's name came up on the screen, guilt blipped through his chest. But he decided he'd better answer.

"This is Wes."

"Do you have something of mine?" she demanded.

He decided to play it cool. "Who is this?"

"You know damn well who this is. You stole your father's file from my cabinet."

"You told me I could look through his files, remember?"

"Only what I decided to show you. Those files are confidential, between attorney and client."

"I only brought them home so I wouldn't have to bother you."

"Bring them back, Wesley. Now. Don't make me come to your house."

A snapping noise in the corner startled him. He looked over to see that Einstein had decided to eat, after all. With a twist of its body, the snake had grabbed the mouse by the neck in a tightening coil. The mouse's tail and feet jerked for a few seconds, then stopped.

Wesley knew how it felt.

"Okay, Liz, calm down. I'll be over in a few minutes."

He could feel her anger vibrating across the airwaves before she disconnected the call. Setting aside his phone, he flipped through the file quickly just to see if anything else interesting caught his eye.

A tan stationery envelope fell out onto his lap. The outside was blank. The tab of the envelope had been tucked inside. He opened it and withdrew a single, folded piece of matching paper. When he opened it, the date made him catch his breath—December of the year his father had disappeared. It had to be just before or around the time that he'd left town.

My darling Liz,

I have to go, you know I do. There are too many things to work out, and I can't do it here. But I'll be back someday, and the people who have done this to me will pay. Thank you for believing in me, and for loving me. I will miss being in your arms every day that I'm gone.

Love, Randolph

White-hot anger whipped through Wesley's chest. His dad had been having an affair? With Liz? How could he have done that to Wesley's mother? Had she known about it?

God, Carlotta would die if she knew. She already didn't like Liz…

Then he straightened. Maybe Carlotta did know, maybe that was why she'd been so upset when he'd called his father's attorney after his arrest for hacking into the city's computer system.

Wesley shook his head. That was Carlotta…always protecting him from the truth. And even though they disagreed about their father's guilt, she'd never said anything about his character to make Wesley think less of him. She had allowed him to form his own opinions of the man as he remembered him.

He refolded the letter and stuffed the file into his backpack, then took a look at Einstein's progress. Killing the mouse was a quick process compared to swallowing it and digesting it. The snake's jaws had unhinged to allow it to draw the mouse into its mouth whole, one centimeter at a time.

Wesley bet that Liz could swallow him whole if she wanted to.

It took him forty minutes to ride to her place. The lights were on in the guesthouse, where they normally rendezvoused. Liz answered the door in a long silky robe, holding a martini. She glared at him and held out her hand.

He pulled out the file and passed it to her. "Why didn't you tell me that you were my dad's mistress?"

She blanched and turned to walk inside. "I didn't mean for you to find out. He wouldn't have wanted that."

Wesley followed her. "How could you do that to my mom?"

"The vows were your father's to break, not mine."

"How long did it go on?"

"Years," she said simply. "You asked me yesterday if I'd ever met the right man."

"You said you did, but he wasn't available. Were you talking about my dad?"

She nodded. "I loved him desperately."

"So did my mom," Wesley muttered.

Liz smiled. "I'm sure she did. But your mom had… problems. She was frail. It was hard for her to take care of herself and your father."

"So you took care of him?"

"It's not what you think," she said. "I never asked your father to leave your mother. I never expected him to. When things got rough, I was a soft place for him to land, that's all." Liz set the file on a table, then lifted her hand to Wesley's cheek. "You are so much like him."

Wesley grabbed her wrist. "Is that why you like screwing me?"

"Yes," she said simply, then tossed back her martini and swallowed. "I'm attracted to you because you're so much like your father. Is that so bad?"

Wesley thought about it. When he realized his cock was as hard as a steel rod, he realized it wasn't so bad being compared to your old man in the sack. In fact…it was kind of cool knowing he could turn on a woman that his dad had turned on.

He pulled her to him and kissed her neck, sliding his hands inside her robe. Underneath, she wore a pink panty and bra set. He rounded his hands over her hips. "I'm still mad at you," he muttered, then pinched her ass.

She shuddered in his arms. "I know. Sleeping with your father and with you was a bad thing. But I can't help myself. What are you going to do to me?"

Wesley swallowed hard, not quite sure he was ready for the power shift that she was suggesting. "I…I guess I'm going to…punish you?"

"Okay," she murmured, then pushed him down on the bed and climbed over his lap in prime spanking position.

Wesley blinked at the woman sprawled over him, trying to take it in. Chance would never believe this.

"I don't believe you, man."

Wesley held up his hand. "Dude, I swear."

Chance threw a leather couch pillow at him. "Liar. It's more likely that she put you over *her* knee, you little tool."

Wesley dodged the pillow and went back to playing Poker Smash.

Chance was revved up, though, high on uppers. "Man, I can't stop thinking about getting punked the other night at that poker game. I'm so pissed off."

"We're lucky we weren't killed," Wesley said.

"I told that bastard Grimes he wasn't getting any more of my money. I can't believe he didn't have security, man."

"He probably figured a shootout would attract attention."

A splintering noise startled Wesley and he looked up to see Chance pulling his bloody fist out of the drywall.

"Dude, are you crazy?" He jumped up to survey the damage. "Can you move your fingers?"

"Yeah, nothing's broken," Chance said, spreading his fingers and shaking off the pain. "I'm just so pissed that you played like a superstar and then we got stripped."

"Find me another game. Tell Grimes he owes us one."

"Yeah, good idea."

Wesley toyed with the idea of telling Chance his suspicions about Leonard being one of the armed robbers, but Chance could be a hothead. Wesley knew that the muscle head could probably kill Chance with a twist of his wrist.

No, he was going to slow-bid his hand for now.

He left after dark, feeling good on the back of another white pill, his head still a little swollen from the earlier session of naughty sex with Liz. The woman was a ball-buster. Who would've guessed she got off on being spanked?

He wonder if E. liked being spanked…or Meg.

Wesley frowned as he unlocked his bike from the rack. Where had that thought come from?

A big hand clamped down on his neck.

And where had this guy come from?

He looked up in the smiling face of Leonard.

"Dude, it's dark out here. You really need to start carrying pepper spray or something. Man could get mugged. Or worse."

"What do you want?" Wesley growled.

"The Carver's upset with you."

"What else is new?"

"You'd said you'd come through on the favor he needed."

"I did the best I could. He said he'd erase my debt. I did my part."

"That's not good enough. The deal's off. I'm authorized to collect a payment right now. You got any cash on you?"

"No. You took it all at the card club."

Leonard blinked. "What the hell are you talking about?"

"I know it was you who robbed the club. Did you share any of that with The Carver, or does he know about your side jobs?"

"You'd better keep your mouth shut, punk."

"Get lost, Leonard. Or I'll tell E. that her boyfriend is a thug."

Leonard pulled him up until they were nose to nose. "You really don't want to bring women into this. They could get hurt." The man released Wesley so abruptly that he stumbled backward.

But he must have touched a nerve, because the bully jogged away.

29

Carlotta glanced at her watch, wondering where Wesley had gone when he'd left the house earlier. Not to Liz's, she hoped. The thought of them together was just too incongruous for her to imagine.

Almost as bad as thinking about her father and Liz together.

Or Jack and Liz together.

Carlotta sank down deeper in the couch and immersed herself in the documentary she was watching about Kiki Deerling's life. The media was still trying to wring out the last bit of newsworthiness from the young woman's death. The only related developments were that Matt Pearson was still barricaded in a Buckhead hotel, and that Kiki's BFF, Naomi Kane, had signed with Kiki's former publicist, Marquita White.

Everyone seemed to be going on with their bad behavior and their careers. Carlotta wondered idly if Matt Pearson *had* given Kiki a lethal dose of heroin. It would definitely explain why he was so distraught over her death. She wished she could figure out a way to talk to him, but had a feeling that even her extensive party-crashing skills would fall short of A-list celebrity security. And she doubted Jack would be in a helpful mood if she got her ass arrested for trespassing.

Hateful man.

Hannah was working tonight. With the night yawning before her, Carlotta considered calling Peter to see if he wanted to catch a movie. The thought of him plucked at her heartstrings…the way his face had lit up when she'd stopped by the office. The man did love her. And he was being so kind, helping Wesley, and giving her the space that she'd asked for. Yet if she was going to "stay close" to Peter, as her father had instructed, she needed to find small ways to interact with him, small ways to help her heart get used to the idea of loving him again.

She picked up her cell phone to call him, and instead it rang in her hand. Hannah's name came across the screen. Carlotta answered, happy for the momentary diversion.

"Hey, I thought you were working tonight."

"I am, but I just found out where—at Diamonds."

"Kayla Deerling's restaurant?"

"Yeah. She's having a private party in her sister's honor. Didn't you say that only the D.A. or the family could request an autopsy?"

"Yes."

"Well, maybe her sister would like to know what you and Coop suspect. If she hates Matt Pearson as much as the tabloids say she does, she might be motivated to find out what really happened to Kiki."

"Can you get me in?"

"Be waiting by the Dumpster in an hour. Wear black."

Carlotta wrinkled her nose. The smell of the rotting food in the Dumpster was almost overwhelming in the summer heat. Where the heck was Hannah? At the sound of approaching voices, she sank into the shadows next to the building. Her black clothing helped to conceal her from the people walking by. The three men didn't even notice her… but she noticed them.

One of the guys was Matt Pearson, she was almost sure. Had Kayla decided to invite him to the private party, after all?

The service door next to the Dumpster creaked open and Hannah emerged, dressed in her culinary smock, wearing a hairnet. "Whip-poor-will, whip-poor-will," she said dryly.

"I'm here," Carlotta said, stepping into the light. "Took you long enough."

"Put this on, and let me have a quick smoke." Hannah handed over a smock identical to the one she was wearing, then pulled out a cigarette and lighter.

"I'll help you with that," Carlotta offered, eyeing the cigarette and shrugging into the smock, buttoning it over the strap of the evening bag looped over her shoulder and across her chest. "If I don't get back to work soon, I'm going to be hooked on these things again."

"Uh-huh." Hannah inhaled to light the cigarette, and took a deep drag.

"What's going on inside?" Carlotta asked, taking the cigarette for a few quick puffs.

Hannah was still exhaling. "The restaurant is closed to the public. Kayla and her boyfriend are holding court in the lounge. There are pictures of Kiki everywhere. It's kind of weird, if you ask me."

"How many guests?"

"We put out food for a hundred."

"Did you recognize anybody?"

Hannah pulled two folded sheets of paper from her sleeve. "The guest list."

"Great—but I'll have to wait until I get inside to read it."

A click sounded and a flashlight came on in Hannah's hand. "You rang?"

"You're a genius." Carlotta took the light and scanned the paper. "Naomi Kane is invited, and the publicist, Marquita White. I'd like to talk to both of them. Wow, Angela Massey…Erin Russell…Cassie Valeo…"

"I don't know who those people are."

"American Idol finalist, the star of that new sitcom on NBC, and shoe designer."

"Which explains why I don't know who any of them are. Ready?"

"Yeah."

"If you want a ride home, let me know. But I have no idea what time this thing will shut down."

"Okay, thanks. Oh, I almost forgot," Hannah said, handing over what looked like a wadded up knee-high. "Your hairnet."

Carlotta pulled it on over her ponytail and followed Hannah inside, through a storage room and office into the kitchen. She made scant eye contact and took Hannah's cue, picking up a tray of sushi that was almost too beautiful to eat. "What is this stuff?"

"Sea urchin caviar sushi," Hannah said over her shoulder.

"Sounds expensive."

"If you drop that tray, you'll have to sell a kidney to pay for it."

Carlotta wobbled. "I'm wearing a cast, you know. You should have given me the less expensive food."

"I did."

They passed a security guard and entered the main seating area of the restaurant. She understood immediately why Hannah described the atmosphere as "weird." The crowd was young and hip and loud, but the poster-size photographs of Kiki all over were downright eerie.

Carlotta and Hannah set the trays on a large skirted buffet table in the middle of the room. Carlotta looked up to scan for Kayla Deerling, and spotted her sitting at a table in the lounge with her boyfriend, her face drawn and puffy as she stared blankly into the crowd.

Then the atmosphere in the room changed suddenly. Heads turned toward the door, and the crowd parted. Matt Pearson walked in unsteadily, looking heavy lidded and high, carrying a long-stem yellow rose. He must have dosed himself just before he came in, Carlotta concluded, since he hadn't seemed so stoned when he'd walked by her earlier.

Security guards stepped up on either side of him, but he shook them off. They looked to Kayla and she shook her head, obviously wanting to avoid a brawl. Matt stopped in front of a picture of Kiki, lifted his hand to touch her face, and teared up. Then he staggered up to Kayla's table and extended the rose to her.

Kayla looked as if she could barely tolerate the sight of him. Carlotta held her breath, along with everyone else in the room, to see if Kayla would throw her drink in his face. Instead, she lifted a quaking hand and took the yellow rose, probably because when the confrontation inevitably leaked to the tabloids, she didn't want to come across looking as unstable as Kiki and her groupies.

It was enough of a gesture for Matt, because he turned around and strolled out of the restaurant. Visibly distraught, Kayla stood up and made a beeline for the bathroom. Carlotta, now trayless, headed back to the kitchen to the employees' bathroom, snagging an empty martini glass with an olive on the way.

Once inside a stall, she removed the white smock and hung it on the door hook. Then she turned her black sleeveless shell to the other side—taupe silk. From her evening bag she pulled glittery earrings and a necklace, then stroked on red lipstick. She lost the hairnet and released her hair from the ponytail, allowing it to fan over her shoulders.

She stepped out of the stall and, when she was sure she was alone, wiped the rim of the martini glass and filled it with water from the sink. The olive gave it the appearance of the real thing. With her heart pounding double time, she left the employee bathroom. The security guard standing between the serving area and the guest area gave her the once-over.

Carlotta held up the martini glass with a little laugh. "I think I'm turned around. Where is the ladies' room for guests?"

He pointed her in the right direction. She thanked him profusely, hoping she hadn't already missed Kayla. When she pushed open the door, a woman she recognized as Marquita White, formerly Kiki's publicist, and currently Matt Pearson's, was standing outside a stall, as if talking to the person inside.

She turned to look at Carlotta. "This is a private moment, do you mind?"

"Sorry," Carlotta said, patting her stomach. "I think the sushi is bad." She ran into the stall next to the one occupied, lowered the commode lid and sat down to listen.

"Honey, you can't let him upset you," Marquita said. "I'm so sorry, he promised me he would stay away. I've decided I'm going to let him go. He can find another publicist. I'm tired of cleaning up his messes. Just remember that this party is to honor Kiki. Come out, dearest, please."

A sniffling noise sounded. "Give me a minute," Kayla murmured.

For her part, Carlotta groaned as if she were sick.

"Okay." Marquita relented. "But don't keep everyone waiting too long."

The woman's high heels tapped across the floor, then the door opened and closed.

"Kayla," Carlotta said.

"Who's there?"

"You don't know me, but I have important information about your sister that you need to hear."

"Is this some kind of joke?"

"No. I was one of the people who brought your sister's body here from Florida. And it's possible that she didn't die of natural causes."

"What? What are you saying? That she was m-murdered?"

"I don't know. But there were track marks on her arm. And bruising around her neck."

"But there was an open casket. She wasn't bruised."

"It was covered with makeup."

"Oh, my God. Are you sure?"

"Yes. I know this is terrible news, but only the family can request an autopsy."

"But...she's already b-buried," Kayla said, her voice cracking.

"It's not too late. A tox screen would still reveal if she had drugs in her system. If so, there would be a full investigation."

"If Kiki *did* have drugs in her system, I think everyone can guess who gave them to her," Kayla said bitterly.

The door opened and, judging from the noise, a group of women entered. *Better to slip out now,* Carlotta thought. She stood and opened the stall door, then casually walked toward the exit.

She felt a hand on her arm, and when she turned, Kayla stood there.

"Thank you," the woman said earnestly, her eyes red-rimmed. "I know everyone thought that Kiki was nothing more than an overexposed, spoiled starlet. But she was my little sister. Thank you for caring. I didn't get your name."

"It's…Carlotta."

"Thank you, Carlotta."

Kayla left the ladies' lounge and Carlotta felt limp with relief. She'd done what she felt was right. Now it was in the hands of the family to decide.

"Are you a friend of Kayla's?"

She turned her head to see Naomi Kane leaning on the counter. From the glazed expression on her face, it looked as if she needed the support.

"Um, no," Carlotta said.

"Who are you?"

"Just a friend…of a friend."

Naomi narrowed her eyes. "You look old. Are you a reporter?"

Carlotta stuck her tongue into her cheek. "No—"

"Because if you are," the young girl slurred, then leaned in, "I have some good scoop."

Carlotta's eyebrows shot up. "What is it?"

"I don't think that Kiki died of an asthma attack."

Carlotta's pulse picked up. "Why not?"

"I was there. I heard her arguing with someone just before Matt found her unconscious."

"Matt found her? I thought her publicist found her."

"They lied," Naomi whispered. "They do that a lot in this business."

"Was the argument with a man or a woman?"

"I couldn't tell, I just heard voices." Naomi laughed. "I was stoned then, too."

"Why didn't you tell this to the police?"

"Because I was stoned?" the girl said as if Carlotta was an idiot.

"Oh. Of course. Do you remember who else was at the party?"

"The regulars. Matt wasn't supposed to be there, but he dropped in to surprise Kiki. She wasn't too happy to see him, though."

"Do you think Matt could have hurt her?"

"I don't know. He has a drug problem, you know."

And you don't? Carlotta thought. That white stuff under the girl's nose wasn't a milk mustache.

"Marquita was there, Kiki's publicist." Naomi laughed. "Oh, I keep forgetting—she's my publicist now, too."

"Could it have been Marquita arguing with Kiki?"

"Maybe. They argued a lot."

"Do you know a guy named Wayne? Red hair, liked to hang around Kiki?"

Naomi went blank for a few seconds, then she brightened. "Oh, the stalker. Yeah, he was there, too, dressed like a waiter. Kiki was pissed. She had him thrown out of the party."

Carlotta got a sinking feeling in her stomach.

"But you didn't hear any of this from me," Naomi said, then brought her finger to her lips in slow motion. "Shhh."

"Right." Carlotta watched the young woman totter away, then shook her head, wondering if Naomi Kane would be the next casualty of an unchecked celebrity lifestyle.

She touched up her lipstick, then left the lounge. A few feet away from the door, Marquita White had Naomi Kane by the arm. The publicist was wearing a rather stern expression and whispering in her client's ear. Naomi looked like a repentant child.

When Marquita White nailed Carlotta with an icy stare, she decided it was time to make her exit. She waved at Hannah on her way by, then walked out the front door and hailed a cab.

When the taxi pulled away, Carlotta settled back in the seat and suppressed a shudder. What she'd seen of the inner workings of the entertainment industry made her skin crawl. It was starting to look as if her suspicions about Kiki Deerling's death might be right. But piercing the cloak of secrecy that surrounded the incestuous industry of Hollywood might prove to be impossible. After all, if Kiki's family thought an autopsy could reveal that she'd taken drugs the night she died, they might opt to just leave well enough alone.

And let a murderer walk.

30

Carlotta sat in a stiff chair, waiting to be called to have her arm x-rayed to make sure it was healing properly. And from the looks of things, it was going to take the better part of the afternoon. She picked up one of the few magazines she hadn't yet read and sighed. Being incapacitated required a lot of time. And patience.

The entertainment magazine she flipped through pre-dated Kiki Deerling's death, showing the young woman out with friends on the beach, at the hottest clubs, at all the red carpet events, her pug, Twizzler, in tow. Matt Pearson was always close by with his arm around her. He'd had "KD" tattooed on his shoulder. They seemed linked at the hip, and she looked happy.

Alive.

Carlotta sighed, glancing at the TV overhead playing an all-news channel. She kept waiting for the announcement that the Deerling family had ordered the body exhumed for a full autopsy, but so far, nothing. And it seemed likely that the more time that passed, the less likely they were to want to bring it back up again.

So she would try to remember the woman as she was in the picture, smiling and happy, rather than stiff and cold, possibly dead by the hands of someone who'd once loved her.

"Carlotta Wren?"

At the sound of her name, she jumped up before they could change their minds. She'd spent thirty minutes being prepped for X-ray, one minute actually being x-rayed, and an additional forty-five minutes waiting for the doctor to review said X-rays.

"You seem to be healing fine," he announced without touching her. "Is the Percocet helping to manage the pain?"

She nodded. "I rarely take them anymore, and I still have half a bottle."

"That's refreshing. I can't tell you how many of my patients use an injury as an excuse to get hooked on painkillers."

"When can I go back to work?"

"How much lifting does your job require?"

"I work retail, at Neiman's, so it depends. Some days I unpack boxes, move inventory around."

"Retail can be physically demanding. My wife has certainly built up her biceps from swiping her card at Neiman's." He laughed at his own joke. "If you still feel good in a week, then maybe you could try going back part-time and see how you feel. But you should wait a full two weeks before going back full-time, okay? Enjoy your vacation."

Easier said than done, Carlotta thought as she left the medical building. She wasn't sure she knew how to have a vacation. The road trip that Coop had offered her was the first time she'd gotten away in years, and that had turned into a nonstop adventure.

Was it possible that she wasn't suited to the pampered, leisurely life that she'd always coveted? Of course, it might be different if she had the money to keep herself well-entertained.

But she was starting to realize that a privileged life—a lot of money and a lot of free time—could be a recipe for disaster.

She walked to the MARTA station and got on the next southbound train. The sets of double doors closed and the train swayed gently as it picked up speed. She looked out the window, enjoying the sunny view. Atlanta was one of the most forested cities in the country. The buildings and trees seemed to cohabitate well.

Someone dropped into the seat next to her. When she looked over, she did a double take, seeing Wayne Barber sitting there.

"You turned me in," he accused, his expression panicked.

Carlotta shrank back. "Are you following me?"

"I can't believe you turned me in," he said, grabbing fistfuls of his own hair.

"Calm down. What do you mean?"

He started rocking in his seat. "Some cop came looking for me, wanted to ask me questions about Kiki's death."

"What did the cop look like?"

"Big guy, tacky tie."

She almost smiled. So Jack was following up, after all. "Did you tell him that you suspected Matt Pearson had given her heroin?"

"No! The cop thinks *I* did." He stood up and punched the air. "Why did you tell him about me?"

"Is there a problem here?" a male passenger a few seats away asked. He stood, eyeballing Wayne.

The train slid to a stop and the doors opened. Wayne darted off and ran through the station, disappearing into the crowd.

"Thanks, anyway," Carlotta said to the passenger.

She was jittery the rest of the ride home. Wayne Barber had a history of mental illness. When Kiki had thrown him out of the party in Boca Raton, had he retaliated by going back and strangling her? Taken her necklace as a souvenir? Was he so grief-stricken by her death because he had caused it himself? And blaming Matt Pearson because the man had what Wayne wanted?

At least Wayne Barber was on Jack's radar. Carlotta toyed with calling Jack to tell him about the encounter with Wayne and the news Naomi Kane had revealed to her last night at the party—about the argument she'd overheard, and that Matt Pearson had found the body, not Marquita White, as had been reported. But then he would only ask her how she'd happened to be at the private party. If he discovered that she'd informed Kayla Deerling her sister might have been murdered, Carlotta wasn't sure what Jack would do.

She was pretty sure that he wouldn't shake her hand, although shaking in general might be involved.

When Carlotta got off the train at Lindbergh, she found herself looking over her shoulder for any signs that Wayne was still following her, but she didn't see anything suspicious along the tree-lined route. By the time the town house was in sight, she had started to relax and anticipate her return to work. Cruise season was in high gear, and Neiman's had lots of in-store fashion events planned.

When she first heard the sound of an engine racing, she thought it was a motorcycle coming toward her. At the sight of a primer-paint-covered car speeding along, her first thought was that she was glad there were no small children living on their street.

Her second thought was, *Oh, my God, that car is going to hit me.*

Carlotta screamed and flailed backward, but the car jumped the sidewalk and grazed her hip, throwing her to the ground. She landed on her back in someone's yard, racked with pain, waiting to hear the sound of screeching brakes a sign that the driver would be running back to see if she was okay. Instead, it sounded as if the car geared up, then the roar of the engine faded as it sped away.

She was afraid to move, afraid something else was broken. She heard the sound of scurrying coming from the opposite direction the car had gone. A tiny black, bizarrely tufted face appeared, and began licking her cheek ferociously, in between rabid fits of barking.

Toofers, Mrs. Winningham's ugly, yappy dog.

Thank goodness the woman wasn't too far behind.

"Toofers, what is that? Haven't I told you not to lick—oh! Carlotta, what happened? Don't move. I'll get Wesley and call 911."

"Visiting you in the hospital is getting to be a regular occurrence," Coop said, standing next to Carlotta's bed in the emergency room ward. "I don't like it."

She smiled. "You heard the doctor, Doctor. I'm fine, just a few bruises." She nodded to Wesley, who was pacing at the foot of her bed like a caged animal. "Why don't you take him to get something to drink. By the time you get back, I should be ready to go home."

He nodded and squeezed her hand, then shepherded Wesley out of the room. In the doorway, they passed Jack.

He came to stand at the foot of her bed and studied her. Had she given him that wrinkle between his eyebrows? She didn't remember it being there when she'd first met him.

"Are you going to shoot me?" she asked finally.

He walked up to the side of the bed and put his face close to hers. "If I did, you'd only come back to haunt me."

"Don't forget that," she murmured.

His golden-colored eyes flashed with anger and passion. He smoothed her hair back from her forehead and ran his thumb over a cut on her cheek. It occurred to her that Jack didn't know what to do about his feelings for her any more than she knew what to do about her feelings for him. They were too confusing, too mired in other circumstances. He straightened and put his hands in his pockets, suddenly all business.

"A uniform picked up Wayne Barber and brought him in, but the guy seems to be on the verge of some kind of breakdown. All he can say is that he didn't mean to hurt you. In his state of mind, I can't count it as an admission, but it's enough to at least hold him for a while."

"That's probably good for his sake, too."

"Do you remember anything about the driver?"

"No. The windows were tinted. I saw nothing."

He sighed. "We have an APB out on the car, and it's pretty distinctive…for now."

"For now?"

"Sometimes primer-painted cars are used to perpetrate a crime, then are immediately run through a paint shop."

"That doesn't sound like something that Wayne Barber would mastermind."

"No. It sounds like a professional job."

"Wesley might be able to help you there," Carlotta heard Coop say.

She looked up to see Wesley and his boss standing in the doorway.

"Do you know something?" Jack asked Wesley.

Her brother didn't say anything, just looked miserable. Coop jabbed him from behind. "Tell them what you did." Coop's voice and body shook with barely controlled anger.

His uncharacteristic behavior toward Wesley frightened her more than the car barreling toward her. "Oh, Wes. What did you do, now?"

31

Even as Carlotta waited for Wesley to confess to whatever was behind his tortured expression, she was sending a silent plea heavenward. *Please, let this be nothing too bad, nothing that will ruin his life.*

Wesley's Adam's apple bobbed. "Last week—"

"Speak up," Coop commanded.

He cleared his throat. "Last week, one of The Carver's guys came to me with an offer. He asked me to, um, help them get Kiki Deerling's body."

"You mean *steal,*" Coop said. "Don't try to dance around with semantics."

"Yeah," Wesley confirmed. "He asked me to help them steal her body."

Carlotta gasped. "Wesley, no!"

"Why would Hollis Carver want the girl's body?" Jack asked, frowning.

"His son Dillon deals to that singing star, Matt Pearson,"

Wesley said. "Dillon provided the heroin for the party in Boca. When they found the girl's body, he split and called his dad, freaking out. His dad told him he'd take care of it."

"By stealing the body?" Jack asked.

Wesley nodded. "He was afraid that if Kiki had overdosed, Dillon would get nailed for providing the dope. He worked it out with someone in her camp that there would be no autopsy." Wesley looked up at Coop. "But they were worried about what would happen once the body got to Atlanta. I told them that Coop would definitely raise questions if he saw anything suspicious, so the plan was to steal the body before we left the morgue."

"And when that didn't work?" Carlotta prompted, feeling sick.

Wesley paled. "I…was supposed to let them know where we were on the road."

She closed her eyes, aching for the trouble Wesley was in, wondering where she had gone so wrong that he could even consider helping with something so heinous. "That's how they knew we were at the restaurant and the rest area."

He nodded miserably. "I was supposed to leave the back door unlocked so they could steal the body at the rest area. But at the last minute, I bailed. It just wasn't right." He looked at them each in turn. "When Coop said he wasn't allowed to own a gun, I thought that meant he didn't have one. So I told The Carver's guys no guns. They weren't supposed to start shooting."

"We all could've been killed," Carlotta murmured. *In front of their father. How Hitchcockian would that have been?*

"Who did Hollis work with from the Deerling girl's side?" Jack asked.

"Her publicist, I think. She said if Kiki went missing, it would guarantee that she would be famous forever."

"Marquita White," Carlotta confirmed. "She was at the party the night Kiki died."

Jack looked at her. "How do you know that?"

"I…just do."

Jack lifted his hands. "So we're looking at an accidental drug overdose, not a strangulation."

"Which means the dealer can be held liable. And if she didn't inject herself, the person who administered it to her is guilty as well," Coop added.

"Matt Pearson," Carlotta said. That news would certainly rock the industry.

"What were they planning to do with the body?" Jack asked.

Wesley shook his head. "I was afraid to ask."

Coop scowled at him. "That's the only smart thing you did."

Carlotta tried not to feel any sympathy for her brother. He'd done a terrible thing. But Wesley looked so distraught, it was hard not to have compassion.

"What was in this for you?" Jack asked him.

Wesley averted his gaze, then looked back when Coop bumped him from behind. "The Carver said he'd clear my debt."

Jack smiled wryly. "I take it since you weren't able to pull it off, The Carver reneged?"

Wesley nodded.

"So what does this have to do with Carlotta's hit-and-run? The girl's already entombed, so The Carver's kid is off the hook unless the family changes their mind about the autopsy and has the body exhumed."

"You said what happened to Carlotta looked like a professional job. I just thought it sounded like something The Carver would do to get to me, maybe keep me quiet."

Carlotta gasped and covered her mouth.

Jack pivoted his head. "What?"

"I might have inadvertently tipped off the publicist that Kiki's death is still being investigated," she mumbled.

Jack frowned. "But it isn't."

She shifted in her bed and glanced around. "Has anyone seen the ice chips?"

"Carlotta…" Jack said, his tone a warning to come clean.

She winced. "I went to a private party last night at Kiki's sister's restaurant, and I might have insinuated to her that Kiki had been murdered."

"You did what?" Coop and Jack shouted in unison.

"You said without more evidence, only the family could request an autopsy. She had a right to know."

"And the publicist was there?"

Carlotta nodded. "She's close to Kayla. Kayla probably confided to her what I said."

"How did you get into a private party?" Jack asked. "Wait. I don't want to know. So last night the publicist, who's in cahoots with The Carver, found out that you're still poking around, and today you almost get run down in the street."

"Sounds like a connection," Coop said.

Jack nodded, making a few notes in a pocket pad.

"What's going to happen to me?" Wesley asked and Carlotta felt a little proud that he at least seemed ready to face his punishment.

Jack looked thoroughly disgusted. "I don't know. The D.A. sure as hell won't cut you any slack. I'll get with your attorney. If you agree to testify, maybe we can convince one of the assistant D.A.s that you came forward on your own and that you were extorted into going along with it."

"Thanks," Wesley said.

"I'm not doing this for you," Jack said pointedly.

"There's one more thing," Wesley stated. "The tall, bald guy at the morgue and in the green van definitely worked for The Carver. I don't know who the other guy was, the beefy one."

"Maybe The Carver was just covering his bets by sending more than one team," Coop said.

"Or maybe there's another ring to this circus," Jack muttered. "I'll have Dillon Carver and Marquita White brought in for questioning. We can at least book them on conspiracy charges, and I'm going to push for attempted murder charges for the hit-and-run."

"Do you think the D.A. will step in now to order an autopsy on Kiki Deerling?" Carlotta asked.

"I doubt it. There's still no motive for murder. And unless someone comes forward to say they saw the girl inject herself, or someone else inject her, she still could've died from an asthma attack. I'll talk to her parents, but if I were them, frankly, I'd leave it alone."

Carlotta bit her lip. It was looking more and more as if Kiki Deerling had overdosed on heroin, that the bruising around her neck had occurred as a result of someone trying to resuscitate her. The circle pendant could have come off at any time, wound up in someone's pocket as a keepsake, or fallen down a street grate when the body was loaded in and out of the ambulance. An autopsy wouldn't be necessary to charge Dillon Carver and Marquita White for conspiring to steal a corpse. Jack was right. No good could come from disturbing Kiki's body now.

She wondered how long it would take for news of the body-snatching conspiracy to hit the wires. The media would be ecstatic for one more juicy chapter in the Kiki Deerling story.

Coop drove them home from the hospital, but they were a morose trio. The tension between Coop and Wesley was so tangible, it was like having a fourth person in the car. As they were pulling into the driveway, Wesley attempted to break the silence with perhaps the worst possible question: "Will you need me for any jobs this week, Coop?"

Carlotta shook her head.

Coop squinted at him in the rearview mirror. "After the stunt you pulled, why should I ever trust you again? You obviously have no concept of the sanctity of the dead."

She willed Wesley not to say anything, to just listen, but no, he couldn't resist.

"I've learned my lesson."

Coop slammed the van into Park, then turned around to face him. "Your lesson? Listen, chief, Kiki Deerling wasn't your lesson to learn. She was a person. A human being. And we were entrusted with her body. You not only broke the law, you broke a moral and ethical code."

"I let you down."

"You let yourself down. Get your issues worked out with the D.A., then we'll talk—if you're not sitting in jail. Or if I'm not picking up *your* body for turning on The Carver. I'm already on the ropes with Abrams at the morgue. Your little stunt will only make things worse. This makes me look bad, Wesley, for trusting you."

"Coop, I'm sorry—"

"Don't tell me you're sorry," Coop interrupted. "Show me. Get your shit together, grow the hell up and stop being such a burden to your sister. Now get out of my sight."

Carlotta sat stock-still while Wesley climbed out word-lessly and closed the door. He walked to the house as if he had the weight of the world on his shoulders.

"Sorry I came down so hard on him," Coop said.

"No, you were right to say those things. He does need to grow up and start thinking about the repercussions of his actions." She sighed. "I haven't been the best mom."

"You're not his mom," Coop said. "And even if you were, he's old enough to start taking responsibility for his own life."

"I know. You're right. This thing with our parents…it's like a cancer. It affects everything we do and everything we don't do."

"So have you told him yet that your father's fingerprints were at a hotel in Daytona?"

"Not yet." Nor had she told Wesley that she'd actually talked to Randolph. "I'm not sure now's the time."

"When is the time? When he's behind bars because his anger at your parents has caused him to let his life spin out of control?"

She looked up at Coop. "You're so smart."

He smiled for the first time in hours. "Don't forget sexy."

She laughed. "How could I?"

"I'll walk you to the door," he offered.

"I'm fine—"

"I insist."

She smiled as he came around to help her out of the van. She was moving pretty gingerly, but it felt good to have his arm to hold on to. The feel of his muscles under his warm skin and the scent of his aftershave brought back strong images of their night in her hotel room, stirring her senses. When they reached the door, she was hoping he would kiss her passionately, like he had the night in the hot tub.

Instead he leaned down and kissed her on the cheek, closer to her ear than to her mouth.

Minus ten.

"Good night, Carlotta."

"Good night," she murmured, her lips left wondering. And waiting.

She frowned and went inside. Wesley was in his bedroom with the door closed, the fan running. She knocked, but he ignored her. She left him alone, thinking there wasn't anything she could say, anyway. He needed to think through what he'd done, and come to terms with it himself.

She took a hot shower to stave off some of the soreness she'd surely feel tomorrow, then climbed into bed to watch TV and relax. A few minutes later, the phone rang. When it became apparent that Wesley wasn't going to answer, Carlotta picked up the cordless handset by her bed.

"Hello?"

"Is this Carlotta Wren?" a woman's voice asked.

"Yes."

"This is Kayla Deerling. We met briefly last night at Diamonds."

Carlotta's pulse picked up. "Yes, of course I remember."

"Detective Terry just notified my family of the conspiracy between my sister's publicist and that drug dealer to steal Kiki's body. It's just…too awful to comprehend. He said that you were instrumental in helping the police. I can't tell you how grateful we are to you."

"You're very welcome."

"Please say you'll come to the restaurant tomorrow night and allow us to prepare a meal for you and a guest, all on us, of course. It's the least I can do to thank you for all that you've done for Kiki."

She could think of worse ways to spend the evening than being comped at a four-star restaurant. "That's very generous of you. Thank you, I'd love to come. What time?"

"Around seven?"

"I'm looking forward to it."

Carlotta hung up the receiver and pursed her lips. What a nice gesture. Now, the real dilemma—who to ask? She mulled over her choices and how that choice might impact the future…or not. After an hour of changing her mind, she picked up the phone and punched in a number.

"Hi, it's Carlotta. I was wondering, are you free for dinner tomorrow night?"

32

Carlotta opened the door and smiled at her dinner date. "Hi."

"Hi," Peter said, his eyes devouring her. She was wearing a short red baby-doll dress and the highest heels she could walk in, considering she was still sore from yesterday. "You look…amazing."

"Thanks," she said, grateful for the body makeup that concealed her scrapes and bruises. She straightened his Pucci tie, which so did not need to be straightened. "You're looking pretty great yourself."

"I'm glad you called."

She nodded. "Me, too." And she meant it. Dinner at Diamonds was the perfect opportunity to spend time with Peter, to try to recapture the feelings they had once shared. "Let me grab my wrap. It's the best I can do to camouflage this horrible cast."

"Which reminds me," Peter said as she locked the door,

"the last time we went out, you wound up dangling from the balcony of the Fox Theater."

She winced. "I know."

They walked down the steps and over to his dark blue Porsche two-seater. He held open the door for her. "I hope it's safe to assume that we're not going to have that much drama tonight."

"Oh, yes," she said, then swallowed a grunt when her aching back twinged from swinging into the low-slung car. "No drama tonight."

He smiled. "Good." Peter closed her door and she nursed a pang of guilt for not sharing more with him. But he would be appalled if he knew she went on stakeouts at the cemetery, crashed upscale parties and was the target of hit-and-runs.

After all, this was a man who would be appalled if he knew she occasionally smoked a cigarette.

When he sank behind the wheel and flashed that sexy grin, though, she decided that if she and Peter became more seriously involved, he didn't have to know every move she made. There was something irresistible about maintaining a certain amount of mystery.

Entering through the front door of Diamonds was certainly more of a pleasurable sensory experience than entering through the door by the Dumpster. A dozen chandeliers reflected like diamonds on the polished black floor. Red carpets ran between tables, creating a vivid Mondrian effect. Live piano music played. Aromas of braised meats and rich wines saturated the air.

When Peter gave their name at the hostess station, the staff seemed to come alive. "Ms. Deerling instructed us to tend to your every need this evening," said the maître d'. "Right this way to your table."

It was the best table in the house, private, but with a stunning view of midtown and downtown. A bottle of Cristal champagne chilled tableside. The linens were exquisite, the flatware was silver and the lighting was romantic. Peter held out her chair, and when he took his, she couldn't help but sigh. It was going to be a perfect night.

The headwaiter removed their napkins from blown-glass napkin holders and placed them in their laps. As a junior waiter filled their water glasses with San Pellegrino, the headwaiter handed them menus. "Everything in our kitchen and our wine cellar is at your disposal. Please enjoy."

When they were left alone, Peter seemed impressed. "Did Kayla Deerling offer a complimentary dinner to Cooper as well?"

"Um, I'm not sure," Carlotta murmured. She hadn't been completely forthright about Kayla Deerling's reasons for extending the dinner invitation, just telling him that it was for handling the details of her sister's transportation with discretion.

"If that was the case, I would've thought that the two of you might have dined together," he said mildly. "Since you handled the job together."

"I know what you're getting at, Peter. And I'm dining tonight with the person I most want to be dining with."

He grinned. "I just wanted to hear you say it. What looks good on the menu?"

"Everything." She closed her menu. "Why don't we let the chef decide?"

Peter closed his in turn. "Excellent idea. Champagne?"

"Absolutely." But she reminded herself to take it easy, considering she'd taken a Percocet a few hours earlier.

He filled both flutes, then lifted his glass. "To new beginnings."

She touched her glass to his, loving the sound of the crystal tinkling. "To new beginnings." The champagne was delicious, sliding over her tongue in a cool shower of bubbles.

They turned the food and the wine selections over to the waitstaff, and soon savory delicacies appeared—figs stuffed with spiced prosciutto, duck with glazed mandarin oranges, lamb with sherry-soaked currants. A plate of exquisite cheeses and fresh fruits came next, then entrées for each of them to choose from—filet mignon, sea bass, pork tenderloin and pheasant. With each course a new bottle of wine appeared. Carlotta tried to keep tabs on the times her glass was refilled, but it all began to blend into a silky haze of happiness.

Peter was delightful company. They talked and bantered while managing to skirt the issue of her father. Peter made her laugh, made her feel desirable, made her feel as if maybe she did have a place by his side. If at times he seemed stiff and predictable, she reminded herself that it was in his pedigree and that he'd had a loveless marriage. He loosened up around her, and she cleaned up around him. They could be good together.

Again.

Kayla Deerling herself made an appearance with their dessert menus. She kissed Carlotta on both cheeks and squeezed her hands. "Thank you again for all that you've done for my family."

Carlotta introduced Peter, who stood to clasp Kayla's hand in his and offered his deepest condolences. Kayla seemed touched, and was pleased that they had enjoyed the food and the service. Carlotta noticed that under the woman's makeup, she looked drawn, her eyes puffy. But each day would get easier.

"Now, what would you like for dessert?" she asked.

"We've been deferring to recommendations all evening," Carlotta said. "Why stop now?"

"I agree," Peter said. "What do you suggest?"

The woman smiled. "How about a chocolate torte for the lady, and crème brûlée for the gentleman?"

"Perfect," they said in unison.

"She's different than I expected," Peter murmured when Kayla walked away.

"Different how?"

He shrugged. "I guess I've heard so much about her sister's antics, I thought she might be a little wild, too."

"No, she's only a few years older, but she appears to be the serious one. The restaurant seems to be doing well. She dates a developer—Reardon, I think is his name?"

Peter nodded. "Jamie Reardon. A wunderkind, I've heard. I'm sure her father approves."

"What do your parents think of me, Peter?"

The question slipped out—it was much too serious for the evening, much too serious for the fledgling state of their relationship.

"I'm sorry, forget it," she said, then lifted her glass for another sip of wine.

"No, I'm glad you asked," he said. "To be honest, I don't know if they would approve of us being together, but I don't care. I married the woman they wanted me to marry, and it was a disaster for both of us. I'm not making that mistake again." He reached across the table to clasp her hand. "I love you, Carly. It's always been you, and only you. Stay with me tonight."

She had trouble swallowing the mouthful of wine. Dinner tonight was supposed to be one of those small steps toward becoming closer to Peter. But it was clear that he wanted to accelerate the dance.

She needed a cigarette—a long one.

"Excuse me," she said. "I think I'll visit the ladies' room before dessert arrives."

He nodded and released her hand.

She grabbed her evening bag and stood a little unsteadily. The wine rushed to her head, and she was sore from sitting so long.

"You okay?" he asked.

She assured him she was and, feeling his gaze on her, walked in the direction of the ladies' room until she knew she was out of sight. Then she pivoted and went through the kitchen, the office and the storage room to the door that led outside.

"Damn nonsmoking ordinances," she muttered, pulling the contraband out of her bag.

She had taken two heavenly drags off the cigarette when she heard the sound of heavy footsteps approaching. She shrank back into the shadows to hide, as she had before. A man walked into the light and she almost swallowed her cigarette. It was Matt Pearson. He seemed nervous, but not high. Loathing filled her chest. If the man had loved Kiki, he wouldn't have gotten her hooked on heroin. He would've left her alone when she'd gotten away from him. He had loved her to death.

Matt shifted from foot to foot and kept glancing around. He was standing about ten feet away, but didn't notice Carlotta. She stood immobile, staring at the door she'd come out of, wondering if she could make it back without drawing attention. He was obviously waiting to score drugs.

Then Matt's head turned and she saw another man approaching, a big man. A finger of alarm trailed up her back, her body reacting even before her mind knew why. And then recognition hit her—it was the Ferragamo Shoes guy from the morgue!

She swallowed a scream and backed up farther into the shadows. The two men started talking. She couldn't hear every word, but Matt seemed agitated and the other man was trying to calm him down. Her mind raced at the implication of their connection—Matt Pearson was behind the other man trying to steal Kiki's body. He'd given her drugs; she'd died. He'd needed to clean up the mess, get rid of the body. And now with his dealer and publicist being questioned, he was likely to be fingered as well.

"Hey, do you smell that?" Ferragamo Shoes held up his hand.

"What?" Matt said.

"A cigarette burning." The big man looked in her direction. "Is someone there?"

She dropped the cigarette to extinguish it, and sparks flew everywhere.

"There's someone back there," Matt said, and both men ran toward her. She bolted for the door, but the big guy caught her and spun her around.

"You!" he said, then looked at Matt. "This is the broad from the morgue, one of the body haulers."

"Dude, she can identify you."

"Oh, no," Carlotta said, shaking her head. "I didn't see anything. I'm nearsighted. I'm just here having dinner. In fact, my dessert is waiting—"

Her protest was cut off by a handkerchief stuffed in her mouth.

Minus ten points.

33

Carlotta struggled against Ferragamo Shoes, but it was like dancing with a refrigerator. He pulled her arms behind her and bound her wrists with a cable tie. She managed to stomp on his instep.

"Ow!" he bellowed.

"Be quiet, man," Matt Pearson said. "Somebody's going to hear us."

"Take off her damn shoes," the big man said.

She resisted, but Matt slid them off and tossed them aside. He looked scared. "Get lost, man. I'll handle this."

"Are you sure?"

"Yeah, I'm sure. Get out of here. Come back and get me in thirty minutes."

Ferragamo Shoes handed her over and jogged away.

So she had less than thirty minutes to live. Regrets and missed opportunities flashed through her mind. There would be no husband, no children, no reunion with her parents.

She thought of the brownies she didn't eat because she was afraid they'd wind up on her thighs—all for nothing. Her thighs were goners like the rest of her.

Carlotta tried to break free from Matt Pearson, but he held on, and her arm hurt like hell. The handkerchief was gagging her, sending tears streaming down her cheeks. Was he going to strangle her? Put her body in the Dumpster? All because she could link him to one of the men who'd tried to steal Kiki's body.

"Stop it! Be still!" he said, forcing her to sit on the ground. "Let me think!" He put his hands to his head and paced. "Jesus, how did everything get so messed up?"

Every part of her ached and she had a feeling her arm might be broken again, but Carlotta marshaled her strength and focused on the door by the Dumpster—she had to get there. Peter was waiting inside, expecting her to come back and eat dessert. He wanted her to stay with him tonight. It was supposed to have been a perfect evening.

She lunged to her feet and took off running, but Matt caught up with her and grabbed her arm. They went down together and pain rolled through Carlotta's body like a tide. She curled up in a ball, moaning.

"Okay, stop," Matt said, sitting up. "I'm going to free your hands if you promise to hear me out."

She nodded, thinking that as long as he was talking, he wasn't killing her. And as soon as he cut the cable tie, she was going for a right hook, if her numb hand would cooperate. He pulled out a knife and reached behind her. She could feel him sawing against her bonds.

Suddenly, thankyouJesus, the door next to the Dumpster opened. Kayla Deerling appeared, along with a man that Carlotta recognized as Kayla's fiancé. Carlotta screamed against the gag and flailed about, trying to stand. Matt pulled her back down.

"They're out here," Kayla said, running toward them. "Get him!"

The men struggled. Carlotta pulled against the sawed cable tie and snapped it. She yanked the handkerchief out of her mouth and struggled to her feet, falling into Kayla for support. After a clicking noise, Matt went limp. Carlotta realized that the other man had got him with his Taser gun, and she sagged against Kayla with relief.

Until Kayla's fiancé pulled out a syringe and stabbed it into Matt's arm.

"What's going on?" Carlotta said. "What's he doing?"

"Matt? He's dying of a heroin overdose." The woman made a rueful noise. "And because you missed dessert, you're going to have to share a similar fate."

"Are you mad?" Carlotta said, clawing at the woman. She ripped her collar, and then she saw it. Kayla was wearing Kiki's diamond circle pendant.

34

Wesley pounded on Chance's door. He was in a foul mood. He was out of OxyContin, but he'd promised himself that was that. He just hadn't counted on wanting more so badly. Since the last pill, every little thing seemed to piss him off.

Like the fact that Carlotta had gone to dinner with Peter. Was it because he had been pushing him at her, as Peter had asked him to do?

Or, rather, had *paid* him to do?

Wes couldn't seem to do anything right these days. And now Coop hated him.

He'd decided to ride over to Chance's to tell him about Leonard. Not because he was hoping to score more pills.

Except now that he was here, he was trying to think of a way to trick Hannah into going out with Chance, just once, for another bag of Oxy. This was a bad time for him to stop taking them. He was stressed over the situation with Coop and about possibly having to testify against The Carver's son.

Then a thought popped into his head. What if he went to The Carver and offered not to testify in return for erasing his debt?

No, something about that logic seemed wrong, but he couldn't put his finger on it at the moment. He felt as if someone were channel surfing in his head.

He pounded on the door again.

Chance opened it and waved him in. "Relax, man. Come the fuck in."

Chance was stoned, and Wesley wondered suddenly why his friend sold tons of drugs, but mostly smoked pot.

Maybe the guy was smarter than he let on.

Chance dropped into a chair, riveted to the TV, where a woman was going down on a guy in a movie that had obviously been recorded on a videocam.

"Man, what's with all the homespun porn lately?"

"Dude, I'm a distributor."

"Of porn? Since when?"

"I've always done it, here and there. But there's a bigger market now for the homemade stuff, and it's usually pretty cheap to come by. I buy a master, and send it off to a shop in Korea. They take care of orders and fulfillment. I get a check every month."

"Why do people buy porn when they can get it free on the Internet?"

Chance lifted his hands. "It's one of the great mysteries of the universe."

Wesley dropped into a chair and squinted. "This one doesn't look that hot to me."

"It doesn't matter, it's that Kiki girl. I paid a hundred grand for it, but it's going to make me a million." He looked up. "Hey, didn't you bring her body back from Florida?"

"Yeah." Wesley leaned in closer. "Who's she with?"

"I don't know." Chance picked up a piece of paper. "The e-mail says it's some developer in Atlanta." He laughed. "Poor schmuck. If he has a wife and kids, he won't have them for long."

Wesley held his head. His mind was chugging away, and he knew he was missing something. He dialed Jack Terry's number, and after a couple of rings, Jack answered.

"Jack, it's Wesley Wren."

"I'm on another call, I'll get back to you."

"Dude, this might be important."

"Don't ever call me dude. Tell me, quick."

"Kiki Deerling's sister, the one who owns the restaurant, what's her name?"

Jack sighed. "Um, Kayla, I think."

"Isn't she engaged?"

"Yeah, to some developer. Why?"

"I'm watching a sex tape with Kiki Deerling and her sister's fiancé. You said you needed motive for murder. Is that enough?"

Jack was quiet for a few seconds. "Ten times over. Where's the tape?"

"I got it. But you need to get to that restaurant. That Kayla chick invited Carlotta to eat there tonight because she was grateful for her help. Carlotta's there with Peter right now."

"I'm on my way."

"I'll meet you there with the tape." Wesley hung up the phone and ejected the DVD. "Dude, I need to borrow this."

"Will I get it back?"

"Maybe. And it'll be worth more."

"Where are we going?"

"You're stoned, you're going nowhere." Wesley punched in Coop's number. After the fourth ring, he picked up. "Hello?"

"It's Wesley."

"This better be good."

"Carlotta might be in trouble."

There was a moment of silence, then, "I'm listening."

"I need for you to pick me up at a friend's house."

"What's the address?"

Wesley gave it to him.

"Be out front in three minutes."

35

Carlotta stared at the pendant hanging around Kayla's neck. "You killed your own sister. You strangled her and took the pendant. Why?"

Kayla's face twisted in hatred. "Because she had everything and it wasn't enough! She had to have the only thing that was mine—Jamie."

Carlotta glanced at the woman's fiancé. He looked guilty. And scared. But he was following Kayla's lead. Was his obedience in exchange for her forgiveness?

"Jamie gave her the pendant," Carlotta guessed. "They were having an affair."

"He made a mistake, and we'll work through this."

"It was you Naomi heard Kiki arguing with. You killed her and let everyone believe it was an asthma attack."

"That's what everyone will go on believing," Kayla said. "After you're gone."

"But why kill Matt?"

"Because the jerk saw me. He was high, but he remembers enough. And you—you should've just minded your own business." The woman grabbed Carlotta by both arms in a steely grip, then looked at her fiancé. "Get her."

Jamie Reardon approached, Taser raised. A little flash of electricity jumped between contact probes. Carlotta screamed as if she'd already been zapped. With what little strength she had left, she swung her cast back into Kayla's stomach, with enough force that the woman relaxed her grip. Carlotta wrenched her arm loose and raised the cast against the Taser.

She heard the clicking noise, waiting for the pain to light up her arm and immobilize her body. Instead, she heard a *thunk* behind her.

"Drop it," Peter said.

She turned to see him standing there in just enough light to reveal the handgun he held pointed directly at Jamie Reardon. Carlotta nearly wet her pants in abject relief. "Peter! Thank God."

"Get behind me," he said, and she did. Kayla Deerling lay on the ground in a heap. Peter must have hit her with the gun.

Reardon dropped the Taser and kept his hands in the air. "This wasn't my idea."

"He injected Matt Pearson with heroin," Carlotta said.

Peter handed her his phone. "Call 911, and go inside."

She called for an ambulance, but the sound of a siren stopped her from going into the restaurant. A familiar dark sedan with a red light roared into the parking lot. Jack was out of the car practically before it was stopped, his gun drawn. "I got him covered, Peter. Put away your weapon."

Peter opened his jacket and put the pistol back into the shoulder holster he wore.

"Where did you get that?" Carlotta asked, still incredulous.

"At the pawnshop when I found your ring. Then I got a permit to carry it concealed."

"And you decided to wear it to dinner?"

He put his arm around her shoulder. "Sweetheart, I wasn't going out with you again unprepared."

She hugged him tightly. "Thank you for coming to look for me."

"I came to apologize for pressuring you. I figured you'd come out here to have a smoke."

"I don't smoke…much."

He laughed. "Okay. And don't worry. I'll always come looking for you," he murmured, and kissed her.

When the kiss ended, Jack was standing there, frowning. "Would you like to give a statement now or later?"

"Later," they said in unison.

"I'm taking her to the emergency room to get checked out," Peter said.

"Good idea. She's been through a lot lately. First the broken arm, then a hit-and-run, and now this."

Peter frowned down at her. "What hit-and-run?"

"Jack," she said, neatly changing the subject, "how did you know I was in trouble?"

"Wes called me. He saw a sex tape that Kiki made with her sister's fiancé and put two and two together."

Two ambulances screamed into view, and Coop's van was

right behind them. Jack directed the EMTs to Matt Pearson and Kayla Deerling. Coop and Wesley jumped out and ran up to the scene.

Wesley hugged her. "Are you all right, Sis?"

She pulled back. "Thanks to Peter…and you…and Jack… and Coop."

"All right, we get the picture," Jack said dryly. "It was a tag-team effort."

Paramedics revived Kayla Deerling, then loaded her into an ambulance. Jack sent a uniform with her. She glared at Carlotta until they closed the ambulance door. The group watched in tense silence as the EMTs worked on Matt Pearson, but at last one of them gave Jack a thumbs-up.

Carlotta exhaled in relief. The man had problems, and she was furious with him for attacking her, but she didn't want to see him dead.

A crowd was gathering fast. An SUV pulled up and a wide-bodied man emerged.

"Ferragamo Shoes!" she said, pointing.

Jack frowned. "Who?"

"It's the other man guy who was trying to steal the body!"

"The man who tried to steal my van at the restaurant," Coop added.

The big man rushed up to the ambulance where they were loading Matt Pearson on a gurney, an IV connected to his arm. "What happened?"

Jack intercepted him. "Who are you?"

"Gregory Young, private investigator." He held up his hands. "I have a .38 on my belt."

"I'll take that," Jack said, then reached inside the man's coat and removed the weapon.

"ID in my breast pocket."

Jack retrieved it, then put it back. "What's your involvement here?"

The P.I. gestured to Carlotta. "Didn't Matt tell you?"

Carlotta glared. "You and Matt bound and gagged me, then you left. He didn't tell me anything."

When Jack made a move to cuff him, he said, "Hang on a minute. Let me explain."

"Make it fast, buddy. Right now you're looking at assault, grand theft auto and tampering with a corpse."

"Matt Pearson came to me a few days ago, said he'd witnessed Kiki Deerling being strangled. But he'd been high on heroin at the time, and knew his testimony wouldn't hold up in court. He needed an autopsy. When the M.E. in Boca Raton decided not to do one, he hired me to take the body for an independent autopsy."

"That's a felony," Jack said.

"To prevent someone from getting away with murder. We were going to make sure the body got back to the family. Matt just wanted the truth to come out, that's all."

"I'll need for you to come down to the station to make a statement. And don't even think about leaving town."

"No problem." He looked at Carlotta. "I'm sorry we scared you, little lady, but we were just trying to keep you quiet until Matt could explain everything."

"I think he was trying," she said to Jack, "before Kayla and her fiancé came out and attacked him."

"What happened to Matt?" the P.I. asked.

"He was injected with heroin," Jack said. "But the paramedics say he's going to make it."

Carlotta gasped. "Jack, I just remembered. Kayla said something about me missing dessert." She looked at Peter. "I'm afraid she might have put something in it."

"I'll go check it out," Jack said. "Peter, get her to the E.R. Do me a favor—put her in restraints once you get her there."

"I'll get the car," Peter said.

"You might need these," Coop said, holding up her shoes. "And is this your purse I found by the Dumpster?"

"Thank you," she murmured. "Although I have no idea how those cigarettes got in there."

He smiled. "Are you really okay?"

"Yeah, I will be. You?"

"Yeah, I will be." Coop winked. "It looks like you're in good hands with Peter."

She nodded. "He is a good man. My cup runneth over lately."

He made a rueful noise of agreement. "So, congratulations, Ms. Wren. Your persistence paid off. Thanks to you, Kiki Deerling will get justice."

"So now there will be an autopsy?"

"Most definitely."

"But if she had heroin in her system, her sister might get off."

"It's possible," he said. "But maybe Kiki was clean."

Carlotta nodded. "I hope so."

Peter came striding up. "The car's ready. Let me carry you."

"Don't be silly. I can walk."

He bent down and whispered, "Do this one thing for me."

Carlotta smiled and relented. She looped her arm around his shoulder and he picked her up. As he carried her to the car, she looked back at Coop. The tight, wounded expression on his face tore at her. It was exactly what she hadn't wanted to happen.

"You'll take Wesley home?" she called, her heart in a bind.

"Of course," he said, then lifted his hand in a little wave, and turned away.

36

Wesley noticed his hand was shaking when he twisted the doorknob to open the front door.

"How was your probation meeting?" Carlotta asked when he walked into the living room. She was lying on the couch, recuperating from the night before. His gut clenched when he thought of how badly the scene at Diamonds could have ended.

"Fine."

"Did Eldora think this situation with the D.A. is going to affect your probation?"

He shrugged. "Maybe. She seems to think they might add on more time, maybe more community service."

"That's not so bad."

"Yeah." He set his backpack on the floor. "I just hope Coop gives me another chance."

"I think he probably will," she said, gingerly pushing

herself up to a sitting position. "He seems like the kind of man who believes in second chances."

"Coop's a good man, isn't he?"

"I think so, yes."

"Do you think that Dad was a good man?"

Carlotta took her time answering. "I think there were some things about Dad that were very good. He was handsome and popular and he was good at his job. He made people laugh. He made people feel good."

"But it's not the same." Now that he knew their dad cheated on their mom, Wes was starting to question a lot of things. If Randolph could justify his affair with Liz, maybe he could do the same for filching a few dollars from the firm.

"Is something on your mind?" Carlotta asked.

"I'm just starting to think that you were right—that our father is no good and has no intention of coming back to clear his name."

"I never said he was no good."

"No, but it's what you've always thought, and I don't blame you. How could he not let us know all this time that Mom's all right?"

Wes watched his sister struggle for an answer, and in that moment, he despised his father for putting her through everything she'd endured.

"Come sit," she said, pulling up her legs to make room on the couch. "I want to tell you something."

Wesley sat, concerned about the serious tone of her voice.

"Part of the reason I went to Florida with Coop was

because Dad's fingerprints were found at a hotel in Daytona that had been robbed."

His heart jumped. "What? When did this happen?"

"Just before we left. Jack told me about it. He was going down to investigate. I wanted to go, but he said no. When Coop asked me to ride along with him, it seemed like the perfect chance to look around myself."

"So you went to the hotel when we were in Daytona?"

"Yes, and I should've told you. You had a right to know. I guess I just didn't want you to get your hopes up. And frankly, I was afraid he was the person who had robbed the hotel."

"Did you or Jack find anything?" Or Liz. Wesley realized that she'd known all along and hadn't told him, either. No wonder she'd missed the file he'd stolen—she was probably adding new material.

"No, we didn't find anything. But…" Carlotta moistened her lips. "But when we stopped at the rest area on the way back home, Randolph came up to me at the vending machines and started talking."

Wes jumped off the couch. "Dad? Dad just came up to you and started talking?"

"Yeah. He was in disguise, but it was him."

"Where was I?"

"Guarding the van," she said dryly.

He jumped around the living room excitedly. "Why didn't you tell me? Why didn't you yell for me?"

She looked away, then back. "I asked if I could, but he didn't want me to."

He stopped jumping. "He didn't want to talk to me?"

"He said not yet."

"What else did he say?"

"He said he'd been keeping tabs on us."

"How's Mom? Did he mention Mom?"

"He said she'd been…sick…off and on."

"But she's okay?"

"Yeah, I guess."

"What's he been doing? Where do they live?"

"All he would say is that he's been gathering evidence to prove his innocence, and that he'd contact us again soon. We didn't even get to say goodbye. When all hell broke loose, he just vanished."

Wesley clapped his hands. "This is fantastic!"

She smiled, a genuine smile. "Yeah, it is."

"I'm going to make a big dinner," he said, pacing the room. "What sounds good?"

"Anything that I don't make," she said, laughing. "Surprise me."

"You got it."

She winced. "But first—do me a favor? Get a Percocet for me out of the bottle on my bedroom dresser?"

"Sure thing."

Wesley loped into her room, so happy he couldn't even be mad at Carlotta for not telling him sooner. She had her reasons. He picked up the prescription bottle and glanced at it to make sure it was Percocet. Then he noticed the refills: two. He unscrewed the cap and removed one of the six tablets for Carlotta…and two for himself. One he swallowed, and one he stuck in his pocket.

It was just to celebrate, that's all. It wasn't as if he was hooked, like those celebrity morons…

37

"Breaking news in the continuing saga of the Kiki Deerling murder investigation."

Carlotta turned up the volume.

"The medical examiner's office in Atlanta, where the body was taken after it was exhumed for a full autopsy, is reporting that there were no traces of heroin or any other drug found in the young woman's bloodstream at the time of her death. Repeating, there were no traces of heroin or any other drug in Kiki Deerling's body."

"Good for you, Kiki," Carlotta murmured.

"The cause of death has been ruled asphyxiation by strangulation, the manner of death, homicide. Sources tell us that the D.A. in Palm Beach County, Florida, will be charging Kayla Deerling with her own sister's murder. Kayla Deerling is also charged with the attempted murder of a woman who visited her Atlanta restaurant, a potential witness in this case, by sprinkling rat poison on the woman's chocolate torte.

And conspiracy to murder pop singer Matt Pearson, her sister's ex-boyfriend, who reportedly witnessed Kiki's murder.

"All this in the wake of not one, but *two* body-snatching schemes, one by Kiki Deerling's publicist and a known Atlanta drug dealer to get rid of the body in an alleged attempt to thwart an autopsy, and one by Pearson himself in an alleged attempt to *secure* an autopsy to prove that Kiki was murdered. Folks, it's going to take a long time to sort this one out. Stay tuned."

"I don't think so," Carlotta said, then clicked off the TV. She stood and stretched, sighing at the pain that still sang out from different parts of her body. It would take a while for all the cuts and bruises to heal, but at least her arm hadn't been broken again.

At the sound of a car pulling into the driveway, she went to the window. Peter had said he might stop by on his lunch hour—to talk. Two words that always put a crimp on her intestines.

But instead of Peter's Porsche, it was Jack's sedan. Her double-crossing heart gave a little lift. Jack emerged from the car and she opened the front door, smiling widely. Damn, did he have to look so devilishly handsome today?

"Hello, Detective."

"Hello. Good to see you up and about."

"I'm a fast healer. I should be back to work in a few days."

"That's very good news," he said matter-of-factly. "Because the more vacation you take, the more work I have to do."

"You sure know how to sweet-talk a girl, Detective. To what do I owe this pleasure?"

He climbed the steps to stand on the stoop, then held up a piece of paper. "One phone tap, cancelled."

She frowned and looked at the paper. "But is it *my* phone tap that was cancelled?"

"You don't trust me?"

"No more than you trust me," she said, verifying the phone number and signatures before she gave him a smile. "Thank you."

He turned and walked back down the stairs. "You're welcome."

"Is that a new suit, Detective?"

He shrugged. "Uh, you know, just something hanging in the back of my closet."

"Looks nice," she said. "And the tie—not bad."

"Thanks." As he approached the car, the passenger door opened and a woman stood up.

In a word, she was stunning. Tall, slim, killer curves, and bushels of wavy caramel-colored hair around a heart-shaped face. "Jack, we just got a call over the radio. We need to get back."

"Okay," he said, then turned. "By the way, Carlotta, meet Detective Maria Marquez, my new partner."

"Nice to meet you," Maria said, then disappeared back into the car before Carlotta could form a sensible word.

Jack gave an extra little wave, then climbed into the car and backed out of the driveway.

Carlotta was still standing there several minutes later when

Peter pulled into the driveway. *Lift, heart, lift,* she commanded.

"Wow, standing at the door. I hope that means you're happy to see me," Peter said when he walked up.

"That's exactly what it means," she said brightly. "Come in. Do you want some iced tea?"

He checked his watch as he walked into the living room. "Actually, I need to get back to the office ASAP."

"Okay. Sit down. What did you want to talk about?"

Peter hesitated, then smoothed his hands over his knees. "Well, you know I've been traveling to New York a lot recently."

"Yes."

"I've been offered an assignment there. If I take it, I'll be moving to Manhattan for a year."

Her heart started to beat faster.

"To be honest, I don't want to leave," he said. "But I also don't want to stay in Atlanta and not be with you."

"Peter, what are you saying?"

He reached for her hands, folding them into his. "I'm asking you to give me something concrete to go on here. I want us to start dating. I want to see you several times a week, heck, maybe even a couple of times a day. I want you to sleep over."

She waited, her vital signs clicking higher.

"You asked for space," he said. "And if you still need more time, then I'll go to New York. I'd rather stay here…but it's up to you. Just say the word."

Stay close to Peter…he's in a position at the firm to help me…I need him…he's the only person there I can trust…then we together again.

She was torn down to her soul. She did want more to sort through her feelings for Peter, but how could she that if he was in New York? And what about the other tw men bouncing around in her heart?

But her father had said he would contact her through Peter, and that wouldn't happen if Peter was out of town. And wasn't reuniting their family the most important thing, for Wesley's sake?

All she had to do was say the magic word.

"Carlotta? Tell me what you want me to do."

She closed her eyes briefly, feeling as if she was making a deal with the devil—her own father. "Stay, Peter…stay."

* * * * *

Don't miss a single move!
Look for books 4, 5 and 6 in the BODY MOVERS series
from Stephanie Bond and Mira Books
released back-to-back in 2009!

www.MIRABooks.com
www.stephaniebond.com

315

'll all be

ime

do

o